# The Terror of Saint Lawrence

Alexander De Chastelaine

Copyright © 2024 A. W. De Chastelaine

All rights reserved.

ISBN: **9798883341945**

# CONTENTS

| 1 | The Minerva Inn | 1 |
| 2 | On Board the Hawk | 25 |
| 3 | The Vixen | 47 |
| 4 | From Nantucket to Newfoundland | 76 |
| 5 | Maria's Rage | 97 |
| 6 | In Liverpool | 116 |
| 7 | Under Attack | 132 |
| 8 | The Capture of the Pollux | 161 |
| 9 | In London | 179 |
| 10 | The Return to Saint Lawrence | 202 |
| 11 | The Terror of Belle Isle | 216 |
| 12 | Home in Plymouth | 233 |
| 13 | Leaving England | 248 |
| 14 | The Chateau in Normandy | 264 |
| 15 | An Act of Piracy | 280 |
| 16 | A Life in France | 304 |
| 17 | Paris | 322 |

# 1 THE MINERVA INN

In the bustling harbor of Plymouth, where ships sailed in and out, and sailors from distant lands mingled with locals, there stood the Minerva Inn. It was a haven for travelers, a place where stories were exchanged over frothy tankards of ale and hearty meals.

The Minerva was nestled in the heart of Plymouth, its weathered wooden façade bearing the scars of centuries of maritime history. From the outside, it appeared no different from any other tavern lining the streets, its windows adorned with flickering lanterns that cast warm pools of light onto the cobblestones below.

To the casual observer, the Minerva was simply a place of revelry and camaraderie. But those in the know were aware of dark secrets within its timeworn walls, lying hidden from the prying eyes of the outside world. Behind the jovial facade of the taproom, where patrons gathered to swap stories and share laughter over tankards of ale, lay a network of hidden rooms and shadowed alcoves.

It was within these hidden chambers that the nefarious practice of impressment thrived—a dark underbelly of the maritime world where unsuspecting young men were snatched from the safety of their neighborhood and pressed into service aboard ships of the Royal Navy or civilian vessels in need of a crew. The Inn was a hunting ground for press gangs seeking to bolster their ranks with able-bodied seamen by any means necessary.

The method was deceptively simple yet devastatingly effective. A friendly captain would approach an unsuspecting young man, striking up a cheerful conversation over a tankard of ale. Unbeknownst to the sailor, a single shilling would be secretly dropped into the bottom of his mug—an unknowing acceptance of payment for services rendered.

If the sailor drank without inspecting the tankard, he unwittingly sealed his fate, by accepting the captain's pay. His destiny was now irrevocably altered as he was hauled off to a ship against his will and pressed into service. It was a cruel and merciless practice, preying upon the vulnerability of those who dared to seek refuge within the walls of the Minerva Inn.

In response to this insidious threat, the tin tankards of the Minerva Inn soon came to be equipped with glass bottoms, allowing wary sailors to peer beneath the surface and check for the telltale glint of silver before taking a sip. It was a small yet crucial safeguard against the dangers lurking within the shadows, a silent warning to those who dared to tempt fate within the confines of the tavern.

In the heart of this shady inn worked Maria, a spirited barmaid with a penchant for adventure.

She was a striking young woman in her early twenties, with lustrous black hair that cascaded in waves around her shoulders like a midnight waterfall. Her almond-shaped eyes sparkled with intelligence and curiosity, framed by long, dark lashes that quivered with every flutter of her gaze. Her skin bore the cold and pale hue of the English shores, rarely kissed by the golden rays of the sun.

Despite her beauty, Maria possessed a strength that belied her youthful appearance. Her slender frame moved with a graceful elegance, yet there was a fiery spirit burning within her that refused to be extinguished. Whether she was serving ale behind the bar of the Minerva Inn or gazing out over the horizon to the sails of a distant ship, Maria's determination and adventurous nature shone through.

Maria was no ordinary barmaid; she possessed a fiery spirit and an insatiable curiosity that set her apart from her peers. She would often listen intently to the tales spun by the sailors who frequented the inn, their words painting vivid pictures of distant lands and daring escapades upon the high seas. She was also known to be not too difficult when a sailor requested more than just a pint of ale and was quick to follow men upstairs, for a Shilling, or two.

One fateful evening, as Maria bustled about the crowded taproom, a rugged figure caught her eye. It was Captain Briggs, a weather-beaten seafarer. He strode purposefully toward her, his eyes gleaming with determination.

"What's your name, maiden?" he asked, his voice carrying the unmistakable authority of a man accustomed to giving orders, "I've heard tales of your adventurous spirit, and I believe you're just the person I've been seeking."

"Maria is the name," the maid replied.

"Briggs, Captain John Briggs," the man introduced himself.

Captain Briggs was a silver-haired man in his fifties, with a rugged appearance that spoke of a lifetime spent at sea. His piercing eyes held the wisdom of countless voyages, and his salt-and-pepper beard was a testament to his years of command. Despite the lines etched upon his face by wind and weather, there was a strength and determination in his bearing that commanded respect from all who crossed his path. He moved with the assuredness of a man who had lived through many storms and emerged unscathed, his presence radiating an air of authority tempered by a quiet sense of friendship.

Maria's curiosity was piqued. "What is it you seek, Captain Briggs?" she asked, her eyes alight with anticipation of a quick coin.

Briggs leaned in closer, his voice lowered to a conspiratorial whisper. "I command The Fly, a sturdy schooner bound for Spain," he explained. "But I find myself in need of a little company tonight to join me. Someone with your spirit and grace."

"There are suitable rooms upstairs, here at the Inn, Captain. I will gladly give you some company there," Maria replied.

"Well, I am more looking for company for a night, my dear, and I am willing to pay a Pound," the man teased.

Maria's heart quickened at the prospect of earning in a night what would normally be a week's pay. But the thought of leaving behind the familiar comforts of the Minerva Inn filled her with hesitation.

"Tell me more," she urged, her mind racing.

And so, over tankards of ale and beneath the flickering glow of candlelight, Captain Briggs explained,

"The Fly is to set sail at dawn, its destination a far-off Spain. If you come to the docks in the evening, and spend the night with me, I will give a Pound. Here is a down pay."

With that, Captain Briggs dropped two Shillings on the

table and left.

As the evening came, Maria stood on the dock, ready to board The Fly, her heart pounding with excitement. The salty sea air filled her lungs, and she felt a surge of adrenaline course through her veins.

As Maria stepped aboard The Fly, she scanned the bustling deck, searching for someone to guide her to Captain Briggs' cabin. Spotting a weathered sailor with a kind expression, she approached him with a polite smile.

"Excuse me," Maria said, her voice steady despite the flutter of butterflies in her stomach. "I'm here to see Captain Briggs. Could you please show me to his cabin?"

The sailor nodded, his eyes crinkling at the corners in a friendly manner. "Of course, Miss," he replied, gesturing for her to follow him. "Right this way."

Maria fell into step behind the sailor, her anticipation growing with each passing moment. As they made their way across the deck, she couldn't help but marvel at the sight of the towering masts and billowing sails stretching toward the sky.

Before long, they arrived at a sturdy door bearing a brass plaque engraved with the name "Captain Briggs." The sailor rapped sharply on the wood, announcing their presence before pushing the door open and gesturing for Maria to enter.

"Captain, there's someone here to see you," the sailor called out respectfully as Maria stepped into the dimly lit cabin.

Captain Briggs looked up from his desk, his weather-beaten features breaking into a short smile as his eyes met Maria's. "Ah, Maria," he said, rising from his seat and crossing the room to greet her. "I'm glad you could make it. Please, come in."

Maria returned his smile, her nerves dissipating in the presence of the captain's easy confidence. As she stepped further into the cabin, she couldn't help but feel a sense of excitement building within her.

As the young woman settled into the chair opposite Captain Briggs, he wasted no time in pouring them each a generous measure of brandy. The rich, amber liquid glinted in the dim light of the cabin, its heady aroma filling the air with warmth and comfort.

"Here you go, Maria," Captain Briggs said, handing her a glass with a gallant smile. "A toast to your presence on board The Fly."

Maria accepted the glass with a grateful nod, her fingers wrapping around the smooth stem as she raised it in a silent salute. She took a sip, savoring the fiery warmth that spread through her chest, fortifying her for whatever lay ahead.

As they stood in companionable silence, Captain Briggs

leaned forward, his gaze lingering on Maria with an intensity that sent a shiver down her spine. Without a word, he reached out and began to unbutton her blouse, his touch firm yet gentle as he exposed the delicate curve of her collarbone.

Maria's breath caught in her throat as she met his gaze, her heart pounding with a heady mixture of anticipation and desire. He slowly unbuttoned her dress and let it fall onto the wooden planks. As she stood in front of him only dressed in her stockings. He bent her over the map table in the cabin and entered her from behind. After a few minutes, the sweating captain was done, and he told Maria to get dressed. The young woman was delighted. "The easiest Pound I've ever earned," she thought, unaware of what was about to come her way.

Maria's heart sank as Captain Briggs abruptly rose from his seat, leaving her alone in the cabin with a sense of unease prickling at her skin. She watched him depart, a knot of apprehension tightening in her stomach as she waited for his return.

Minutes stretched into an eternity, and just as Maria's anxiety threatened to overwhelm her, the door swung open once more. But instead of Captain Briggs alone, he returned accompanied by his crew of nine men, their rough-hewn faces set in grim expressions.

Confusion turned to alarm as Maria realized that something was terribly wrong.

"She is yours," the captain said with a sneer.

Before she could react, the men advanced upon her, their movements swift and coordinated. With a cry of protest, she tried to back away, but it was too late. Strong hands seized her arms, pinning her to the rough wooden table with a force that knocked the breath from her lungs.

"What—what is the meaning of this?" Maria demanded, her voice trembling with fear and indignation. "Captain Briggs, release me at once!"

But the captain remained silent, his expression inscrutable as he watched his men restrain Maria with an iron grip. Panic surged within her as she struggled against their hold, her mind racing with a thousand unanswered questions.

It was then that she realized the true nature of Captain Briggs' intentions. She had been lured into a trap; her trust had been betrayed by a man she had dared to place her faith in. As the realization dawned upon her, a cold fury ignited within her veins, banishing her fear and replacing it with a steely resolve.

Though outnumbered and overpowered, Maria refused to surrender to despair. With every ounce of strength she possessed, she fought against her captors, her spirit unbroken even in the face of overwhelming odds. However, there was little she could do. One man held her hands stretched out behind her head, while two sailors held her legs, one each. Another took his turn. One by one the rough sailors violated her, as Captain Briggs looked on without emotion.

All but one young ship's mate, who silently stood in the corner, violently ravished the young woman. Maria noticed him. His eyes, filled with fear, met hers. He would have stopped the brutal ordeal, but there were 8 against him and the captain. The ordeal lasted an hour. Then the captain threw her dress at her and told her to get off the ship.

"The two coins I gave you at the inn should be more than enough," he joked, as his crew cheered. "That's all you're worth."

It was the last word she heard from the brutal captain. Trembling, she stood in the dimly lit cabin, her dress ripped, bruised, and bleeding from her nose. But Maria knew that no matter what trials lay ahead, she would never relinquish her dignity. And as she met the captain's gaze with a defiant stare one last time, she vowed to herself that she would find a way for revenge, no matter the cost.

With trembling hands and a heart heavy with indignation, Maria made her way to the constable's office in Plymouth. She recounted her harrowing ordeal to the officer, her voice quivering with emotion as she detailed the violation she had endured at the hands of Captain Briggs and his crew aboard The Fly, anchored in the harbor.

The constable listened to her story with a dispassionate expression, his features betraying no hint of sympathy for her plight. When Maria finished speaking, he looked at her with a half-smile, dismissing her ordeal as nothing more than a trivial inconvenience.

"It seems to me, it was just a bunch of sailors wanting to have a good time," he remarked callously.

Maria's eyes flashed with anger as she retorted, "It was not just a 'good time.' I was violated, and it is against the King's law."

But the constable's response only served to further fuel her frustration. "You are a bar wench," he said dismissively. "What do you expect?"

"I expect that the King's laws are being upheld," Maria shot back, her voice trembling with righteous fury.

The constable's next words cut through the air like a knife, leaving Maria reeling in disbelief. "Look, Miss," he said with a sigh, "The Fly is owned by the Duke of Devonshire. What do you want me to do? Arrest the entire crew and have them hanged? This ship is a trade ship, bringing goods from the continent to our shores. There are thousands of pounds at stake."

With that callous dismissal, Maria's anger boiled over, her resolve hardening like steel. Without another word, she turned on her heel and stormed out of the constable's office, her determination unshaken despite the injustice she had faced. She may have been just a barmaid in the eyes of the constable, but she refused to let anyone diminish her worth or deny her the justice she deserved. And as she walked away, her heart ablaze with justified fury, Maria vowed to fight.

With determination etched upon her features, Maria returned to the familiar confines of the Minerva Inn, her refuge from the harsh realities of the world outside. As she climbed the creaking stairs to her modest room, her mind raced with thoughts of the challenges that lay ahead. She knew that she needed to get back to work if she was to pay her rent to the landlord and avoid the looming threat of eviction.

After taking a few moments to clean herself up and tend to her bruises and the dried blood around her nose, Maria emerged from her room with renewed resolve. Stepping back into the taproom of the tavern, she squared her shoulders and set to work with a steely determination.

Despite the lingering ache in her body and the heavy weight of injustice pressing upon her soul, Maria threw herself into her duties with new dedication. She moved among the rough patrons of the tavern, serving ale with a practiced efficiency and a warm smile that belied the turmoil raging within her.

As the hours passed and the evening wore on, Maria found a bit of solace in the rhythm of her work, the familiar tasks providing a welcome distraction from the turmoil of her thoughts. And though the bruises on her skin served as a painful reminder of the injustices she had endured, she refused to let them break her spirit or dampen her resolve.

Maria knew that she was stronger than the hardships she faced and that as long as she had the power to stand tall and the courage to face each new day with determination, she would overcome whatever obstacles stood in her path.

As the last patrons trickled out of the Minerva Inn, leaving behind an air of quietude, Maria found herself drawn to the corner where a young man, not much older than herself, sat watching her with an intensity that sent a flutter through her heart.

"You seem to have had a rough day, Maid," he remarked, his voice gentle and concerned.

Maria offered him a weary smile. "It wasn't my best day," she admitted, feeling a strange sense of comfort in his presence.

The young man seemed to exude a warmth and kindness that set him apart from the grizzled sailors who frequented the pub. His boastful offer to spend the night aboard his ship sparked a flicker of interest in Maria, but she couldn't shake the lingering memories of her past experiences at sea.

"I've had bad experiences with going on ships, rather

not," she replied, her voice tinged with regret.

Eric's expression softened, understanding flickering in his eyes as he nodded in acceptance. "Aww, that's too unfortunate," he said sympathetically. "By the way, I'm Eric Cobham, Captain Eric Cobham."

"Maria Lindsay," she replied, offering him her name in return.

As the two exchanged introductions, Maria couldn't help but feel a sense of companionship blooming between them, a connection that transcended the boundaries of their disparate worlds. And as Eric mentioned that he was willing to pay for a room upstairs, Maria perceived a spark of curiosity igniting within her—a glimmer of possibility that hinted at the promise of new beginnings and unexpected adventures yet to come.

Eric Cobham was a strikingly young captain, his boyish features, aged only slightly by a well-trimmed brown beard, were belying the weight of responsibility that rested upon his shoulders. Despite his youth, there was an air of confidence and competence about him that spoke volumes of his capabilities as a leader.

With tousled chestnut hair that framed his face in unruly waves and clear, earnest eyes that shimmered with determination, Eric possessed a charm that was as undeniable as it was disarming. His smile was infectious, lighting up his features with a warmth that drew others to him like moths to a flame.

Dressed in a well-worn captain's coat that bore the marks of his past voyages, Eric carried himself with a grace and poise that belied his years. His movements were fluid and purposeful, each gesture imbued with the quiet strength of someone who had earned their place at the helm through hard work and dedication.

But perhaps most striking of all was the apparent kindness and compassion that radiated from Eric like a beacon in the night. Despite the rough and tumble world of seafaring in which he navigated, he remained steadfast in his commitment to treating others with respect and understanding, a quality that endeared him to both friends and strangers alike.

In the dim light of Maria's small room, the atmosphere was thick with tension and unspoken secrets as Eric and Maria sat together, their conversation mingling with the swirling tendrils of pipe smoke that filled the air. With a pitcher of ale from the tavern and glasses in hand, they shared stories and laughter, finding solace in each other's company amidst the chaos of their troubled lives.

But as their conversation took a more intimate turn, Eric's gentle kiss sent a shiver down Maria's spine, igniting a spark of desire that still smoldered within her, despite her recent endeavor on the ship Fly. With trembling hands, he began to unbutton her dress, his touch both tender and passionate as he sought to unravel the layers of her pain and uncertainty.

Concern flickered in Eric's eyes as he noticed the bruises marring Maria's delicate skin, a silent testament to the abuse she had endured the night before.

"Where do the bruises on your body come from?" he asked softly, his voice laced with a mixture of anger and concern.

But Maria's response was guarded, her walls firmly in place as she shook her head in refusal to divulge the source of her pain. "I don't want to talk about it," she replied, her voice barely above a whisper.

A flash of determination crossed Eric's features as he vowed to seek vengeance on Maria's behalf, his words dripping with a promise of retribution. "Whoever did this to you, he'd better not come across me, because I'll send him to the bottom of the ocean," he declared fiercely.

But Maria's doubts lingered, her disbelief palpable as she struggled to come to terms with Eric's revelation.

"You're not teasing? There were nine sailors and a captain. What could you possibly do?" she asked incredulously, her eyes searching his for any sign of deception.

"No," Eric replied solemnly, his gaze unwavering. "There is a lot I can do. I will be a captain of a pirate ship, and they would not be the first sailors I have sent to the bottom of the sea."

Maria's mind reeled with the weight of his confession, her world spinning on its axis as she struggled to reconcile the image of the kind-hearted young man before her with the fearsome reputation of a pirate captain.

"But you are not a captain yet?" Maria asked with disappointed doubt in her voice. "And you don't actually command a ship, as you claimed?"

"Not quite yet, but I am about to purchase a new ship," Eric replied.

With that, he produced a purse filled with gold coins and laid them on the table, Maria's fingers trembled as she reached out to touch them, her heart racing with a mixture of awe and disbelief.

"That must be three hundred pounds," she murmured, her voice filled with wonder and uncertainty.

In the hushed intimacy of Maria's small room, Eric's embrace enveloped her with a warmth and tenderness that banished the shadows of doubt and uncertainty. As their lips met in a tender kiss, the world outside faded into insignificance, leaving only the two of them entwined in a cocoon of desire and longing.

He tried to move his hands under her skirt. She pinned his hands down, and he feigned resistance, his movements suggestive of a struggle. Then, he swiftly unbuttoned her blouse. As she allowed her breasts to brush against his face, a surge of desire coursed through him, igniting a primal urge. With fervor, he thrashed against her grasp, consumed by a wild, insatiable passion. They were becoming one in body and soul.

With each caress and whispered endearment, their passion grew, igniting a fire that blazed brightly within their hearts. The confines of the room melted away as they surrendered to the intoxicating rhythm of their shared longing, lost in the timeless dance of love and desire.

Their bodies molded together as they sank onto the soft embrace of the bed, their kisses deepening with each passing moment. At that moment, nothing else mattered but the overwhelming rush of sensation that pulsed through their veins, binding them together in an unbreakable bond of passion and desire. Forgotten was the brutal encounter on the small schooner at the pier. Forgotten was her anger at the merciless response of the constable.

As they lay entangled in each other's arms, their hearts beating as one, Maria felt a sense of completeness wash over her—a feeling of belonging that transcended the boundaries of time and space. And in the tender embrace of the man she had come to desire, she knew that she had found her sanctuary, her refuge from the storms of life that raged outside, on the streets of Plymouth. She knew Eric was strong enough to protect her from the dangers lurking in a rough harbor town. And Eric seemed to have the means to take care of a woman like her.

As the clock struck midnight, Maria's curiosity got the better of her, and she found herself unable to resist the urge to ask Eric about his life as a pirate. With a knowing smile, she posed the question that had been weighing on her mind.

"How does one become a pirate? Isn't it a dangerous trade?" she inquired, her voice tinged with curiosity.

Eric's expression softened, his gaze turning inward as he contemplated the memories that lay buried beneath the surface of his consciousness. With a sigh, he nodded, acknowledging the complexity of his past and the journey that had led him to his current path.

"Dangerous, it is! It's a long story, though," he began, his voice filled with a hint of melancholy. And with that, he launched into the tale of his life—a narrative of adventure, betrayal, and redemption that unfolded like a map charting the course of his destiny.

Eric spoke of his poor childhood, spent in the coastal town of Poole in Dorset. As his tale unfolded, Maria listened in rapt attention, her heart heavy with empathy for the young man who had endured such hardship at the hands of fate.

He had been pressed into the service of a fishing vessel bound for Newfoundland, with a dozen of other young boys from his hometown. She felt a lump form in her throat as he recounted the brutal realities of life aboard the fishing cutter bound for the New World—a journey fraught with danger and despair, where innocence was stripped away and replaced with the harsh realities of survival.

The image of young boys, barely out of childhood, being pressed into service aboard the unforgiving vessel struck a chord within Maria's soul. It was not too different from her own story. She had started her life as a bar wench at age 11, and Maria could only imagine the terror and helplessness they must have felt as they were torn from their homes and families and thrust into a world of cruelty and brutality.

Her heart ached as Eric spoke of his best friend, Peter, whose fate had been sealed by the callous indifference of a captain and his crew at the age of 14. Peter's hand became ensnared in a pulley on the ship, severing several of his fingers.

Helpless and in excruciating pain, he lay immobilized under deck, and weeping incessantly. His suffering seemed unending until he simply disappeared one day. Some said that he had jumped overboard, others alleged that the captain and two crewmen, annoyed by his cries, callously cast him overboard into the frigid waters off the Newfoundland coast.

It was at that moment of abandonment and despair that

Eric resolved to flee the tyranny of the ship and carve out a better future for himself. The memory of Peter's cries of pain and fear echoed in the recesses of her mind, a haunting reminder of the injustices that lurked within the shadows of a sailor's life.

But amidst the darkness, there was also light—a flicker of determination and resilience that burned brightly within Eric's heart. The resolve, audible in his voice as Eric spoke of his determination to escape the clutches of oppression and forge his own path forward, filled Maria with a sense of admiration and respect.

As Eric fled the fishing vessel upon its return to Poole, he found himself adrift in a world filled with uncertainty and desperation. With few prospects and even fewer resources at his disposal, he struggled to find a foothold in a society that offered little in the way of opportunity for a young man of humble origins. Eric soon stood at a crossroads, grappling with the weight of his circumstances and the daunting challenges that lay ahead.

Born into humble beginnings, he was the son of poor parents, his father a sailor who had served in the Royal Navy before losing an arm in battle. Eric's mother now bore the heavy burden of providing for their family of seven in the wake of her husband's unsuccessful struggle to make ends meet.

But fate intervened in the form of a local smuggler, a shadowy figure who ran goods from the French coast to the shores of England and who offered Eric a chance to escape the cycle of poverty and hardship that had plagued him since childhood. With the promise of easy money and a taste of the forbidden allure of life on the wrong side of the law, Eric seized the opportunity with both hands, throwing himself headlong into a world of danger and intrigue.

For a time, Eric thrived in his new role as a smuggler of brandy, his pockets lined with ill-gotten gains and his heart filled with the thrill of adventure. But the fleeting sense of prosperity was short-lived, shattered by the harsh realities of life as a criminal in a world governed by ruthless ambition and unforgiving justice.

Caught in a web of betrayal and deceit, the ship's smuggling operation was discovered by the Royal Navy, leading to a swift and brutal reckoning for all involved. The smuggler's crew was caught on the River Thames with 5,000 gallons of ill-gotten brandy. The crew members, including Eric, were subjected to a public flogging and sentenced to two years of imprisonment in the notorious Newgate Prison in London—a punishment that would test their resolve and almost break their spirits.

For Eric, the true cost of his crimes went far beyond the physical pain of the lash or the confines of a prison cell. As he watched his captain swing from the gallows, the weight of his choices bore down upon him like a millstone, crushing his dreams of a better life.

Following his release from Newgate, Eric had sought refuge in the city of Oxford, where he had found employment at a local inn. It was there, amidst the hustle and bustle of travelers and patrons, that fate would cast him into a fateful encounter with a wealthy merchant.

One night, while serving at the inn, Eric was tasked with attending to the needs of a particularly affluent guest. The weapons and tools dealer, weary from his long journey and indulging in the comforts of the inn, had imbibed more wine than was prudent and soon succumbed to a deep slumber.

As Eric entered the merchant's chamber to replenish his wine, he noticed the telltale glint of gold emanating from the man's belt. Temptation gnawed at Eric's conscience as he beheld a weighty purse dangling before him, brimming with the promise of wealth and opportunity.

Eric yielded to the lure of temptation and deftly liberated the purse from the merchant's belt. Its contents, a fortune of three hundred pounds in gold, whispered of a life beyond the confines of poverty and hardship.

With his heart pounding in his chest, Eric fled the inn under the cover of night, his footsteps echoing in the empty streets as he made his escape. By the time morning dawned and the merchant awoke to discover the loss of his purse, Eric was already on his way to Plymouth, his mind consumed by the possibilities that lay ahead.

Yet, unbeknownst to Eric, his actions had set into motion a chain of events. The merchant, upon discovering the theft, wasted no time in pointing an accusatory finger at the innkeeper, casting a shadow of suspicion and mistrust upon the unsuspecting host, who was held liable for the theft.

As Eric journeyed toward Plymouth, his mind heavy with the weight of his transgression, he knew that he had irrevocably altered the course of his fate. There was no going back. For this, if caught, he would get hanged.

## 2 ON BOARD THE HAWK

As the first light of dawn filtered through the window of Maria's small room, Eric and she lay entwined in a tender embrace, the warmth of their bodies mingling with the soft rays of morning sunlight. As they basked in the quiet intimacy of their shared moment, Eric's words hung in the air like a lingering promise of possibility.

"Why don't you come with me on the ship?" he asked softly, his voice filled with a mixture of hope and longing. "What do you have to lose here?"

Maria paused, her gaze meeting Eric's with a mixture of uncertainty and determination. She knew that her life at the Minerva Inn offered little in the way of security or fulfillment, her days filled with the monotony of serving ale to rough sailors and enduring their leering advances. And yet, the thought of leaving behind the familiar comforts of home filled her with a sense of apprehension.

She did not have much, but she had more than some. Then she reconsidered.

"I have indeed nothing to lose," Maria replied, her voice saturated with resignation. "Other than being manhandled by rough sailors every day," she added with a rueful smile.

Eric's expression softened, his eyes brimming with empathy as he reached out to brush a stray lock of hair from Maria's face. "You deserve better than that," he said earnestly. "Come with me, Maria. Together, we can forge a new life for ourselves—a life filled with adventure and possibility."

Maria hesitated, torn between the safety of the life she knew and the tantalizing allure of the unknown. But as she looked into Eric's eyes, she saw a reflection of her own hopes and dreams—the promise of a future defined not by the constraints of society, but by the boundless potential of their shared journey.

With a nod of determination, Maria made her decision. "Yes," she said softly, her voice filled with newfound resolve. "I'll come with you, Eric. Let's see what lies ahead, together."

As the morning sun cast its rays over the bustling harbor of Plymouth, the innkeeper's insistent knocking broke through the tranquility of Eric and Maria's tender embrace. With a sigh, Maria reluctantly rose from the comfort of their shared bed, knowing that the reality of their situation could not be ignored.

Opening the door, she was met by the stern gaze of the innkeeper, who demanded payment for the week's rent with an air of impatience. But before Maria could respond, Eric stepped forward, his hand reaching into his pocket to produce two shining Shillings, which he promptly dropped into the innkeeper's outstretched hand.

"There you go," Eric said with a charming smile, his eyes twinkling with mischief as he ushered Maria past the bemused innkeeper and out into the crisp morning air.

Together, they made their way to the docks to meet with a weathered captain who was eager to sell his ship—a small 39-foot lugger called Hawk, with a single mast, perfectly suited to their needs.

As they inspected the vessel, Maria couldn't help but feel a sense of excitement building within her chest. The ship may have been modest in size, but it held the promise of freedom and adventure that she had longed for all her life.

After a brief negotiation, Eric and the captain reached an agreement on a price of £250—an investment that would set them on a course toward a future filled with possibility and opportunity.

With the deal sealed, Eric turned to Maria with a grin, his eyes shining with anticipation. "Well, Maria," he said, extending his hand to her. "Are you ready to set sail on our new adventure?"

Maria's heart swelled with excitement as she took Eric's hand in hers, her gaze fixed on the horizon as she nodded eagerly. "I am, Eric," she replied with a smile. "Let's make some waves."

As Maria settled into the cramped captain's cabin of the small ship, Eric wasted no time in setting his plans into motion. With a sense of purpose burning bright within him, he made his way to The Pennycomequick Pub—a sinister establishment nestled close to the imposing walls of the old Devonport prison.

There, amidst the dimly lit interior of the pub, Eric reunited with two men from his old smuggler's crew, who had served time with him in the notorious Newgate Prison of London. Alongside them were two sailors who had recently been released from the confines of Devonport prison, their eyes filled with a hunger for opportunity.

"I have a ship," Eric explained, his voice low and measured as he outlined his plan. "A small 39-foot lugger. It's fast and has a shallow draft. And it's armed with two guns."

The cutthroat sailors nodded in understanding, their expressions hardened by years of hardship and adversity. But as Eric laid out his proposal, their interest was piqued, their eyes gleaming with the promise of riches and freedom.

"What's in it for us, Eric?" his old mate Tom asked, his voice tinged with skepticism.

"We will prey on merchants in the Irish seas," Eric replied, his tone unwavering. "And split the proceeds. I will take 40 parts of the booty for me and the ship, and the crew splits 60 parts."

The sailors, weary of the constant threat of impressment by the Royal Navy, weighed their options carefully. But in the end, the allure of adventure and the promise of riches proved too tempting to resist, and they agreed to join Eric's crew without hesitation.

With Eric at the helm and his newly assembled crew by his side, the ship was ready to set sail on a voyage that would take them beyond the confines of the law and into the treacherous waters of the Irish seas. And as they prepared to embark on their daring adventure, Maria's presence aboard the ship raised questions.

As Eric's crew gathered on deck, their eyes turned to Maria with a mixture of curiosity and skepticism. One man, voicing the unspoken question that lingered in the air, asked bluntly, "Why do we have a wench on board?"

Eric, recognizing the potential for discord that a single female presence could bring aboard a ship, especially among a crew of rough sailors, chose his words carefully.

With a steady gaze, he replied, "That is not a wench, it is Maria Cobham, my wife. She will cook for us and will be a part of the crew."

The sailors exchanged glances, their expressions shifting from uncertainty to understanding. The prospect of having decent rations and a capable cook on board outweighed any concerns they may have had about having a woman among their ranks. With a collective nod of agreement, they accepted Maria's presence as a valuable addition to the crew.

And so, with Maria officially welcomed into the fold, Eric's crew prepared to set sail on their daring adventure, united by a common purpose and a shared determination to seize their destiny on the seas. As the ship slipped away from the safety of the harbor and into the vast expanse of the open ocean, Maria's presence served as a beacon of stability amidst the uncertainty of their journey, a reminder that even in the face of adversity, they were stronger together than they could ever be apart.

The Hawk sailed, her water barrels filled and her pantry well-stocked. Soon, her sleek hull cut through the choppy waters of the English coast. Eric and his crew had embarked on a daring voyage. Guided by the steady hand of their captain and fueled by the promise of adventure that lay ahead, they charted a course eastward around Land's End, the rugged coastline of Cornwall fading into the distance behind them.

With the wind at their backs, they turned northward toward the coast of Wales, the towering cliffs and sweeping vistas serving as a dramatic backdrop to their journey. As the sun dipped low on the horizon, casting a fiery glow over the sea, the crew of the Hawk worked tirelessly to keep her course true, their eyes fixed on the distant horizon and the promise of the Irish Sea beyond.

They sailed onward into the gathering darkness, and the thrill of the unknown coursed through their veins, driving them ever forward toward their destiny. And as the first stars began to twinkle in the night sky, casting their silver light upon the restless waves, Eric and Maria knew that their adventure had only just begun.

When evening descended upon the Hawk, Maria set to work in the ship's cramped galley, her skilled hands weaving culinary magic as she prepared a hearty meal for Eric and the four sailors. The savory aroma of stew filled the air, mingling with the salty tang of the sea as it wafted through the small confines of the ship.

Maria served up with a warm smile, her eyes alight with pride as she watched the hungry sailors eagerly dig in. The hearty fare was well received, the sound of satisfied murmurs filling the air as they savored each mouthful with gusto.

Once the meal was finished and the crew's bellies were full, Maria withdrew into the tiny captain's cabin, seeking refuge from the chill of the night air.

As Eric stepped into the cozy cabin, his eyes fell upon Maria reclining on the modest single bed tucked into the corner. She lay on her back, her legs stretched outwards, straddling the wooden panels that flanked the alcove on either side. Her thighs were exposed.

Moving closer, Eric approached Maria, his presence filling the room. With a gentle touch, he shifted the pillows on the bed and joined her, turning her body slightly. Her feet now dangled over the edge of the bed, her toes curling over the wooden frame.

Through the soft fabric of her cotton night dress, Eric delicately placed two fingers of his right hand between her legs, a silent gesture of connection and intimacy in the quiet sanctuary of the cabin.

Eric's movements became more deliberate as he closed the distance between them, his body shifting above Maria's. With tender care, he reached out and brushed his fingertips against her breasts, tracing the contours of her features with a gentle caress, as he slipped into her ripping-wet vulva.

Soon, enveloped in the warmth of each other's embrace, the couple drifted into a peaceful slumber, their bodies entwined on the snug confines of the cushioned space provided by the small bed. As the soft glow of moonlight filtered through the window, casting gentle shadows upon their intertwined forms, Eric and Maria were lulled into dreams by the rhythm of their beating hearts.

The sea roared around them as Captain Eric's ship sliced through the waves of the Irish Sea, a predator seeking its prey. The crew's eyes were sharp, scanning the horizon for any signs of a lucrative target. But it wasn't just wealth they sought; it was the thrill of the chase, the rush of the plunder, that drove them forward.

After days of fruitless searching, Captain Cobham's keen instincts led him to order a change of course. They set sail toward St. Davids on the Pembrokeshire Coast, hoping to intercept unsuspecting vessels along the way. But there was no ship in sight, other than a few fishing boats. Then, with the taste of potential riches still lingering, they turned southward, eager to prowl the waters of the Bristol Channel.

It was on the sixth day that fortune smiled upon them. Silhouetted against the horizon, like a prize waiting to be claimed, was the unmistakable outline of an East Indiaman, laden with cargo and moving sluggishly through the water, trying to make its way to the busy port of Bristol. The crew licked their lips in anticipation, their eyes gleaming with greed.

The vessel moved at a sluggish pace, visibly burdened by its cargo, boasting a substantial tonnage of over 300 tons. As dusk descended, the ship began to veer eastward, navigating approximately two miles off the coast of Hartland Point. The Hawk, a considerably faster ship, swiftly closed the distance, unleashing a shot from one of her two cannons at a mere 60-yard range.

As the sun dipped below the horizon, casting an orange hue over the sea, the Hawk closed in on her prey. With practiced precision, they unleashed another shot from one of their guns, the sound of cannon fire echoing across the waves. The East Indiaman, unarmed and defenseless, was caught off guard.

Howard, a seasoned member of Captain Cobham's crew, led the daring boarding party onto the merchant ship. But to their surprise, they were met not only with frightened crewmen but also witnessed Maria, now with the appearance of a fierce woman brandishing a cutlass and a pistol. She had joined the pirates on their raid of the merchant ship.

Defenseless and unarmed, the Indiaman found itself at the mercy of Eric, Maria and their four companions, who had thrown grappling hooks onto the ship's rigging and boarded the vessel. Stricken by misfortune, the merchant ship housed a mere ten crew members, with the majority having succumbed to a fever during their voyage along the treacherous Coast of Africa.

With swift efficiency, they subdued the remaining crew, binding them and the captain as they set about raiding the cargo holds. The hold was a treasure trove, filled to the brim with exotic goods from distant lands. Silk, spices, and precious metals gleamed in the dim light, a testament to the wealth of the East India Company.

As the crew set about pillaging the cargo, Maria fixed her

gaze upon the captain. "I'm aware that there's gold aboard this vessel. Where is it?" she demanded, brandishing a small dagger beneath his chin.

"There's no gold, I swear it," the captain protested.

"Let's make a deal," Maria proposed, her tone cold and unwavering. "You disclose the whereabouts of the gold, and we'll allow you to sail away unharmed. But if you deceive us and we discover the gold later, we'll scuttle this ship with you still aboard."

Despite the captain's continued denials, Maria remained unconvinced. The small crew of the Hawk, assisted by 2 sailors from the East Indiaman, loaded up their small vessel with looted goods. Determined to unearth the truth, Maria ventured below deck into the captain's cabin, methodically overturning every conceivable hiding spot.

Suddenly, a faint creaking noise caught her attention as she inadvertently stepped on a loose plank. With swift precision, she pried the plank away, revealing a concealed compartment housing an iron box brimming with thousands of gleaming gold coins. Yet, her discovery didn't end there; nestled alongside the gold lay another trunk, this one laden with shimmering silver. Maria's eyes widened with satisfaction as she realized the extent of their bounty, knowing that their fortunes had just taken a lucrative turn.

"Come on down," Maria beckoned to Eric, who was

overseeing the loading process. "Take a look at this."

Eric's eyes widened as he beheld the treasure before him. "This looks like thousands of pounds. You've outdone yourself, my love," he exclaimed with a mix of awe and admiration.

"I knew he was lying, I just knew it," Maria smiled.

With efficient coordination, they began transferring the plundered gold and silver onto their small vessel, each clinking coin and gleaming ingot a witness to their successful endeavor. Once the transfer was complete, they turned their attention to the East Indiaman, its fate sealed by their actions.

Without hesitation, the crew of the Hawk punctured holes in the hull of the now-desolate vessel, ensuring it would soon find its resting place at the bottom of the sea. As the water began to flood in, engulfing everything in its path, including the stubborn crew who had dared to oppose them, Maria and Eric watched with a sense of grim satisfaction, knowing that they had emerged victorious and enriched from their daring exploits.

"Dead cats don't meow, I guess," Eric muttered as he turned around to attend to his ship.

As the pirates gathered around the table aboard their small ship, Maria treated them to a hearty dinner complemented by rum salvaged from the sunken East Indiaman. The mood was jovial, filled with the comradeship of shared triumph and the anticipation of new-found and ill-gotten wealth.

"Let's set sail for Plymouth and offload this treasure," one enthusiastic sailor declared.

But Eric, ever the pragmatist, interjected with caution. "Selling this cargo in England poses too great a risk. By now, news of the Indiaman's disappearance has likely reached our ports. Any attempt to sell its cargo would raise suspicion."

A chorus of concern rippled through the crew. "What's our plan then?" another sailor queried.

"We need to make for a port on the mainland," Eric explained, his tone resolute. "We'll dispose of the cargo there and return with only the gold and silver. I've no desire to face the gallows in England, or to see Newgate Prison from the inside ever again."

The sailors nodded in agreement, recognizing the wisdom in Eric's strategy. With their course of action decided, the ship set sail for Gibraltar, a strategic waypoint on their journey to Marseille along the French coast. In the French port, Eric knew from his captain on the smuggler's ship he once sailed, there were traders who asked no questions about the provenance of goods.

Eight days later, after navigating the waters of the Bay of Biscay, clearing Gibraltar, then traversing the Mediterranean, and evading any potential pursuers, the ship finally arrived at its destination. The crew wasted no time in offloading their illicit cargo, exchanging it for gold and silver that would fetch a handsome price without attracting unwanted attention. As they sailed away from Marseille, their pockets heavier and their consciences lighter, they knew they had successfully evaded the long arm of the law, at least for now.

As Eric and Maria strolled through the busy port of Marseille, their eyes alighted upon a modest shop bearing the sign *Courtier en Fret* - Cargo Brokers. Eager to explore their options, they stepped inside, where they were greeted by a Frenchman who spoke English with admirable fluency. Accompanied by the broker, they made their way back to the Hawk, where the cargo was meticulously assessed and tallied by the experienced man.

After a thorough evaluation, the broker extended an offer: £15,000 for the precious cargo from India, coupled with the bounty of gold and silver coins, their total earnings amounted to a staggering £40,000.

Gathering his crew together, Eric addressed them with a proposition.

"Lads. We now possess a total of £40,000," he began. "If I were to distribute each of your shares now, you'd each walk away with £6,000 upon our return to Plymouth. That's a handsome sum, no doubt. However, I urge you to consider an alternative. I propose that each of you receives an advance of £1,500 immediately, and together, we invest in a new ship back home. Let's put it to a vote."

The crew deliberated amongst themselves, weighing the options before them. Would they opt for immediate gratification, or would they seize the opportunity to secure a more prosperous future? The decision hung in the balance, awaiting the outcome of their democratic process.

After careful consideration, the sailors weighed their options, cognizant of the fact that while £6,000 would certainly provide a significant windfall, it might not guarantee lasting financial security for the remainder of their lives. With this in mind, they recognized the potential for greater long-term prosperity in Eric's proposal of investing in a larger vessel.

Taking into account the potential for expanded opportunities and increased earnings afforded by a new ship, each sailor cast their vote in favor of the collective investment. While the allure of immediate wealth was undeniable, they understood the wisdom in prioritizing future stability and growth over fleeting riches.

Two weeks later, the Hawk glided into the familiar harbor of Plymouth once more, its sails billowing in the salty breeze. True to his word, Eric and Maria disbursed the agreed-upon sum of £1,500 to each member of the crew, fulfilling their part of the bargain.

A new, unanimous decision had been reached. The crew

stood united in their resolve to embark on a new venture together, trusting in the promise of greater fortunes that lay ahead aboard their larger vessel.

With their earnings securely in hand, Eric and Maria wasted no time in seeking out the Minerva Inn, the familiar place steeped in memories of their former lives. However, this time, Maria entered the establishment not as a humble bar wench, but as a patron in her own right, her stature transformed by the success of their recent endeavors.

As they approached the inn, the innkeeper's surprise was palpable at the sight of Maria, now exuding an air of confidence and prosperity. Without hesitation, Eric and Maria secured a room -the largest at the inn- for themselves, eager to rest and regroup after their journey, their newfound status as successful entrepreneurs marking a significant milestone in their shared journey.

Soon, Maria walked down the cobbled street, her steps echoing softly against the ancient stones. She made her way to a modest bathhouse nestled discreetly between two buildings, its sign swaying gently in the breeze. Pushing open the heavy wooden door, she stepped inside, greeted by the warm embrace of steam and the faint scent of lavender.

An hour passed, during which Maria found herself in a small, dimly lit room, the air heavy with humidity. She stood there, completely unclothed, her skin bathed in the soft glow of candlelight and hot water. It was perhaps an imprudent choice, knowing there were male guests bathing in the nearby rooms, but Maria paid it no mind. Then, all that mattered was her own pleasure. Soon, her steps lead her back to the Minerva, where Eric lay on the bed without any clothes on.

With a graceful movement, Maria slipped into bed beside Eric. She turned to him, her breasts bared, a silent invitation hanging in the air. Eric, sensing her desire, responded eagerly, allowing himself to be swept up in the passion of the moment.

He began by exploring her breasts with his mouth, tracing delicate patterns across her skin as if he were an artist painting a masterpiece. Maria surrendered herself to the sensations, her hands weaving through his hair, her breath coming in soft, ragged gasps.

Eric began to probe her with a sense of urgency, swiftly immersing himself in the intricate wetness of her labia. As he traced his fingers through her lips, he found himself captivated by the delicate fragrance from the bath that enveloped her, a heady blend of jasmine and rose.

But as his attention lingered on her hair, he felt a subtle shift in her demeanor. Her thighs spread wider, a silent indication of her growing impatience, urging him to redirect his focus to where she desired it most.

As their lovemaking intensified, Maria's thighs tightened

in a silent protest, prompting her to sit up and grasp Eric's face in her hands. "Just do it," she whispered, her voice husky with desire, her eyes smoldering with passion. And at that moment, words became unnecessary as they surrendered themselves to the primal rhythm of their bodies entwined in ecstasy.

The morning sun cast a golden glow over the foggy streets of the harbor town as Eric and Maria sat down for a hearty breakfast at the Minerva Inn. The aroma of freshly baked bread and sizzling bacon filled the air, invigorating their senses as they savored the simple pleasures of a hot meal after the night's embraces.

Their conversation was lively as they discussed their plans for the day ahead. With the profits from their latest venture weighing heavy in their pockets, they were determined to make the most of their newfound wealth. Their first order of business: selling off their current ship, The Hawk, and acquiring something bigger, faster, and more formidable. Something that could hold a lot of cargo, but would also be fast enough to escape into shallow waters where the warships of the Royal Navy could not go.

Leaving the comfort of the inn behind, they made their way to the harbor. It didn't take long for word to spread that Captain Eric and Maria were in the market for a new vessel, and offers came flooding in from eager sellers.

One captain, in particular, caught Eric's eye. He had a

ship named The Vixen for sale down at the docks. The seller presented a sleek schooner to Eric and Maria, 70 feet in length and nearly new, with a shallow draft, which was ideal for navigating the treacherous waters of coastal channels and estuaries. The ship boasted impressive cargo capacity, capable of carrying 190 tons while still maintaining remarkable speed with a minimal crew.

Negotiations ensued, with Eric haggling fiercely to secure the best possible deal. The captain initially demanded £30,000 for the schooner, but Eric's shrewd bargaining skills saw the price lowered to £20,000, with him ultimately agreeing to part with £22,000 to seal the deal.

With the transaction complete, Eric wasted no time in investing further in their new acquisition. As Maria walked back to the Minerva, he sought out a ship outfitter and commissioned the installation of ten naval guns, strategically positioned to maximize firepower and ensure their dominance on the high seas. Four 16-pounders would be mounted on each side of the main deck, with a formidable 8-pounder placed at the rear and the stern each, ready to repel any would-be attackers from the back and front.

The Minerva Inn buzzed with activity as Maria stepped through its weathered doors, the familiar scent of ale and tobacco swirling in the air. She had come for a moment of respite, seeking solace from the chaos of the world outside. But her brief reprieve was shattered when she found herself accosted by none other than Captain Percy, a notorious figure among the pubs at the ports of the Southern Coast.

Percy, with his grizzled countenance and reputation for violence, was no stranger to the inn's corridors either. He was an old Liverpool captain, commanding a sizeable brig, The Lion, and was known for manhandling and beating wenches at the pubs if they would not entertain him. His presence sent a shiver down Maria's spine, and she instinctively recoiled as he pulled her into a dimly lit hallway, his intentions clear. But Maria, emboldened by her newfound status as an apparently married woman, refused to succumb to his advances.

"I am not a bar wench anymore, Captain," she protested, her voice tinged with defiance. "I am a wife now, and my husband will not be amused by your advances."

But Percy was undeterred, his grip tightening on her arm as he attempted to force himself upon her. "Ah, to hell with your bloody husband, he knew he married a harlot, I suppose," the captain snickered.

"Have you no shame, Captain? At any minute patrons could walk in," Maria exclaimed.

"Why suddenly so full of shame, you dirty sloven," the captain replied with anger.

Maria's instincts set in, and with a swift kick, she lashed out, catching the captain off guard, and landing her foot between his legs. The assailant hesitated for a split second. Bu then, in retaliation, Percy struck her with a brutal blow, leaving a painful mark as a cruel reminder of his dominance.

"Don't be so feisty, you filthy wench," he snarled, his words dripping with contempt. "You won't fool me. Once a pub harlot, always a pub harlot."

Suddenly, the captain froze. From behind, a man had approached him, and the tip of a sharp dagger was suddenly visible on his neck, puncturing the captain's throat just a bit, drawing a tiny amount of blood. Just as Maria feared the worst, salvation had arrived in the form of Eric. With a steely resolve, he had intervened, his presence commanding respect as he brandished the sharp dagger which normally rested securely in his boot. The weapon's glinting blade was now pushed firmly against Captain Percy's throat.

"Let go of my wife, drop your weapons," Eric's voice was firm, his gaze unwavering. "I could end your life here, Captain. But I will be merciful, as I do not wish to be charged with cleaning up the mess of your blood in the hallway."

Though his words were laced with menace, Eric knew the consequences of taking a life, especially within the boundaries of the city. With their plans to set sail looming on the horizon, they could ill afford the scrutiny of a lengthy investigation, which would certainly raise questions about the provenience of Eric's newfound fortune.

"Hold still, Sir, no offense, I will be on my ship and off to Newfoundland in the morning," Percy now muttered.

Reluctantly, Captain Percy backed away as Eric's blade eased off his throat. As soon as Percy believed himself in a safe distance, the old captain's face contorted with rage as he spat curses at Maria and Eric.

"You wench, I will surely see you again, and I will gut you both alive," he threatened, his words echoing down the hallway like a dark omen.

As Percy picked up his cutlass and slunk away into the shadows, Maria clung to Eric, her heart racing with a mixture of fear and relief. Together, they now stood united against the dangers that lurked in the murky depths of the seafaring realm, their bond now stronger than ever, as they prepared to face the challenges that lay ahead on their journey into the dangerous world of piracy.

# 3 THE VIXEN

Weeks passed by, but eventually, the day arrived when the guns were installed on The Vixen. As the sun reached its zenith in the sky, Eric and Maria stood proudly aboard their newly acquired schooner, their eyes sparkling with anticipation for the adventures that lay ahead. With their pockets full, their ship armed to the teeth, and the wind at their backs, they were ready to embark on their next daring escapade, forging their destiny on the unforgiving sea. They moved their few belongings onto the ship, and Eric started looking for a larger crew. He now needed to hire 6 more sailors.

Their first night on the schooner was nothing short of luxurious. Eric had invested a good amount of money to make this cabin home for himself and Maria. The captain's cabin, a vast expanse compared to their cramped quarters on board the Hawk, enveloped them in comfort and opulence. The spaciousness was staggering, with ample room for a double bed, expertly crafted by a skilled carpenter at Eric's request.

In one corner of the cabin stood a stately writing desk, where Eric could attend to his duties as captain with ease. A large chart table occupied the center of the room, its surface adorned with navigational maps and tools, a testament to the meticulous planning that lay ahead of them. To one side, a small wash closet provided the convenience of freshening up without having to venture far from the comforts of their cabin.

Maria had brought two bottles of Spanish wine from the inn, their deep red contents adding a warm glow to the intimate atmosphere of their cabin aboard The Vixen. As they savored the rich flavors of the wine, the air between them crackled with anticipation, fueled by the shared excitement of their new adventure and the undeniable chemistry that simmered beneath the surface.

With a gentle touch, Maria leaned in to kiss Eric, her lips meeting his with a passion that ignited a fire within them both. Eric responded eagerly, his hands moving with purpose as he guided her, his touch deliberate yet tender, each caressing a symphony of desire and longing.

Eric's touch seared her skin, sending shivers down her spine, while his cool fingertips trailed along her legs as he deftly undid the buttons of her dress. Each movement was electric, sending waves of anticipation through her body. Despite the dizzying sensation threatening to overwhelm her, she remained steadfast, her senses heightened by the intensity of his touch. With a confidence that bordered on arrogance, Eric explored her body with an expert touch, his hands tracing the curves of her form with practiced precision. Maria surrendered to his touch, her senses overwhelmed by the intensity of their connection, the sheer force of his desire leaving her breathless and exhilarated.

He opened his pants. As they fell away, revealing his hardened desire, she felt a surge of arousal coursing through her veins. Without hesitation, she reached out, her hand trembling slightly as she grasped him firmly. In mere moments, he shifted her position, rolling her over and entering her once more, as though the brief pause were merely a prelude to their fervent union. This time, her response is unrestrained, her passion unleashed in full force, as she screamed under his thrusts. The sturdy captain's bed beneath them creaks and strains under their fervent movements, bearing witness to the intensity of their union.

As her breath quickened, she became consumed by a primal need, her body arching with abandon as waves of pleasure washed over her. With each powerful thrust, he delved deeper into her, igniting a fiery passion that left them both utterly consumed by desire. Bracing himself against the wall for support, he hooked his knees outside her legs, driving himself further into her, lost in the intoxicating ecstasy of their union.

In the heat of the moment, Maria found herself swept away by the intensity of their fusion, her body responding to his with a fervor she had never known. With a shudder of release, she surrendered to the pleasure that enveloped her, her senses overwhelmed by the sheer force of their connection.

Eric and Maria came together; the boundaries between them were blurred. With each movement, Eric led her to the edge of ecstasy and back again, a master of his craft, his hips made known to the raw power that pulsed through him.

As they sunk into the sheets, spent and sated in each other's arms, the world outside faded into insignificance, their shared intimacy a sanctuary from the chaos of the world. With a tender kiss on her cheek, Eric whispered a soft goodnight before drifting off to sleep, leaving Maria to bask in the afterglow of their passion, her heart full and her spirit soaring on the wings of their love. Their new ship had become their home.

They lay embraced in their new surroundings, and Maria couldn't help but marvel at the transformation. Gone were the days of cramped quarters and rough living; now, they were captains of their destiny, sailing toward new horizons aboard the magnificent Vixen. And as they drifted off to sleep that night, the gentle sway of the ship beneath them whispered promises of adventure and freedom.

The following morning, Eric embarked on a quest to assemble a new crew. While the four sailors from the Hawk awaited a new adventure, he still needed six more.

Once more, he ventured to the dark taverns of Plymouth, starting with the Pennycomequick Pub, the place where those released from the King's prison would often hang out. Within half a day, he had successfully recruited five additional sailors. It was at the Fisherman's Arms pub where he encountered the sixth recruit, a weathered seaman who had served as a quartermaster in the Royal Navy, and had recently been discharged from the King's Devonport prison.

Approaching the seasoned sailor, Eric initiated the conversation. "Recently set free from the King's prison, I hear," he remarked.

"If that's what they say, it may very well be so," the sailor responded curtly.

"Captain Eric Cobham," Eric introduced himself.

"James Bancroft," the sailor replied in kind. Bancroft bore the countenance of a man who had weathered storms both at sea and in life. His face, etched with lines of experience, told stories of battles fought in his time in the Royal Navy, and hardships endured. Sun-weathered skin hinted at long days spent under the harsh glare of the maritime sun, while his salt-and-pepper beard spoke of years spent at sea.

His eyes, deep and piercing, held a quiet intensity, betraying a wisdom gained from a life lived on the edge of danger. Despite the weariness that clung to him like a second skin, there was a resilience in his gaze, a spark of determination that refused to be extinguished.

Clad in worn sailor's garb, James moved with the sure-footed grace of a man who had spent a lifetime on deck. Every movement spoke of a quiet strength and confidence, honed through years of navigating treacherous waters and facing down formidable foes.

Though his years in the King's prison had left their mark, James Bancroft remained a formidable presence, a seasoned sailor ready to brave the high seas once more.

Curiosity piqued, Eric inquired, "What were you in the brig for, James?"

"Killing a man in anger," James replied bluntly. "He beat a wench and I went in between. I laid him out after he attacked me."

Undeterred, Eric stated, "I am in need of an experienced quartermaster for my ship, The Vixen, a 70 ft. schooner with 10 guns."

Eyeing Eric with interest, James asked, "Where is she headed to?"

"The Channel, at first, perhaps the Bay of Biscay later, depending on where the King's ships patrol most," Eric replied with a smile.

"I take it she isn't an ordinary merchant, with 10 guns and that route", the old sailor smirked.

"No, she isn't. Let's say we are looking for cargo of other ships. But my raids are lucrative," Eric responded with a smile. "Last time we went out, my men came back with £1,500 each, in less than a month."

"That's more than what I made in my entire career in the Royal Navy," Bancroft replied, a hint of surprise mingling with admiration in his voice. With a wry smirk playing on his lips, he extended his weathered hand to Eric and gave it a firm shake.

"I am on board, Captain," he declared, his tone resolute and determined. At that moment, it was clear that James Bancroft was ready to embark on a new chapter of adventure and challenge under Eric's leadership.

At the port, Maria went to purchase provisions for the galley of The Vixen. She knew well that a crew's contentment depended vastly on a full stomach, as well as a heavy purse.

Before Maria made her way back to the ship, she paid a visit to a tailor's shop to commission new attire for herself. As she perused the selection, her gaze settled on a striking blue uniform coat—the very emblem of a Captain in the Royal Navy. Intrigued, she tried it on, only to find it too large for her frame.

"Can you make me two of these, master, but in black wool instead of dark blue? With silver buttons in the front and on the sleeves?" Maria inquired; her voice was resolute despite the tailor's hesitation.

"Certainly, I can," the tailor responded, though he couldn't help but express his concern. "But you must understand, this is a Captain's coat from the Royal Navy, not typically tailored for women."

"Leave that to me," Maria assured him, placing two gold coins on the counter as a sign of her determination. "In addition to the coats, I'll also need five linen blouses, three sets of pantaloons, skirts, and a waistcoat."

Though the tailor shook his head in disbelief, he accepted the payment, recognizing Maria's resolve to have her way. With a mixture of curiosity and reluctance, he began the task of tailoring the unconventional garments according to Maria's specifications.

Maria sauntered back to the ship, her eyes catching a glimpse of a pair of exquisite, small double flintlock pistols displayed in the window of a nearby gunmaker's shop. Intrigued, she stepped inside.

"These are the newest models from France," the gunsmith explained proudly as Maria inspected the pistols, feeling their weight and balance in her hands.

"How much for both of them?" Maria now asked, her interest piqued.

"£30 for both, with gun powder flask, a leather holster for two pistols, and ample ammunition," came the gunsmith's reply.

Maria hesitated at the hefty price tag. "That's enough to outfit an entire crew with guns," she mused aloud.

"True, My Lady," the gunsmith acknowledged, "but consider this – with these double pistols, you have four shots in total, offering a significant advantage in any confrontation. And they're compact and elegant, perfect for a lady such as yourself."

Maria mulled over the offer. "Still a hefty sum for just two guns," she countered. "A musket barely costs £3."

The gunsmith paused, considering Maria's reluctance. "Alright, how about £26, and I'll throw in this lady's dagger with an ivory handle," he proposed, hoping to seal the deal.

After a brief negotiation, Maria emerged from the shop armed with two finely crafted French pistols and a sleek lady's dagger, ready to return to the ship with her newfound treasures.

They were ready to set sail. Maria strolled along the pier, resplendent in her new black captain's uniform. A sailor, sitting on a barrel, couldn't resist taunting her. "You're a wench dressed like a man!" he jeered, his words dripping with mockery.

Unfazed by his remarks, Maria shot back, "What business is it of yours?" The sailor approached, further mocking her appearance.

"This is the most riotous thing I've ever seen," he continued, laughing. "A wench dressed in a captain's uniform? You don't even look like a woman! You look like a lad!"

Maria's anger flared at his insolence. Swiftly, she drew one of her newly acquired pistols from her coat and pressed it firmly under the sailor's chin. "How's that, bigmouth?" she asked, her voice steady despite her rising fury.

"I am more of a man than you will ever be, and I am more of a woman than you will ever have," she hissed. With a confident smile, she delivered a swift kick to the sailor's knee with her heavy boot, causing him to grimace in pain before she turned and walked away, leaving him to ponder his foolishness.

A week had passed since The Vixen had weighed anchor in Plymouth and set sail, her sleek silhouette cutting through the waves of the English Channel with purpose. Captain Cobham and his crew, with a hunger for plunder, were on the prowl for merchant vessels ripe for the taking. However, their plans were soon thwarted by the presence of several Royal Navy ships patrolling the waters, forcing Cobham to rethink their strategy.

With a calculated decision, the captain steered The Vixen

southward, toward the vast expanse of the Bay of Biscay, north of Spain. Here, amidst the rolling waves and endless horizon, they sought out their prey, waiting patiently for unsuspecting vessels to cross their path.

For days on end, the crew crisscrossed the waters north of the Spanish port of A Coruña, their eyes sharp and their senses heightened as they scanned the horizon for any signs of movement. Despite their vigilance, the only ships they spotted were French vessels, their imposing stature and heavy armaments making them formidable adversaries for The Vixen and her crew.

As the days stretched on, fatigue began to set in among the crew, the monotony of waiting taking its toll on their morale. But just as hope began to wane, a glimmer of opportunity appeared on the horizon in the dim morning light—a schooner flying the British flag, its course set northward.

Excitement rippled through the crew as they sprang into action, preparing to intercept their quarry with ruthless efficiency. With the wind at their backs and the thrill of the chase coursing through their veins, they set their sights on their next target, eager to reap the rewards of their exploits.

As the schooner drew closer, its lack of armaments belied the weight it carried, hinting at the valuable cargo nestled within its depths. The Vixen, sleek and menacing, closed the distance under the cover of dawn, its crew poised for action.

On the deck of The Vixen, Maria stood tall in her new black captain's coat, one of her French pistols gleaming in the fading light. With gun ports open and cannons primed, they glided alongside the ponderous merchant vessel, their intentions clear.

Surender, the mate of The Vixen, signaled, but the sailors on the merchant ship stood defiant, armed to the teeth with guns and cutlasses. Undeterred, The Vixen's mate relayed Captain Cobham's offer of mercy, but still, there was no response from the stubborn crew.

"Portside guns, fire!" Eric's command rang out across the deck, and with a deafening roar, The Vixen unleashed a devastating broadside from her formidable 16-pound cannons. The thunderous barrage tore through the air, shredding the mast and sails of the merchant schooner and punching a jagged hole in its hull.

Amidst the chaos, a white flag soon fluttered weakly from the broken mast of the stricken vessel, a silent acknowledgment of defeat. With precision born of years of experience, Eric ordered his crew to throw the grappling hooks, securing their prize and bringing the captured ship under their control.

As they boarded the crippled schooner, the pirates wasted no time in subduing the remaining resistance, their victory assured. With the spoils of their conquest within reach, they set about plundering the cargo hold, their laughter mingling with the creaking of the timbers as they claimed their prize on the unforgiving seas.

Maria stepped onto the deck of the captured ship. A shiver ran down her spine, a cold dread settling in the pit of her stomach. There was something unsettlingly familiar about this vessel, something that stirred memories she had long buried deep within her.

Her heart raced as she read the ship's name, emblazoned in faded letters upon its bow: The Fly. The realization struck her like a thunderbolt, sending shockwaves of horror coursing through her veins. This was no ordinary merchant vessel; it was the ship of Captain Briggs, the man who had deceived her back at the Minerva Inn in Plymouth and had subjected her to unspeakable horrors at the hands of his crew.

Memories flooded back with brutal clarity, about the nightmarish ordeal she had endured at the hands of Briggs and his vile sailors. The betrayal, the violation, the crushing sense of powerlessness—all of it came rushing back, threatening to engulf her in a tidal wave of anguish.

Maria's hands trembled as she stood frozen on the deck, her mind reeling with a maelstrom of emotions. Anger, fear, and a profound sense of betrayal warred within her, each vying for dominance as she grappled with the magnitude of the situation.

Amidst the turmoil, a steely resolve ignited within her, a flickering flame of determination born from the ashes of despair. No longer would she be a victim of her past; no longer would she allow the ghosts of her trauma to haunt her every step.

With a defiant glare, Maria squared her shoulders and steeled herself for the task at hand. Though the sight of The Fly had threatened to unravel her resolve, she refused to be cowed by the demons of her past. With each step forward, pistol in hand, she reclaimed a piece of her strength, her courage burning bright against the darkness that threatened to consume her.

She joined her crewmates in securing the captured ship. Maria's gaze scanned for the captain. She spotted him sitting among his crew, along the reeling with his hands tied, guarded by a pirate.

With steely resolve, Maria stepped forward, her gaze locked on her tormentor. "Having a good day, Captain?" she asked, her voice tinged with a cool detachment.

The old captain, his face twisted into a sneer, glanced up at her. "Best day of my life, it seems," he replied, his tone dripping with arrogance.

"Do you remember me?" Maria pressed, her voice steady despite the roiling emotions within her.

The captain's gaze flickered, and suddenly, recognition seemed to dawn in his eyes. "I do," he admitted grudgingly. "You're the maid I tricked onto my ship back in Plymouth."

He paused, a bead of sweat forming on his brow as the weight of his crimes hung heavy in the air. "And I did far worse than trick you," he added, his voice barely above a whisper.

Maria's jaw clenched with suppressed fury as she stared down at the man who had inflicted so much pain upon her. But beneath the anger, there was a glimmer of satisfaction, a sense of justice finally being served.

With a cold smile, Maria turned away from the captain, leaving him to stew in his guilt and shame. She had faced her demons and emerged victorious, reclaiming her power and her dignity in the process.

As the crew of the Vixen finished unloading the precious cargo from The Fly onto their ship, Maria wasted no time in issuing her commands. Stepping back onto the quarterdeck of the captured vessel, she directed the sailors to take down the main sail and spread it out on the deck.

With efficient precision, the crew of the Vixen followed her orders, unfurling the sail until it lay flat against the wooden planks. Then, with a steely gaze, Maria turned to the sailors of The Fly, her voice cutting through the air like a whip.

"Stand up and lay onto the main sail," she commanded,

pistols in hand, her tone brooking no disobedience.

Without hesitation, the nine sailors and their captain obeyed, arranging themselves on the sail as instructed. But as Maria surveyed the scene before her, her eyes fell upon one young shipmate who had not participated in the encounter on The Fly, back in Plymouth.

"Not you," she said, a hint of recognition softening her voice. "You can join our crew if you wish."

With a sense of satisfaction, Maria watched as the remaining eight men plus the captain of The Fly lay like sardines on the main sail, their faces contorted with fear and confusion.

Captain Briggs, sensing the impending doom, pleaded for mercy, his voice trembling with fear.

"We just wanted to have a little fun that day," he stammered. "You weren't harmed. There is gold hidden in my cabin, I can pay you."

Maria's laughter rang out like a clarion call, her amusement at his pathetic attempts at bargaining evident. With a mocking grin, she tossed two shillings at his feet. "Here, take this," she taunted. "This is all you're worth."

She nodded to her crew, who swiftly lifted the four ends of the sail and tied them together with a rope, ensnaring the sailors within like cats in a sack.

With a flick of her wrist, Maria signaled for the sailors to hoist the sail, their captives dangling precariously over the edge of the ship. And as the sea claimed them with a splash, the sailors screamed and fought, but to no avail. After a minute, the sail was gone, swallowed by the dark green sea.

The captain's gold was found in his cabin, regardless. It was a nice sum totaling almost £2,500. Maria turned her back on The Fly, as another broadside from the guns of the Vixen sent the ship to the bottom of the ocean. Her heart was light with the satisfaction of a debt repaid and justice served. As she returned to her duties aboard the Vixen, her spirit soared with the knowledge that she was no longer a victim, but ready to face whatever challenges lay ahead with unwavering strength.

The Vixen set sail toward Marseille, to sell the plundered cargo; the mood aboard the ship was buoyant with anticipation. Their successful plundering of The Fly had yielded a handsome profit, with the precious cargo fetching another £14,000 at the broker's market, on top of the gold that was pilfered from the captain's cabin of the unfortunate ship. With each sailor's purse now bulging with over £1,000, the crew's spirits soared, their pockets heavy with riches.

Captain Cobham, the mastermind behind their latest conquest, basked in the adulation of his crew, his skill and cunning once again leading them to victory. With a satisfied smile, he steered the ship toward their next destination, his sights set on the fabled West coast of

Africa.

Whispers of ivory and precious goods laden upon ships hailing from Africa tantalized their imaginations, fueling their hunger for more plunder. The promise of untold wealth lay on the horizon, a siren song beckoning them onwards into the unknown.

As the Vixen sliced through the waves, her sails billowing in the wind, the crew's excitement grew with each passing mile.

Night descended upon the ship, casting a warm glow over the deck. The crew gathered in the mess room for a well-deserved meal. The scent of freshly cooked provisions filled the air, mingling with the rich aroma of brandy poured liberally from one of the ill-gotten barrels.

Laughter filled the cramped space as the crew swapped tales of past adventures and shared jests over hearty portions of stew and bread. The brandy flowed freely, warming their spirits and lifting their moods as they reveled in the spoils of their latest conquest.

Amidst the jovial atmosphere, Eric and Maria stole away from the festivities, retreating into the sanctuary of the captain's cabin. Behind closed doors, they found solace in each other's arms, their bond strengthened by the trials they had endured together.

A kiss from Eric, delicately fragile yet bursting with sensation, sent a shiver down Maria's spine, momentarily suspending her sense of self. In that fleeting moment, everything she had ever known about herself seemed irrelevant, overshadowed by the overwhelming rush of sensation that enveloped her.

There were no words, only the smooth caress of their lips against each other, tender and gentle like the playful lick of a kitten. Maria felt herself succumbing to a power beyond her control, a voluntary surrender to the intoxicating allure of Eric's kiss.

They stood together in the middle of the cabin, lost in the timeless dance of giving and receiving kisses, each one a whispered echo of the passion that burned between them. Eric explored her lips, her mouth, her tongue with a fervent hunger, savoring each taste as if committing it to memory.

Maria, her hands trembling with desire, traced the contours of Eric's loins, marveling at the softness of his skin beneath her fingertips. In return, Eric's touch was gentle yet possessive, his fingers sweeping across her thighs, tracing the delicate arc of her pelvis, before allowing his fingers to dive into her.

Surrounded by the hushed intimacy of the cabin, Maria and Eric were lost in each other, their bodies and souls intertwined in a symphony of desire and longing. And as they surrendered themselves to the passion that consumed them, they knew that in each other's arms, they had found a love that transcended time.

As The Vixen sailed forth from the Mediterranean Sea, leaving the iconic silhouette of Gibraltar behind, her prow slicing through the azure waters with purpose, the watchful eyes of her crew scanned the horizon for signs of potential prey. It wasn't long before their keen senses caught sight of a looming presence on the horizon—a massive ship, its imposing bulk hinting at the valuable cargo it carried.

As they drew closer, it became apparent that the ship was a Guineaman, its unarmed state offering a tempting target for the keen crew of The Vixen. With gun ports open and cannons primed, they closed the distance, pulling alongside their unsuspecting quarry with ruthless efficiency.

Despite the irate protests of the ship's captain, the tired crew of his ship put up no fight and surrendered with hands in the air. The men of The Vixen wasted no time in asserting their dominance, overwhelming the outnumbered sailors with ease. With guns trained and swords drawn, they swiftly subdued the crew of 25 men, binding them on deck.

But as they ventured below deck to inspect their prize, a wave of horror washed over the hardened men, accompanied by a stench so vile it turned their stomachs. Rows upon rows of black men, women, and children lay shackled in chains, their hollow eyes staring back at their captors with a mixture of fear and resignation.

The realization hit Maria like a blow to the gut, her heart heavy with despair at the sight of the enslaved. The air was thick with the stench of sweat, urine, and despair and the stench of human suffering hung heavy in the air, threatening to overwhelm her senses. Maria fought to contain the bile rising in her throat.

The Vixen's crew faced a stark truth—a candor that spoke of the depths of human depravity and the brutality of the slave trade. And as they grappled with the enormity of their discovery, Maria, Eric, and their comrades knew that they could not turn a blind eye to the injustice before them.

Below deck, in the suffocating hold, hundreds more enslaved individuals were soon found, crammed together like sardines in a tin, their bodies pressed against one another in the dim light filtering through the cracks in the planks above.

Some of the people looked emaciated. Food and water seemed scarce commodities on this ship. The slave ship's crew, now securely tied up on deck, must have seen the enslaved individuals not as fellow human beings, but as mere cargo to be transported and sold for profit, leaving their weakened bodies wasting away before their eyes.

Among them, there was no distinction between man, woman, or child—all were reduced to mere commodities, shackled and chained, stripped of their humanity and their dignity. Their eyes, hollow with despair, stared into the darkness, haunted by memories of home and loved ones left behind.

The moans and cries of the sick, their bodies wracked with disease, resonated through the hull of the ship. The enslaved clung to whatever scraps of humanity remained within them, some lowering their eyes in fear as the group of pirates entered their realm.

On a wall, two heavy, braided whips were hanging. Any sign of disobedience seemed to have been met with swift and brutal punishment.

The most insidious aspect aboard the Guineaman seemed the mental torment inflicted upon its passengers. Cut off from their homes and their freedom, they were forced to confront the harsh facts of their existence—a reality defined by cruelty, suffering, and hopelessness.

Eric's mind was consumed by questions about the destination of the cursed Guineaman. The timing and trajectory seemed off—too far north for a transatlantic passage to the New World. Could these enslaved individuals be destined for somewhere else?

His brow furrowed in deep contemplation, Eric pondered the possibilities. Perhaps the ship was bound for the Eastern Mediterranean, where demand for labor was high and the slave trade thrived. It would explain the deviation from the usual transatlantic route and the sense of urgency in their journey. Or perhaps even London?

With a resolute command, Eric ordered the crew to turn the ship around and set course for the shore visible in the distance. With practiced efficiency, the men maneuvered the Guineaman toward land, grounding the vessel as high tide approached. The Vixen followed but stayed in deep waters. As the sea receded, the slave ship lay stranded, listing to one side, its fate sealed.

Eric inquired of the captain whether there were any cargo or valuables aboard the ship. The captain adamantly denied it. "Very well," Eric responded firmly. "Release the slaves."

The crew, gripped by fear at the thought of confronting the enslaved individuals they had mistreated, began to plead desperately. "Please, anything but that!" they cried out in distress.

As tensions simmered on the deck of the ship, Eric's demand hung heavy in the air. The crew of the slave ship, their faces etched with fear, pleaded for mercy, their voices trembling with desperation. Even the captain, an arrogant figure of authority, appeared shaken by the gravity of the situation.

But Eric remained resolute, his eyes fixed on the captain as he made his demand.

"Release the slaves," he repeated, his voice firm and unwavering. There could be no compromise, no half-measures—the enslavement of innocent lives could not be tolerated, no matter the cost.

Reluctantly, the captain relented, his resolve crumbling under the weight of Eric's determination. "There is a purse with 2,000 gold coins in my cabin," he admitted, his voice barely above a whisper. It was a meager offering, a pitiful attempt to buy his way out of the impending confrontation.

With a nod from Eric, the quartermaster was dispatched below deck to retrieve the money. As he returned with the purse clutched tightly in his grasp, the crew watched in silent resignation, knowing that their fate was sealed.

With a sense of grim satisfaction, Eric took hold of the purse, his fingers closing around the cool metal coins within. It was a small victory, but a victory nonetheless—a sign that justice would prevail, even in the face of adversity.

Turning to the captain, Eric's gaze was steely as he delivered his final command. "Release the slaves," he said again, his voice echoing with authority. It was his final command. And with that, the chains that bound the enslaved would now be cast aside, their freedom restored at long last.

The crew of The Vixen were hardened pirates, each of them a cutthroat, a thief, and a scoundrel. Some were even murderers. But the pitiful scene below the deck the of the slave ship had softened even their hardened hearts.

With steady hands, the sailors unshackled the enslaved men, women, and children, pulling lengths of chain through their bonds and guiding them up onto the deck.

With resolve, the crew herded the freed slaves onto the deck, signaling for them to make their way ashore. For many of the slaves, the realization that they were finally free was a moment of profound disbelief, their eyes wide with wonder and uncertainty.

Before the liberated stepped into the water to wade ashore, a wave of emotion swept over them, their hearts swelling with gratitude and hope. Some fell to their knees, kissing the ground beneath their feet, while others prostrated themselves before their rescuers, their voices raised in what seemed to be unknown prayers and thanks.

With a sense of closure, Eric ordered his crew to return to The Vixen, leaving the bound crew of the slave ship in the hands of those they had once held captive.

The somber mood aboard The Vixen cast a pall over the ship as it sailed northward. The once jovial atmosphere was now replaced by a reticent silence that weighed heavily upon the hearts of all who sailed upon her decks. Eric and Maria, once inseparable, now found themselves lost in their thoughts, the spark of joy between them extinguished by the weight of what they had just witnessed.

"Do you think God is real?" Maria's voice broke the

silence, her words hanging heavy in the air like a lingering fog.

Eric's response was measured, his tone tinged with bitterness born from years of disappointment and disillusionment. "If God is, I have not seen him, and he hasn't seen me," Eric replied, his voice tinged with resignation.

"My father, a proud man who served in the Royal Navy, lost an arm in battle, leaving him unable to carry out his trade. We were left destitute, forced to scrape by on the meager earnings he could muster by collecting animal dung on the streets of Poole, selling it to local tanneries just to put food on the table."

Maria listened in silence, her heart aching for the hardships Eric had endured in his youth. His plight mirrored her own.

"I once prayed fervently every day," Eric continued, his voice heavy with the weight of his memories.

"Morning and night, I begged God to ease my father's suffering, to lift us out of poverty just a tiny bit. But despite my prayers, it seemed as though we were met with only silence."

Maria nodded in understanding, her faith shaken by the harsh realities of life. "There is no God for people like us," she declared, her voice firm with conviction. "The poor are here to be consumed by the rich."

"If you can spend half a decade on your knees, praying with all your heart, only to be met with the deafening silence of your own echo in your head, then it is clear: there is no God," Eric concluded.

Maria's words hung heavy in the air, each syllable laden with the weight of a lifetime's worth of sorrow and hardship. As she spoke, her voice trembled with the pain of memories long suppressed, her eyes glistening with unshed tears.

"My father, a quartermaster on the King's ship, died at sea when I was barely seven years old," she recounted, her voice barely above a whisper. "Left to fend for ourselves, my brother and I struggled to make ends meet. The meager payments from the King's paymaster ceased, leaving us destitute and alone."

A heavy silence descended upon the room as Maria continued her tale, each word a painful reminder of the cruel hand fate had dealt her family. "My brother, just eleven years old became an apprentice at a bakery, so we had at least bread. But one day, he was taken by a press gang on his way to work, leaving us with nothing," she recounted, her voice tinged with bitterness.

"My mother, once the picture of beauty and grace, was reduced to selling her love to the highest bidder on the streets of Plymouth," Maria continued, her voice cracking with emotion. "For fifteen long years, she walked those harbor streets, her once radiant beauty fading with each passing day."

Tears welled in Maria's eyes as she spoke of her mother, her voice choked with grief. "Weakened by consumption, her body ravaged by disease, she languished in agony, her cries for help falling on deaf ears," she whispered, her heart heavy with regret.

"While others went to school, I worked as a maid cleaning tankards at the inn since age 11. It's a miracle I am even able to read and write. Even then, as a child, I had to fight off the advances of drunk sailors. But it's hard to preserve your honor if someone holds a coin under your nose, and you haven't eaten in two days," she whispered.

"What has become of your mother?" Eric asked.

"Our meager coins could barely afford the services of a quack at the barber shop, let alone a proper doctor," Maria lamented, her voice now barely audible above the sound of her sorrow.

"And so, I watched helplessly as my mother faded away before my eyes, her beauty and spirit extinguished by the cruel hands of fate."

As Maria's words trailed off into silence, the weight of her lot hung heavy in the air, a poignant reminder of the harsh reality on the streets of an English harbor town.

Maria's words echoed with a newfound determination,

her resolve steeling against the injustices of her past. "But now, I won't stand for it anymore," she declared, her voice firm with conviction. "I will take what's mine."

A flicker of defiance danced in her eyes as she spoke, a fire ignited within her soul by the burning desire for justice.

"It feels good when you are suddenly the one beating, and not the one taking the beatings anymore," Maria proclaimed, her words ringing out with a sense of strength.

Eric, moved by her words and determination, rose from his seat and embraced her, pressing a tender kiss to her forehead. Amidst the darkness of the night, the ship sailed onward, guided by the light of the stars above.

# 4 FROM NANTUCKET TO NEWFOUNDLAND

As The Vixen made her way back to the port of Plymouth, a looming silhouette appeared on the horizon—a warship of the line belonging to His Majesty King George's Royal Navy, donning 60 heavy 36-pound guns. With no chance of escape, Captain Cobham and his crew braced themselves for the inevitable encounter.

"What's your destination?" the warship signaled, its imposing presence casting a shadow over The Vixen.

"Captain Cobham commanding the schooner Vixen, empty, on our way to Plymouth to load a cargo of hides," came the reply from The Vixen.

"Stop here, and hold still," the response came swiftly from the warship, leaving the crew of The Vixen with no choice but to comply.

As the warship drew alongside, two officers followed by three men boarded The Vixen, their sharp eyes scanning the empty hull for any sign of stolen cargo. Despite their thorough search, the officers found nothing unusual, the hold of the ship was devoid of any illicit goods. The Vixen's loot had been sold at the harbor of Marseille.

With a curt nod, the officers acknowledged the empty state of The Vixen and made their way back to their vessel. The tension aboard The Vixen eased as the warship departed, leaving Captain Cobham and his crew to continue on their journey unimpeded.

Though the encounter had been fraught with tension, The Vixen emerged unscathed, her reputation untarnished by the scrutiny of His Majesty's Navy. And as she sailed onward toward Plymouth, her crew breathed a sigh of relief, grateful to have escaped unharmed from the watchful gaze of the authorities.

In the aftermath of the encounter, the concern aboard The Vixen was palpable. Eric addressed the gathered crew in the dimly lit mess hall. With the Royal Navy patrolling the waters of the British Channel and the Sea of Ireland fraught with danger, the risks of remaining in European waters were too great to ignore.

"We can continue to skirt the coast of France or linger in the British Channel, but sooner or later, we'll find ourselves staring down the barrels of a warship belonging to His Majesty," Eric warned, his voice grave with concern. The crew murmured in agreement, their expressions reflecting the gravity of the situation.

Drawing upon his own experiences as a young sailor, Eric proposed an alternative course of action.

"As a boy, I sailed the waters of the New World on a fishing vessel. While the hunting grounds there may be treacherous, certain routes remain unprotected by naval patrols," he explained, his words resonating with the gathered sailors.

"We should set sail for the coast of the Americas," Eric concluded, his tone resolute. After a brief discussion amongst themselves, the crew reached a unanimous decision. The risk of encountering pirate hunters and warships in European waters was too great, and the promise of unguarded routes in the New World offered a glimmer of hope amidst the uncertainty that lay ahead.

They stopped one last time in the familiar port of Plymouth to take on water and provisions. Then, Eric set course 285° northwest. With their resolve steeled, the crew of The Vixen prepared to embark on a new chapter of their journey, setting course to the distant shores of the Americas. After 19 days, they arrived at the coast of the New World, dropping anchor in the harbor of Sherburne on an island 30 miles southeast of the city of Boston.

On the remote island, where only a handful of farms dotted the landscape and a solitary pub stood by the harbor, the crew of The Vixen found a welcome respite from their seafaring adventures. Despite the limited amenities, the crew eagerly set about replenishing their provisions and enjoying a well-deserved rest on solid ground.

Maria, standing tall on the quarter-deck of The Vixen, watched with keen interest as a heavy merchant sloop docked nearby, its crew unloading a diverse array of merchandise onto the dock of the quiet harbor. From guns and pots to linen and tools, the cargo held the promise of wealth and opportunity.

Drawing Eric's attention to the scene unfolding before them, Maria proposed a bold idea.

"Look, they are unloading all types of goods," she remarked, her voice tinged with excitement. "They must be getting paid handsomely for their services and sailing away with a fortune in gold."

Eric nodded in agreement, his mind already racing with possibilities. "Perhaps we should follow them when they pull out of the harbor," Maria suggested, her eyes alight with anticipation. "It's always better to take gold than merchandise."

As the sun rose on the following day, Maria made a subtle change in attire, exchanging her black captain's coat for a flowing dress that billowed gently in the sea breeze. With a newfound air of femininity, she strolled purposefully down the pier, her gaze fixed on the merchant sloop that had captured her attention.

Approaching the ship with confidence, Maria engaged in conversation with the captain, her demeanor charming and disarming. "Where do the seas take you, maiden?" the man inquired, his curiosity piqued by Maria's presence.

"We hail from Plymouth and will be setting sail back soon," Maria replied with a winsome smile, her voice carrying a hint of mystery.

"And you, captain?" she continued, turning the conversation back to the man supervising the unloading of his ship. "Where does your journey lead?"

With a grin, the captain leaned in, eager to share his plans. "Ah, we are preparing to depart in three days' time, bound for Bristol," he revealed, his eyes alight with excitement at the prospect of adventure on the open seas.

"I hope your purses will be well-filled when you return home," Maria laughed.

"These trade routes to the New World are very lucrative; our purses will be heavy when returning home," the captain boasted in an attempt to impress the pretty woman.

Maria nodded thoughtfully, her mind already whirring with possibilities. As she bid the sailor farewell and made her way back to The Vixen, a plan began to form in her mind. With the promise of departure looming on the horizon, she knew that the time for action was drawing near, and she was determined to seize the opportunity that lay before her.

In the dimly lit confines of the captain's cabin, Maria, Captain Eric, and Mr. Bancroft, the quartermaster, huddled together, their minds ablaze with the fervent desire to outmaneuver their elusive quarry.

"This sloop is faster than The Vixen, especially when empty," Eric remarked, his brow furrowed with concern. "We need a plan if we're to catch her."

Maria's eyes widened with apprehension as she considered the challenge before them. "What can be done? How are we going to catch her?" she asked, her voice tinged with uncertainty.

James Bancroft, ever the pragmatist, interjected with a suggestion. "We could pull out the night before and wait for her," he proposed, his voice steady with confidence.

Eric's gaze shifted to a map spread out on the table before them, his mind already calculating the possibilities.

"We could lay at Cape Sable Island," he mused aloud, tracing a route with his finger. "She will sail 65° northwest and then alter course at Cape Sable to 53°, I assume. It's the shortest route to Bristol and the safest."

With their plan set in motion, The Vixen sprang into action. Anchor raised and sails unfurled, she cut through the waves with purpose, her crew united in their mission to capture their elusive prey.

As they sailed toward Cape Sable east of Acadia, anticipation hung heavy in the air. With each passing moment, the tension aboard The Vixen grew, each member of the crew keenly aware of the stakes that lay before them.

They finally reached their destination at Cape Sable Island and lay in waiting. The crew of The Vixen braced themselves for the inevitable confrontation that awaited them.

In the harbor, on the morning of day three, the telltale sounds of activity aboard the merchant sloop signaled its imminent departure. As Eric had predicted, the captain set his ship on the shortest and safest course to the Harbor of Bristol, at 65°, planning on altering course around Cape Sable, to cross the North Atlantic.

With the steady south wind propelling them forward at a brisk pace of 14 knots, Eric had calculated that the empty sloop would reach Cape Sable in approximately 48 hours. As the clock struck midnight on the fifth day, the appointed hour had arrived, and Eric wasted no time in issuing his command to the crew, to get The Vixen ready.

"Raise anchor," he ordered, his voice cutting through the

stillness of the night like a clarion call to action.

The crew sprang into motion, their movements synchronized as they worked in tandem to prepare The Vixen for departure. Lines were secured, sails unfurled, and the ship's course set for Cape Sable, the designated rendezvous point for their daring plan.

Soon, The Vixen glided through the moonlit waters, her hull slicing through the waves with effortless grace, the tension aboard the ship was palpable.

As the morning sun cast its golden rays over the waters of the Northern Gulf of Maine, the vigilant lookout stationed atop The Vixen's mast spotted a ship on the horizon, sailing northward just as Eric had predicted. With their quarry in sight, Eric wasted no time in putting their plan into action.

"Set course south," he now commanded, his voice resolute as The Vixen altered her trajectory, zigzagging against the prevailing south wind with expert precision.

The crew adjusted the sails and maneuvered the ship with practiced skill as they raced to intercept the approaching sloop. With each passing moment, the distance between The Vixen and her target grew smaller, the tension aboard the ship mounting with each heartbeat.

As they closed in on their quarry, the crew of The Vixen stood ready, their eyes trained on the ship ahead, anticipation coursing through their veins. With every maneuver, they drew closer and closer, until finally, they had the sloop in a distance of 1/8 of a mile to the port side.

Their prey now within reach, Eric and his crew executed the final phase of their daring plan. The gunports of The Vixen flew open, and a thunderous roar echoed across the waves as she unleashed a devastating broadside from all four starboard guns.

The sloop, caught off guard by the sudden attack, was left reeling as the boom of her mainsail was split in half, sending the sail crashing down onto the deck. A modest hole marred the ship's hull above the waterline, a testament to the destructive power of The Vixen's cannons.

With her speed severely diminished, the sloop now relied solely on her head sail to propel her forward. As The Vixen turned around in pursuit, her crew brimming with anticipation, the gap between the two vessels narrowed again with each passing moment.

With precision and skill, grappling hooks flew from The Vixen, latching onto the sloop's deck as the pirate crew boarded their prey. Among them stood Maria, her presence commanding respect as she set foot on the deck, a pistol gripped firmly in her hand.

To their surprise, the merchant crew offered no resistance, their faces etched with defeat as they realized the futility of defiance. With little effort, Eric and Maria soon uncovered an expected but well-hidden stash of gold and silver coins in a secret compartment of the captain's cabin, a glittering treasure trove worth over £8,000.

With the sloop now stripped of her valuable cargo and rendered incapacitated by the cutting of her tiller ropes, the pirates departed, leaving the empty vessel to drift aimlessly upon the waves. Though they left the sloop behind, her fate sealed by their actions, the crew of The Vixen sailed on, their spirits buoyed by the promise of more wealth.

Their purses were heavy with newfound gold, and the crew of The Vixen now faced a tantalizing question: where to venture next in pursuit of further riches? The waters of England were too dangerous. It was only a matter of time until they would face an English warship there, either sending them to the bottom of the ocean, or to the gallows.

The harbor of Boston was busy, perhaps too busy, and the coast of the mainland was too sprawled out to guarantee a permanent supply of ships. Eric, drawing upon his childhood experiences sailing the waters of Newfoundland as a pressed deckhand on board a fishing vessel based in his hometown of Poole, recalled the bustling trade routes that crisscrossed the region.

"Between Cape Breton and the southern tip of the Island

of Newfoundland, there lies a narrow gap of merely 110 miles," Eric explained to his eager crew, his eyes alight with the prospect of adventure.

"There is the Cabot Strait going between. This is the main thoroughfare for all sea traffic to and from Europe, with ships from France and England delivering wares and returning with valuable cargo of fur and other goods bound for Europe. It's a never-ending supply of ships. Then, there is the Strait of Belle Isle, coming down from the northern tip of Newfoundland as well."

"Are there plenty of ports to get rid of cargo," James, the quartermaster asked.

"There's Port aux Basques on the southern tip of Newfoundland, many harbors along the coast of Cape Breton Island, and plenty of smaller ones scattered along the coastline of Newfoundland," Eric elucidated, his voice carrying a note of excitement. "And let's not forget about the French city of Quebec, situated upstream along the St. Lawrence River."

As he spoke, the crew of The Vixen listened intently, their imaginations ignited by the prospect of the myriad opportunities that lay ahead. With each destination offering more potential for plunder and adventure, the possibilities seemed endless.

"How far is all that from here? How long will it take us to get there?" Maria asked.

"We are less than 400 miles away from these thronging trade routes, four or five days, perhaps even less with the current favorable winds," Eric continued, his voice brimming with excitement as his finger showed the spot on a map laid out on the table.

"If we sail north and find a suitable hiding spot along the shores of Newfoundland, we can lie in wait and prey upon these unsuspecting ships. They will pretty much sail into our traps, without us having to cruise for prey."

The crew nodded in agreement, their spirits buoyed by the promise of further plunder and adventure.

"We'll need to carefully consider our options and choose our hiding spot wisely, a place where French warships cannot go," Eric continued, his gaze sweeping over the eager faces of his crew.

"But one thing is for certain: wherever we decide to make landfall, there will be no shortage of opportunities for us to reap the rewards of our endeavors. I can guarantee you that."

With their course set and their destination in mind, The Vixen surged forward, her crew united in their determination to seek out fortune and glory on the untamed shores of the Gulf of Saint Lawrence. En route to the northern reaches of Newfoundland, The Vixen forged ahead, her sails billowing in the wind as she embarked on a new chapter.

As The Vixen sailed northward along the rugged coastline, her crew keeping a keen eye out for any signs of a suitable hiding spot, they soon reached the northern tip of Cape Breton on the third day of their journey. Crossing over to the Island of Newfoundland, their hopes were high as they scanned the horizon for any signs of potential prey.

Within hours, their diligence was rewarded as they spotted three ships heading southward, confirming Captain Eric's earlier assertions about the bustling trade route in the area. The sailors knew now that their captain hadn't lied when he was predicting plenty of prey. With renewed determination, the ship continued its journey northward, their anticipation growing with each passing moment.

Navigating the treacherous waters along the western coastline, The Vixen's crew remained vigilant, their eyes peeled for any signs of danger lurking beneath the surface. With their shallow 8-foot draft providing them with a clear advantage, they pressed on, their hearts set on finding a secure hiding spot to serve as their home base.

After another day and a half of sailing, they reached the bay of Saint George, and in its midst, a long, wooded island known as Flat Island. On its east side, there was an elevation, Sandy Point, leading into a shallow bay. East of it, the shallow cove was dotted with several smaller islands and treacherous sandbanks. They presented both challenges and opportunities for the resourceful crew.

Flat Island's rugged shores and the hidden bay on its east side seemed to offer the promise of seclusion and safety, as the few ships making their way up and down the western coast of Newfoundland, would rarely dare to navigate into the shallow waters to the east of Flat Island. There was little incentive for them to do so, as there was nothing to be had, and larger vessels could easily run aground on one of the treacherous sand banks. The majority of fishing vessels in general stayed on the cod-rich East of Newfoundland Island anyway.

With only a few natives residing on Flat Island and no signs of human habitation on the Newfoundland Coast to the east, Eric and The Vixen's crew immediately saw the potential for a secure hideaway.

As two sailors checked the depth with a lead line, the vessel cautiously made its way around Flat Island, each member of the crew filled with a sense of anticipation for the adventures that lay ahead in their newfound sanctuary. As long as they were discreet when slipping out from their spot behind the wooded island, they were pretty much non-existent.

As Eric, Maria, and three sailors from The Vixen made landfall on Flat Island, they were soon greeted by a small group of natives, identified as Micmac, who had established a settlement on the island. Despite the initial language barrier, several of them seemed to speak broken French, allowing for communication to take place.

The Micmac were native to the northeastern part of North America. They had lived there for a long time. In what is now Newfoundland, the Micmac lived long before European settlers arrived. Skilled hunters, fishers, and gatherers, the tribe lived in harmony with the land, their survival intertwined with the ebb and flow of the seasons. With reverence, they fished, hunted, and gathered the bountiful gifts bestowed by the earth.

But when Europeans arrived on big ships, things changed. They wanted land and power. Some Micmac welcomed them, but others were worried about losing their way of life and traditions. Existence turned hard for the Micmac They had to fight to protect themselves against the settlers. Frequent clashes with the white newcomers and they unknown customs ensured.

Despite these challenges, the Micmac remained strong and refused to give up their culture or identity.

With Eric acting as the spokesperson, he explained to the Micmac people that they had come in peace and sought to anchor their ship in the bay on the eastern side of the island. There seemed to be only very few of them, perhaps less than five dozen. To the sailor's relief, it became apparent that the natives were receptive to their request, indicating their willingness to accommodate the arrival of The Vixen in their waters.

With gratitude for the warm welcome extended by the Micmac, Eric and Maria, sent the sailors back to the ship to gather some supplies for the natives. Loading several cast iron pots, knives, and a dozen blankets onto a small boat, they made their way back to Flat Island.

Upon their return, they presented the gifts to the Micmac people, who received them with joy and gratitude. The sight of the pots, sturdy knives, and warm blankets brought smiles to their faces, and they expressed their thanks in a language of gestures and nods.

As the exchange took place, a sense of mutual respect filled the air, bridging the gap between the crew of The Vixen and the few indigenous inhabitants of Flat Island. Through this simple act of generosity, early bonds of friendship were forged, laying the foundation for a harmonious coexistence between the newcomers and the native people of the island.

Flat Island proved to be strategically situated close to the bustling trade routes in the south, making it an ideal base of operations for The Vixen and her crew. Despite its proximity to the main sea lanes, the treacherous sand banks and shallow waters surrounding the island would serve as a natural barrier, deterring large warships from pursuing them.

Hidden between the rugged western coast of Newfoundland and the protective embrace of Flat Island, The Vixen lay concealed from view, shielded from the prying eyes of any passing ships that might venture northward along the coastline. With the island offering both seclusion and security, the crew could rest easy knowing that they were safely hidden from sight, free to conduct their activities without fear of detection or interference.

The Vixen left the hideout to sail south and zigzag through the Cabot Strait, scouring the waters for potential prey. They eventually found themselves anchored in the bay of the Codroy Valley on the tip of the Island of Newfoundland. With each passing day, they spotted numerous ships passing through the strait, but Captain Eric remained patient, unwilling to board the first vessel they encountered.

It wasn't until the third day that they spotted a two-masted brig flying the French flag. The sight of the heavily laden ship promised a bountiful cargo, prompting Eric to order his crew to prepare for pursuit. With determination, they set off in pursuit of their quarry, closing the distance until they were able to pull alongside, gunports open and ready for action.

To their surprise, the crew of the brig offered little resistance, clearly intimidated by the sight of The Vixen's 10 formidable guns. With the pirates swiftly boarding the deck, the captain of the brig was quickly identified and subjected to intense questioning by Maria and Quartermaster James.

Under pressure, the captain soon divulged the location of the ship's hidden stash of money, leading the crew to uncover another £9,000 in loot, which the captain had likely gained by selling goods brought over from France at the shores of the colony.

Despite the comparatively small size of The Vixen, the crew managed to secure a significant portion of the brig's cargo, loading their vessel with as much as it could carry before setting sail once more, their hold filled with valuable furs from the inland.

With their pockets lined with plunder and their ship laden with valuable cargo, they sailed on, now looking for a harbor to unload and sell the Vixen's loot.

Eric poured over the maps spread out on the table in the captain's cabin of his ship, his brow furrowed in concentration. After careful consideration, he identified a promising harbor on the east side of Cape Breton known as St. Esprit. It appeared to strike the perfect balance between being small enough to allow for discreet unloading of their ill-gotten loot, yet bustling enough to attract potential buyers without arousing too much suspicion.

With their course altered, The Vixen made its way toward St. Esprit, the anticipation mounting among the crew as they approached the busy harbor. As the ship moored at the pier, Eric and Maria wasted no time in disembarking, eager to seek out a suitable buyer for their cargo.

Making their way through the busy streets of the small

harbor, they soon came across a small office that appeared to be a brokerage. Stepping inside, they were greeted by a man seated behind a ledger, who listened attentively as they explained their offer.

To their delight, the man seemed interested and agreed to accompany them back to The Vixen to inspect the cargo firsthand. After a thorough examination, he made them an offer of £12,000 for the furs, a sum that exceeded their expectations and left them both pleased with the outcome.

With the deal struck and the furs sold, Eric and Maria returned to The Vixen, their pockets lined with gold and silver from the successful transaction. With their purses filled, they set sail for Flat Island, to lay low for a while and to better outfit their hiding place.

The pirates frequently returned to Flat Island with captured goods such as tools and fabric, which they generously shared with the local Micmac natives. In gratitude for their assistance, the tribe aided them in constructing three small log huts and a small storage building. Eric and Maria took residence in one of the smaller huts, while the crew divided themselves among the two larger buildings, with five men in each.

The men of the Vixen began to forge bonds with the Micmac women, fostering a sense of familial connection between the two groups. Eric and Maria, determined to make their log hut a home away from home, adorned it with furniture salvaged from captured ships. Each evening, they would gather around the fireplace in their cozy log abode, enjoying the warmth and companionship as they shared stories and hatched plans.

As Maria settled onto the modest bed made of pine, the softness of the beaver furs enveloping her in a cocoon of warmth and luxury, she felt a sense of contentment wash over her. The furs, taken from the plundered ships, served as a reminder of the riches that still awaited them on the open seas.

Eric followed suit. As he settled onto the bed beside her, his strong arms encircling her in a protective embrace, Maria felt a sense of peace—a sense of belonging that she had never known before.

In the flickering light of the lantern that cast dancing shadows upon the walls of their tiny cabin, Eric and Maria lay in each other's arms, their bodies pressed close as they savored the warmth and intimacy of their embrace. With each gentle touch and whispered word of affection, they forged a stronger bond.

And as she closed her eyes and surrendered to his embrace, she whispered a silent prayer of gratitude to the fates that had brought them together.

As Eric's lips and tongue moved along Maria's skin, igniting flames of passion that flickered and danced within her, she couldn't help but marvel at the intensity of the sensations coursing through her body. His touch, though on her thighs, and rough with the hint of his beard, sent shivers of pleasure cascading down her spine, awakening a hunger that had long lain dormant within her soul.

With each caress, each whispered word of devotion that escaped his lips, Maria felt drawn deeper into the fiery embrace of desire, her senses ablaze with Eric's scent and sweat mingled with the heady aroma of arousal. At that moment, all thoughts of the past faded into insignificance, replaced by the overwhelming ecstasy of being desired by a man who knew just how to touch her in all the right places.

For Maria, the experience was cathartic—a release from the burdens of her past, a validation of her worth and desirability in the eyes of another. In Eric's arms, she found sanctuary from the harsh realities of her former life as a barmaid in Plymouth, where so many men had failed to understand the depths of her desires and the intricacies of her pleasure.

Eric continued to tease and tantalize her, and Maria couldn't help but surrender to the overwhelming tide of sensation that threatened to consume her. She knew that she had found her salvation in the arms of the man she loved.

And as the waves of pleasure crashed over her, washing away the last vestiges of doubt and insecurity, Maria clung to Eric with a fierce determination, knowing that they would forge a path forward—a path defined not by the shadows of the past, but by the light of their desire.

# 5 MARIA'S RAGE

Over the summer months, the crew of The Vixen sailed the waters of the Cabot Strait with cunning and determination. Day after day, they hunted their prey, crossing the stormy waters north of Cape Breton, where a constant stream of ships sailed to and from the shores of the Old World, laden with goods and treasure.

Their efforts were rewarded handsomely as they successfully intercepted five more ships sailing the Cabot Strait. Four of these ships were heavily laden with furs, their holds overflowing with the pelts of beavers, foxes, and other precious animals coveted by traders and merchants alike. The fifth ship, coming from the Old World, carried a different kind of treasure—tools from France, a valuable commodity in the burgeoning colonies of North America.

With each successful raid, The Vixen's crew grew

wealthier. Their plunder always fetched a hefty profit at the harbor of Saint-Esprit, where eager buyers awaited their precious cargo with open arms.

Each time they sailed into the quaint harbor, the crew of The Vixen wasted no time in offloading their plunder, and their pockets were soon bulging with the weight of gold and silver. The furs were sold to their trusty cargo trader who marveled at their quality, while the tools from France were snapped up by a warehouse eager to sell them to local workshops and craftsmen.

Back on Flat Island, with their coffers filled to the brim, the pirates celebrated their success with raucous laughter and hearty meals, their voices raised in triumph as they reveled in the spoils of their daring exploits.

As the crew of the Vixen gathered around the crackling campfire in their hiding spot on the east side of Flat Island, the glow of the flames casting flickering shadows upon their faces, the conversation turned to the hefty sum of money that had accumulated in their pockets over the summer months of plundering the shipping routes of the Cabot Strait.

"What are we going to do with all this money?" one sailor mused aloud, his voice tinged with a hint of uncertainty.

"It's kind of pointless having your purse full of gold coins but nowhere to spend it," another chimed in, echoing the sentiment of the group.

"We could make our way to Quebec," suggested one, his eyes glinting with the promise of adventure.

But Eric, ever the pragmatist, shook his head in response. "It's October already, and cold," he pointed out. "In six weeks, we will be freezing here. Why not sail back to England and stash our money in the bank, and then return in spring? That would also spare us the cold and rough winter here."

Maria, seated beside Eric, nodded in agreement. "I could use a little holiday from these hostile shores," she admitted with a wry smile, her thoughts already drifting to the comforts of home and the promise of warmer days ahead.

"And if we sail back to Plymouth, we could also have the ship tarred and cleaned at a boatyard. She needs it badly," Mr. Bancroft, the quartermaster, added, his practicality earning nods of approval from the rest of the crew.

"I agree with you, James," Eric nodded in response to the suggestion.

"But then, Plymouth is too familiar territory for us now. We need to lay low for a while, be careful, and let the heat die down. So far nobody has identified us, but it will be clear what we are doing to those who know us in Plymouth and at the South Coast of England. Liverpool or Bristol would offer us more anonymity, a chance to blend in with the crowds without drawing undue attention."

The crew murmured their agreement, recognizing the wisdom in Eric's words. After months of successful plundering along the Cabot Strait, and returning home with bags of money, it was only a matter of time before their exploits caught up with them, and facing the gallows in England for piracy wasn't a good prospect. Moving to a less conspicuous harbor would provide them with a much-needed respite from the constant scrutiny of old friends and jealous acquaintances.

"It may indeed be safer," the quartermaster added, his tone grave. "We've grown accustomed to living on the edge, but we must exercise caution after adventures like these."

And so, as the flames of the campfire danced in the night, casting their warm glow upon the faces of the crew, a plan began to take shape—a plan that would see them safely home to England, their pockets lined with plunder and their ship restored to its former glory. They toasted on their return to their home shores.

With a unanimous decision made to fill The Vixen's cargo holds one final time before returning to England, the crew wasted no time in making preparations for their next venture into the waters of the Cabot Strait. Two days later, the sleek ship set sail once more, her sails billowing in the wind as she sliced through the choppy waves with purpose and determination.

As they navigated the familiar waters of the strait, the crew kept a sharp lookout for any signs of potential prey, their eyes scanning the horizon for the telltale silhouette of a merchant vessel ripe for plunder. With each passing hour, their anticipation grew, fueled by the promise of one final haul to line their pockets with gold and silver.

And then, on the third day of their journey, their patience was rewarded as they spotted their quarry—a merchant ship laden with valuable cargo, coming from France, its sails billowing in the breeze as it made its way through the narrow channel.

With practiced precision, The Vixen closed in on her target, her crew springing into action as they prepared to board their unsuspecting prey. The air crackled with tension as they drew nearer, the thrill of the chase coursing through their veins as they prepared to unleash their fury upon their hapless victim.

With a thunderous roar, the guns of The Vixen disabled the unarmed merchant vessel. The pirates, their grappling hooks in hand, struck the listing ship, their cries echoing across the waves as they stormed the merchant ship with all the ferocity of a pack of hungry wolves.

The ship's hull was filled with new and shining arms and guns from France. In a matter of hours, the cargo holds of The Vixen were filled to bursting with the spoils of their latest conquest, her crew reveling in the thrill of victory as they set course for Flat Island once more.

As The Vixen sailed homeward with her latest prize, her cargo holds groaned under the weight of their plunder. Among the treasures seized from the merchant ship were 2,500 French Model 1728 Infantry Muskets from Saint Etienne, renowned for their quality and precision craftsmanship. These muskets were prized by soldiers and militias alike for their reliability and accuracy, and their acquisition promised to fetch a handsome sum on the black market in England, fetching perhaps four or five pounds each.

In addition to the muskets, the crew had also seized 500 French cavalry pistols model 1733, each one in new condition. These pistols, with their elegant design and deadly accuracy, were highly sought after, and their presence in The Vixen's cargo hold promised to bring in a substantial profit upon their return to England.

As The Vixen drew closer to Flat Island, the man in the lookout called, "ship ahead." Soon, the crew's eyes were drawn to a sloop, roughly 70 feet in length, anchored off the island's west coast. A sense of unease settled over them. Had someone stumbled upon their carefully guarded hiding place?

"This is not good, I hope they're not venturing to the east, where our storage is located," Eric murmured to James, the quartermaster, his voice tinged with concern.

The gravity of the situation was not lost on the crew. The presence of the sloop posed a clear threat to their hidden sanctuary, and they braced themselves for the impending confrontation.

As The Vixen neared the sloop anchored off the coast of their little island, tension hung heavy in the air. The crew exchanged nervous glances, their hearts pounding with the anticipation of what lay ahead. Had someone discovered their secret hideout? Were they facing an enemy intent on disrupting their operations?

"Let's give her a weak broadside and maim her," Eric whispered to the quartermaster, his voice low and urgent.

"Agreed. Let's approach her with open gun ports," Mr. Bancroft suggested, his eyes narrowing as he surveyed the scene before them.

The crew knew that they needed to be prepared for whatever lay ahead, their instincts honed by years of navigating the seas.

"Why don't we be safe and send her to the bottom of the ocean?" Maria interjected, her voice laced with a hint of desperation.

But Eric shook his head, his expression grim. "Because the water isn't deep enough here," he explained, his tone somber. "Her masts will still be showing if she sinks. It may draw the attention of wreckers and of passing ships."

As they sailed alongside the sloop, Eric issued the command to fire, and the guns of The Vixen roared to life, unleashing a barrage of cannon fire that tore holes into the hull of the merchant ship. The crew worked with practiced efficiency, their movements fluid and precise as they disabled their adversary without sinking the ship outright.

And as the smoke cleared and the echoes of gunfire faded, the lookout's urgent cry pierced the air, "Hold fire! There seem to be some locals from our shores aboard that ship!"

Eric swiftly raised his telescope and scanned the scene, confirming the presence of indigenous people on the shore, their gestures filled with anger. His heart sank at the sight of two bodies lying lifeless in the sand.

Reacting swiftly, the pirate crew boarded the merchant ship, their weapons at the ready. The crew of the vessel, realizing the dire situation they were in, raised their hands in surrender. Their expressions were a mix of fear and resignation, as they dropped the few muskets they carried onto the planks of the ship's deck.

As the pirates cautiously explored the ship, their hearts heavy with dread, they stumbled upon a grim scene. Several young, nude Micmac girls lay bound and helpless on the planks, their eyes wide with fear and confusion. The sight filled the pirates with anger.

Venturing further into the hull, they discovered another young, stripped naked girl lying on a table, bound and bleeding, her frail form trembling with fear. The pirates wasted no time in freeing her from her restraints.

In the ship's kitchen, a large pot of stew bubbled away on the stove, its savory aroma filling the air. But the pirates paid little attention to the tantalizing scent, their minds consumed by the harrowing discovery they had just made. Determined to bring justice to those responsible for such heinous acts, they set about securing the ship and ensuring the safety of the rescued girls.

Eric and Maria rowed the johnboat with four young girls to shore, their hearts heavy with sorrow and indignation. As they approached the angry natives, a man who spoke French stepped forward to convey their grievances.

He explained that the sailors from the ship had come ashore in the morning, committing acts of violence and brutality. They had mercilessly taken the lives of several men and women with their muskets, leaving behind a trail of death and devastation. Worse still, they had hunted down the young girls, capturing them and taking them back to their ship, leaving behind a wake of anguish and despair.

Eric and Maria listened as the man recounted the atrocities committed by the sailors. Maria, with grim resolve, vowed to exact revenge, as her and Eric returned to the ship.

Standing back on the deck of the captured vessel, Maria

approached the captain, her dagger held firmly in her hand as she confronted him. He was held at gunpoint by one of her crewmates, his expression defiant as he met her gaze.

"What is this all about, Captain?" Maria inquired, her voice laced with determination.

The captain's response was callous and dismissive. "What do you mean? My men were just having a bit of fun with these savages," he replied nonchalantly, a sneer playing at the corners of his lips.

Maria's grip tightened on her dagger, her patience wearing thin. "It appears to me that you are the savages here. You have murdered two women and three men ashore, and you have violated four young girls, one still a child," she retorted, her voice sharp as she pressed the blade under the captain's chin.

The captain, caught off guard by her boldness, attempted to defend his actions. "What do you care? These are just heathens," he protested. "We were simply having some harmless fun."

Maria's eyes flashed with anger at his words. "Perhaps I should show you what real 'fun' feels like," she replied icily, her tone dripping with disdain. "It seems you are heathens as well. You are not following the teachings of Christ too closely yourself, it seems," she added, her words a biting rebuke to the captain's hypocrisy.

"We did not break any laws of the crown," the captain protested, his tone defiant. "Nowhere is it written that you can't hunt yourself some Indians."

Maria fixed him with a steely gaze. "But King George is far from here, in England," she responded coolly. "And we here follow our own laws. My laws."

"Why would you turn against a countryman and a fellow Christian, Lady?" the captain challenged.

Maria paused, considering his words carefully. "You are right, Sir," she conceded, her expression softening slightly. "Perhaps I am a little too harsh on you. After all, you seem to be good English folk."

"We indeed are, from the shores of Portsmouth we hail," the captain replied proudly, his chest puffed out with a hint of arrogance.

"Oh well. Let's feast together," she added, her voice ringing with false warmth. "I will retrieve some bottles of good port from my ship."

With a gracious smile, Maria turned and made her way back to The Vixen, her heart pounding with anticipation as she prepared to set her plan into motion.

With that, Maria stepped back on board her ship, her mind already racing with a plan. She swiftly retrieved a can of arsenic used as rat poison from its spot below deck, hiding it in her black captain's coat. Then, she grabbed two bottles of port wine looted during their recent exploit. With a sly smile, as she ascended again.

Returning to the captured ship, Maria made her way into the galley, where the large pot of stew simmered enticingly. With a deft hand, she poured the contents of the arsenic can into the stew, stirring it well to ensure it was thoroughly mixed.

Whispering something to Eric, she then instructed her crew to lower their weapons and prepare for a feast. As the captured sailors descended into their dining area below deck, Maria discreetly whispered to each of her men, "Don't eat anything, just act as if you were eating." The sailors nodded with a murmur.

The pirate crew, their weapons still within reach, mingled with the sailors of the captured ship below deck, each of them taking a bowl of soup. However, the pirates refrained from tasting any of it, while the sailors of the merchant eagerly dug in, devouring the stew along with slices of bread.

"Let's help ourselves," Maria told the captain who stood nearby, her tone casual yet calculated. "Sit down, Captain," she instructed, using a ladle to scoop both of them a bowl of the stew.

As the captain and his crew began to eat, Maria sat in silence, her eyes keenly watching their every move, while Eric and the quartermaster stood guard at the door, ready to intervene at a moment's notice.

The effects of the arsenic-laced soup quickly became apparent. The first sailor began to cough, his breath growing short and labored. Soon after, a second sailor clutched his stomach in agony, doubling over in pain. A third sailor started vomiting violently, unable to contain the poison wreaking havoc on his body.

Chaos erupted as more sailors succumbed to the poison, writhing in agony on the floor, some even soiling themselves in their desperate struggle against the deadly toxin. Maria watched in grim satisfaction as her plan unfolded before her eyes, the pirates of The Vixen spared from the poison by her forewarning.

Eric and the quartermaster remained vigilant at the door, ensuring that none of the sailors attempted to escape or retaliate amid the chaos. With each agonized cry and pained groan, Maria's resolve only strengthened, knowing that justice was being served for the lives that had been taken on their island, and the young girls who had been cruelly violated, before the eyes of their families.

As the captain succumbed to the effects of the poison, Maria's laughter rang out, a chilling echo in the chaos unfolding around them. The captain's distressed gaze met hers, accusing her of the treachery that had brought them to this grim fate.

"You crafty wench, you have poisoned me and my crew,"

he accused, his voice filled with anguish.

Maria's laughter only grew more frenzied in response.

"Oh, we're just having a little fun, good Sir. We're good Christian people, after all. But a little fun never hurt anybody, right?" she replied, her tone dripping with sarcasm as she reveled in the captain's torment.

The sailors writhed in agony on the pantry floor, soiled in their own throw-up and excrements, their cries of pain drowned out by Maria's laughter and the clamor of the pirates watching on.

With Eric's command, the crew of The Vixen sprang into action, setting sail and towing the doomed ship into open waters. Several miles offshore, where the water was deep and cold, the guns of The Vixen thundered, sending the sloop and its cursed crew to the murky depths of the Gulf of Saint Lawrence.

As the ship disappeared beneath the waves, Maria's laughter echoed across the ocean, a chilling reminder of the price paid for crossing the wrath of those who called the shores of Flat Island home.

The Vixen sailed deftly between sandbanks, navigating the shallow waters to reach their hidden spot behind the island. The devastation left by the violent merchant crew among the once-peaceful natives was evident at every turn. Huts lay in smoldering ruins, the air thick with the scent of charred wood. Some men lay injured on the ground, while others mourned over the bodies of their fallen loved ones.

Feeling a deep sense of shame and remorse for the havoc wrought by his countrymen, Eric sought to make amends. He called for the chief of the native tribe, to convey his sincere regret for the destruction caused by the crew of the merchant ship.

As a gesture of reconciliation and solidarity, Eric then called all the native men to gather at the shore. They assembled solemnly around the log homes of the pirates, their expressions a mix of curiosity and apprehension. Three crates filled with muskets were brought forth from The Vixen, and the pirates distributed them among the men, along with ample ammunition.

The native men looked upon their new prized possessions with awe and gratitude, marveling at the firepower they now possessed.

"This should give you enough firepower to protect yourselves from future raids," Eric declared, his voice filled with sincerity as he sought to right the wrongs committed by his countrymen.

As November approached and the night temperatures dipped below freezing, the crew of The Vixen prepared to set sail back to England. Each member of the small pirate crew carried a hefty sum of over £6,000 in their purses. The ship, already laden with French muskets from their recent exploits, was further loaded with water and provisions for the journey ahead.

Before departing, the crew spent one last night in their log huts ashore, surrounded by the native inhabitants whom they had befriended during their time on the island. They reassured the natives that they would return in the spring, promising to continue their friendship and cooperation.

With the break of dawn, The Vixen set sail, her crew eager to begin the journey homeward. They sailed eastward through the Cabot Strait, then around the islands of Saint Pierre and Miquelon. From there it was still over 2,000 miles home, and Eric plotted a course to northeast 63°, setting the ship's heading toward the southern tip of Ireland. Their ultimate destination: the bustling port of Liverpool, where the comforts of rustic harbor pubs and the promise of a new chapter awaited them.

The Vixen, laden with a valuable cargo of guns and arms, struggled to make swift progress, averaging a speed of 9 knots on a good day. It took two weeks of arduous sailing to complete the crossing of the vast expanse of the Atlantic.

On the fifteenth day of their journey, weary but determined, the ship finally pulled into the busy harbor of Liverpool on the west coast of England. As they approached the docks, the crew breathed a collective sigh of relief, their hearts filled with anticipation at the prospect of returning to their home shores after a long and dangerous voyage.

The port of Liverpool was a busy hub of maritime activity, teeming with ships of all shapes and sizes from around the world. The strategic location of the port made it a vital center for trade and commerce, particularly with the American colonies, the Caribbean, and Africa.

The waterfront was lined with warehouses, wharves, and dockyards, abuzz with activity as cargo was loaded and unloaded from ships. Tall masts of sailing vessels dotted the skyline, their sails billowing in the wind as they arrived and departed from the port.

The streets surrounding the port were always crowded with merchants, sailors, and dockworkers, bustling with the energy of trade and commerce. Taverns and alehouses, filled with sailors and merchants exchanging stories of their voyages over pints of ale, were busy day and night.

The port also had shipyards, needed to clean and tar the beaten hull of the Vixen. She needed it baldly. Almost two years in the water had left her hull laden with barnacles, reducing her speed significantly.

With the ship safely moored in the harbor's docks, the pirate crew, now camouflaged as unsuspicious merchant sailors, began the task of unloading their precious cargo, ready to reap the rewards of their daring exploits on the high seas.

As they set foot on solid ground once more, they looked forward to the comforts of home and the promise of new adventures that awaited them in the vibrant port of Liverpool.

## 6 IN LIVERPOOL

The next morning, Eric wasted no time in attending to the business of selling the cargo of looted arms. Making his way to a merchant's office near the busy docks of Liverpool, he approached the man in charge and quickly arranged for the inspection of the valuable load.

As the merchant examined the guns, pistols, and blades, Eric watched intently, eager to secure a favorable deal. After careful scrutiny, the merchant offered a total of £15,000 for the entire lot, a generous sum that exceeded Eric's expectations.

With the successful sale of the cargo adding almost another £6,000 to Eric and Maria's already considerable fortune, their total wealth now stood at an impressive £45,000. The windfall provided them with newfound financial security and opportunities for future endeavors.

As they counted their earnings, Eric and Maria couldn't help but feel a sense of satisfaction and excitement for the possibilities that lay ahead. With their coffers now overflowing, they could afford to pursue their dreams with even greater ambition and confidence.

Meanwhile, Maria, now back in the civilized surroundings of Liverpool, seized the opportunity to transition from her trusty captain's frock to a more feminine dress. Shedding the attire of the sea for the elegance of land, she embraced her newfound femininity with grace and poise, ready to embark on the next chapter of her journey.

The crew, relieved from their duties and eager to embrace the pleasures of shore leave, soon found their way into the lively taverns of the port. With pockets filled with their share of the plunder, they reveled in the freedom and indulgence that came with their newfound wealth.

Eric wasted no time in attending to the necessary tasks to prepare The Vixen for her next voyage. Securing a shipyard to clean and waterproof the vessel's hull, he ensured that she would be in prime condition for their future adventures in spring.

With their immediate responsibilities taken care of, Eric and Maria seized the opportunity to embark on a journey of their own. Renting a comfortable carriage, they set off on the long journey to London, located 210 miles to the southeast.

Ensuring the safety of their precious cargo, a chest filled with gold securely hidden in the carriage, with Eric and Maria both well-armed, they made their way to Threadneedle Street in the capital. Their destination: the Bank of England, where they intended to deposit their hard-earned loot.

After two weeks of leisurely travel, Eric and Maria arrived in the bustling metropolis of London. Waste no time, they made their way to the esteemed Bank of England to deposit their considerable fortune of £42,000, a substantial sum that ensured their financial security for the foreseeable future. They retained £2,000 in their purse, keeping a prudent reserve for any unforeseen expenses in the coming months, and to pay for the overhaul of their ship, The Vixen, in the port of Liverpool.

Eager to escape the hustle and bustle of the city, Eric and Maria wasted no time in setting out to explore the countryside in search of a place to settle down or even purchase. Their journey took them from the urban sprawl of London to the tranquil landscapes of Oxfordshire, where Eric had once engaged in a daring act of thievery, stealing a purse with 300 gold coins from a wealthy merchant.

From Oxfordshire, they turned their sights northward, venturing into the picturesque regions of Leicestershire and Derbyshire. Surrounded by rolling hills and idyllic countryside, they sought out the perfect spot to establish roots and build a future together. With each passing mile, they felt a sense of excitement and anticipation for the adventures that lay ahead, ready to embrace whatever opportunities awaited them in their quest for a new home.

In the picturesque parish of Mapleton in Derbyshire, west of Ashbourne, only 80 miles east of Liverpool, Eric and Maria stumbled upon a charming property that immediately caught their eye – Mapleton Manor. Nestled amidst the rolling hills and verdant countryside, this small two-story manor exuded an air of timeless elegance and rustic charm.

The front facade of Mapleton Manor boasted five windows, each framed by intricate stonework that added to its quaint allure. Surrounding the manor was an enclosed courtyard, where the gentle sounds of nature mingled with the tranquility of the countryside.

Flanking the courtyard stood additional buildings, including a sturdy stable and two smaller houses, all interconnected to form a cohesive and inviting space. The manor's surroundings were adorned with lush greenery and colorful blooms, creating a picturesque setting that beckoned Eric and Maria to explore further.

As they stood before the Manor, Eric and Maria couldn't help but feel a sense of excitement and possibility. With its idyllic location and charming architecture, this quaint estate seemed to hold the promise of a new beginning – a place where they could finally put down roots and build the life they had always dreamed of.

Eric and Maria, captivated by the allure of Mapleton Manor but still in need of temporary accommodation, found themselves a cozy room at The Horns, a charming inn located in Victoria Square, Ashbourne.

Nestled in the heart of the small town, The Horns Tavern welcomed weary travelers with its warm hospitality and an inviting glow from the windows.

Inside, Eric and Maria were greeted by the comforting scent of a crackling fireplace and the soft murmur of conversation from other guests. The innkeeper, a friendly figure with a welcoming smile, showed them to their room, which boasted a comfortable bed and all the amenities they needed for a restful stay.

As they settled into their accommodations, Eric and Maria couldn't help but feel a sense of contentment wash over them. Their riches were secured at the Bank of England, their ship was being overhauled, and their crew was eager to set sail again in the spring. Despite the uncertainty of their future, they took comfort in the warm hospitality of The Horns as they planned to explore the surrounding lands in the morning.

As Eric reclined on the bed at the small room, which was now bathed in soft shadows, his gaze lingered on Maria's beautiful, naked form. She stood by the closet door, her skin glistening with sweat and the glow of happiness. Just the sight of her filled him with a profound sense of joy and desire.

"Come over here, to me," he beckoned to Maria, his voice husky with desire.

Maria remained standing. Her hands traced the curves of her body, caressing her breasts with a tantalizing touch that sent shivers down her spine. With practiced ease, her palms circled her nipples, igniting a fiery sensation that coursed through her veins. As her hands glided down her sides, she felt a surge of heat pooling between her thighs.

With each gentle stroke, she teased her hips, feeling the tension building within her. Her movements became fluid, and rhythmic, as if she were dancing to a silent melody, only she could hear. Her feet pointed elegantly, tippy-toeing like a ballerina in pleasure as she surrendered to the intoxicating sensations washing over her.

Across from her, Eric watched with rapt attention, his gaze fixed on her with an intensity that sent a thrill coursing through her. At that moment, she felt desired, empowered by the raw passion that simmered between them.

"Come on now, I need you," he whispered.

Without hesitation, Maria now joined him on the bed, the tangled sheets pulled up to cover them both. Their bodies intertwined eagerly, each movement sending waves of pleasure coursing through them. Then, Maria straddled him. She ground her damp cheeks of her butt against Eric's loins, belly, and mouth, their lips meeting in passionate kisses that left them breathless.

In the dim light filtering through the window, Eric's arousal was evident, his penis thick and dark like a sturdy tree branch. It rose between his legs, carried by a powerful flow of his blood that seemed to explode in his body, reaching upwards like the branches of a spreading tree. Aiding it with his hand, he entered her, and she was so ready.

With strands of Maria's dark hair cascading between them, they surrendered to the rhythm of their lovemaking. Maria rode Eric, rocking back and forth in a dance of desire that ignited a fire within them both. As their bodies moved in harmony, their hearts beat as one, their passion building to a finale that left them both spent and satisfied.

Exhausted yet content, they lay entwined in each other's arms, their lovemaking a symphony of love that echoed through the night, a melody that spoke of their deep connection and boundless affection for one another.

The next morning, Maria's heart swelled with affection as she wandered the halls of Mapleton Manor, envisioning her future as a lady within its storied walls. An eager broker led them through the premises, highlighting its grandeur and charm, but Eric, ever the pragmatist, cautioned against hasty decisions.

"We have more opportunities awaiting us in the Gulf of Saint Lawrence," Eric reminded Maria, mindful of their ongoing adventures as pirates. Despite her longing for a permanent home, Maria understood the wisdom in his words. Besides, she had learned to cherish the rough pirate life with all its dangers and bloodthirsty exploits.

Reluctantly, they informed the broker of their decision. "We will be off to a business adventure in the New World, but If Mapleton Hall is still available in a year's time, we will certainly consider it," Maria assured, her gaze lingering wistfully on the grandeur of the estate.

With their promise made, Eric and Maria bid farewell to Mapleton Hall, their hearts heavy with the weight of uncertainty yet buoyed by the hope of future possibilities. As they ventured back into the world, they knew that their voyage was far from over and that the allure of Mapleton Hall would continue to beckon them in the years to come.

The journey back to Liverpool was a slow and leisurely one, the carriage making its way through the picturesque countryside over the course of six days. Eric and Maria, nestled comfortably inside, watched the passing scenery with a sense of contentment and peace.

With each passing mile, the harbor town drew closer, yet Eric and Maria were in no hurry to reach their destination. They took delight in the journey itself, finding joy in the simple pleasures of the open road and the beauty of the natural world around them.

As they finally arrived back in Liverpool, weary but content, Eric and Maria stepped out of the carriage and onto the bustling streets of the city, in a quest to find an inn for the coming weeks.

Ye Hole In Ye Wall, a pub and inn, was nestled in the heart of Liverpool. Located on a quaint cobblestone street, the pub exuded charm and character, drawing visitors from near and far to its welcoming doors. It offered comfortable accommodations for weary travelers, with cozy rooms and plush beddings, providing a peaceful retreat for guests seeking a restful night's sleep.

As Eric and Maria stepped inside, they were greeted by the comfortable interior of the pub, with its low ceilings, exposed brick walls, and warm, inviting atmosphere. The space was filled with the comforting scent of wood smoke and the murmur of friendly conversation, creating a welcoming haven from the hustle and bustle of the city outside.

As the sun rose over Liverpool, Eric's footsteps led him to the busy shipyard where The Vixen awaited her captain's inspection. With a sense of anticipation, he approached the vessel, eager to assess the progress made on his beloved ship.

To his satisfaction, Eric found the ship in a state of considerable improvement. The shipyard workers had toiled diligently to clean the hull of barnacles and repair any damage, sealing it with a fresh coat of tar. Improvements to the cabins had been made. The ship stood tall and proud, ready to take on the open seas once more.

With just a week or two left, until The Vixen was ready to set sail again, Eric felt a surge of excitement. It was late in February already, and the voyage to Flat Island would take three weeks, or perhaps less with favorable winds. Soon, he, Maria, and his crew would embark on yet another journey, their spirits buoyed by the promise of new loots and plunders in the Gulf of Saint Lawrence.

Gathered together in a cozy pub at the swarming harbor of Liverpool, Eric and his crew discussed their plans for the future. The camaraderie among them was palpable, each member of the crew eager and ready for the next adventure of plunder in the Gulf of Saint Lawrence.

As they raised their tankards in a toast to new beginnings, Eric outlined their proposed timeline. The crew agreed unanimously to set sail in the first week of March, eager to once again feel the wind in their sails and the thrill of the open ocean beneath their feet. This would take them to Flat Island in early April, the latest, just at the right time for a new hunting season at the Strait of Cabot.

As they parted ways for the evening, the excitement and

anticipation of the upcoming voyage hung in the air, filling their hearts with a sense of purpose and determination.

Before long, The Vixen found herself once more moored at the busy Liverpool dock, her sleek form rocking gently on the sparkling waters, refreshed and revitalized.

Eric and Maria bid farewell to their temporary abode at Ye Hole In Ye Wall and made their way aboard their beloved ship. Their captain's cabin, newly furnished and welcoming, awaited them, a sanctuary amidst the bustling activity of the harbor.

With provisions ordered and the ship's guns meticulously checked, Eric and Maria prepared for their upcoming voyage. As they traversed the pier, Eric's sharp eyes caught sight of a two-masted brig moored nearby—the Lion, the ship of their old nemesis, Captain Percy.

"Ah, that wretched scoundrel," Eric muttered, his disdain evident in his voice. Maria echoed his sentiment with a resigned sigh, fully aware of the trouble Percy had caused her in the past, the last time when he tried to violate her in the hallway of the Minerva Inn in Plymouth.

"I am well aware that Liverpool is his home port, but let's see if we can gather some information about his cargo and destination," Eric proposed, his curiosity piqued.

Approaching a carpenter disembarking from the Lion, Eric inquired about the ship's intended journey. The carpenter's response was curt and dismissive, but Eric's offer of a gold coin quickly loosened his tongue.

With newfound eagerness, the carpenter divulged that the Lion would be setting sail in a week, laden with tools, wool fabric, and clothes, bound for the colonies in the New World. Eric thanked the man with a nod, the glint of determination in his eyes belying his calm demeanor.

As the carpenter scurried away, Eric and Maria exchanged knowing glances. Armed with valuable information, they began to formulate their plans.

"The Vixen is empty and faster than the Lion," Eric mused, his mind already plotting their course of action. "If we follow him down the Mersey, in a three-hour distance, we will catch him around Fastnet Rock in Southern Ireland, before he turns to the West."

"Then we take his cargo and send him to the bottom of the ocean," Maria declared, her eyes gleaming with excitement.

"It is a good plan. Not only will it rid the world of a scoundrel, but we will also not have to sail empty, and can start the new season with half-filled purses already," Eric concurred, nodding in agreement.

With their plan firmly in place, Eric gathered his crew together and outlined their strategy. Within a week, they were all on board The Vixen, prepared and eager to set sail. Now, they simply awaited the departure of the Lion to set their plan into motion.

Eric had stationed a sailor on the docks every morning, strategically positioned across from The Lion. Soon, a flurry of activity erupted on the ship as it prepared to set sail. Eric waited patiently, timing their departure two hours after the Lion cast off. With practiced precision, The Vixen slipped away from the dock, gliding down the Mersey and into the expansive waters of the Irish Sea.

Unbeknownst to the crew of the Lion, The Vixen trailed behind, silently shadowing its plotted course.

After two and a half days of stealthy pursuit, The Vixen unfurled her full sails, harnessing the wind to increase her speed. As they neared the southern tip of Ireland, just two miles off the coast, they closed in on their unsuspecting prey, closing the distance until The Vixen sailed alongside the Lion.

"Open gun ports," Eric commanded, his voice carrying across the deck. The crew swiftly obeyed, readying the cannons for action. "Fire," Eric ordered, and with a deafening roar, the guns of The Vixen unleashed a volley of cannonballs, tearing through the Lion's rigging and hull.

"Reload," Eric commanded once more, and the crew sprang into action, quickly preparing for another round of devastating firepower. The Lion, now defenseless and crippled, was swiftly boarded by the pirates of The Vixen.

A few of the Lion's crew, armed with muskets, hesitated briefly before dropping their weapons at the sight of the approaching pirates, realizing the futility of resistance against such overwhelming force.

On the quarterdeck, Captain Percy stood in disbelief as Maria, pistol in hand, jumped on the deck of the Lion and approached him with steely determination.

"You said we'd meet again, Captain," Maria began, her voice dripping with scorn. "I see, you were right! I reckon you recognize me."

"You're that wench from the pub in Plymouth," Captain Percy snarled, his anger palpable.

"Not in the mood to gut me today, I assume," Maria retorted, her tone laced with defiance.

"Shut up, wench! This is piracy in the King's waters. You will hang for this, of that I will make sure," the captain spat, his fury mounting.

"Oh, is that so? I guess I shall gut you then," Maria replied coolly, her gaze unwavering.

"Tie him to the mast, or what's left of it," Maria commanded, her authority ringing clear.

Two sailors swiftly seized the struggling captain, binding him securely to the battered stump of the mast. As his curses grew muffled, Maria's resolve remained unyielding, her eyes glinting with satisfaction.

Maria sliced open his shirt with her lady's dagger, extracted from her boot. She then ran the razor-sharp blade along the outline of his belly. With a steady hand, she ran the blade over his skin, scoring it deeply before plunging the sharp dagger firmly into the captain's gut, slicing his belly open with a swift upward motion. Percy screamed in pain.

"This is what pirates do, my dear captain," she said with a smirk. With a swift motion, she drove the dagger into his heart with full force, looking sternly into his eyes as his life expired.

Meanwhile, the crew of The Vixen, assisted by the forced sailors from the Lion, began transferring the cargo onto the pirate ship. Despite the Lion's size, not all of it could be accommodated. After ransacking Captain Percy's cabin and absconding with a crate of the best brandy and a purse of £800, they swiftly cut the lines and retrieved their grappling hooks.

With one final broadside from the guns of the Vixen, causing the ship to list and eventually sink, they set sail for the New World, as the sailors of the once proud Lion jumped overboard, trying to swim ashore.

18 days later, the pirate ship sailed into the small harbor of St. Esprit once again, where they sold the looted cargo of fabric, clothes, and kitchen utensils at the familiar brokerage, fetching £8,000. Maria kept a small number of shirts, pantaloons and coats as well as some kitchenware.

This was her welcoming present for the Micmac tribe on Flat Island. The next morning, they set sail, headed to their old hideout around the shores of Sandy Point.

As the ship sailed past Flat Island the next evening, the natives on the island immediately recognized the familiar silhouette and stood ashore, waving enthusiastically. Eric turned the ship to the east and navigated between the sandbanks to the eastern backside of the island, dropping anchor in the bay. The crew found the shores untouched, in the same condition they had left them in the fall.

The three small log homes stood intact, just as they had left them. The Micmac tribe, now gathered around the beach, was thrilled, especially when Maria handed out coats, shirts, trousers, pots and pans from their recent loot of The Lion.

Soon, the crew settled into their familiar abodes, lighting fires in the fireplaces of the log huts. Goods and small furniture brought from England now added to the comfort of the dwellings.

# 7 UNDER ATTACK

Eric and Maria sat at the table in their small summer home, looking at a bottle of brandy from Captain Percy's cabin.

With a nod of agreement, Eric fetched two glasses and poured a generous amount of the brandy into each. As they raised their glasses, the warm aroma of the amber liquid filled the air, inviting them to savor its richness.

"This is good Brandy, it seems. To new adventures," Eric toasted, clinking his glass against Maria's.

"May they always be as hot as this brandy," Maria added, her eyes sparkling with anticipation.

Together, they took a sip, allowing the smooth warmth of the brandy to wash over them, savoring the moment and the companionship they shared amidst the tranquil surroundings of their tiny summer home, hidden in the bay of Flat Island.

From the fire, there was little light in the room. Loosened by the alcohol, Maria was bolder and far more loquacious.

"Today nothing is off-limits, you can touch where you like, she smiled at Eric. Eric came over and unbuttoned her blouse."

"You are in a mood, my dear," Eric replied as he fondled her breasts.

"Would you like to suck my breasts?" Maria asked in a sassy voice.

"Perhaps I will," Eric answered, as he lowered his lips on her nipple and ran his hands between her legs.

"Use your mouth and your tongue," Maria begged. "Go ahead. Is that nice! Good!"

"Eric was a little shocked, bemused, almost physically winded by this sudden acceleration into a tabooless candor of word and gesture with Maria. But he was elated too. "We need to make love now," he said sternly, as he turned the willing Maria around and pushed her onto the table.

"I need you to make love hard, Eric," she said, as he complied, entering her from behind, holding her head on the chart table. Maria succumbed to his thrusts, letting herself fall, guided by the strong hands gripping her shoulders.

With the comforting warmth of the brandy still lingering in their veins, Eric and Maria soon nestled into their bed, wrapped in each other's arms. The gentle sound of the waves outside the window and the soft glow of the moonlight cast a serene ambiance over their small sanctuary.

As they drifted into slumber, their hearts were filled with contentment for the adventures they had shared and the peace they had found in each other's company.

After settling in with the Micmac natives on Flat Island, the crew of The Vixen embarked on another raid into the waters of the Cabot Strait. Their friendship with the islanders revived, the pirates ventured out in search of plunder once more.

Their vigilance paid off when, after two days of waiting at Port aux Basques, they spotted a sloop heading eastward. Swiftly, they seized the opportunity and captured the vessel, securing a valuable cargo of furs. With their prize in tow, The Vixen set sail southward, bound for the trusty port of St. Esprit. There, they would sell their bounty for a good return.

After the successful raid on the sloop, The Vixen sailed back to Flat Island, the purses of the pirates heavy with gold and silver coins. The furs they had looted had fetched a handsome profit at the port of St. Esprit, adding to their growing wealth.

Eric, ever mindful of the dangers of piracy, implemented a strategic approach to their raids. He ensured that they did not linger in the strait for too long, spacing out their expeditions by four to six weeks. They knew that any hint of piracy in the Gulf of Saint Lawrence and the Cabot Strait could spell discovery. Therefore, the crew of The Vixen operated with precision and stealth on rare occasions only, ensuring that their actions went unnoticed by the authorities.

By sinking captured ships and maintaining a low profile, they avoided arousing suspicion and scrutiny. It was quite normal for ships to vanish sporadically, and authorities seldom raised immediate alarm. Given the lengthy voyages typically undertaken to reach England or France, it could take weeks or even months for a missing vessel to be noticed. Consequently, many of the plundered ships were simply presumed lost at sea.

By spacing out their raids and sinking the captured ships, the crew of the Vixen avoided the notion that an abundance of ships went missing in the same area in a short period of time. This way, they could minimize the risk of raising suspicion and being discovered and hunted down by warships.

Maintaining this façade of innocence was therefore paramount for the survival of the pirate crew. Any indication of their illicit activities could provoke a swift and deadly response from warships protecting the interests of the French crown, or the English, for that matter. Thus, discretion and cunning were the greatest assets of the pirates as they continued to navigate the busy waters of the Gulf of Saint Lawrence and the Cabot Strait.

The crew settled back into their routine on Flat Island, and Eric and Maria discussed their future plans. Despite the dangers they faced as pirates, they were determined to continue their adventures and make the most of their newfound wealth. With each successful raid, they grew more confident in their abilities to outsmart their adversaries and secure their place on the island.

On Flat Island, where the tree lines of the island hid The Vixen from the crew of passing ships, the pirates had long considered themselves masters of their domain. Led by Captain Eric, they had devised numerous strategies that outwitted many a navy patrol and a few rival buccaneers. Yet, even the best-laid plans could falter under the scrutiny of unforeseen circumstances.

Port aux Basques, a quaint colony of fishermen nestled on the main island's southern shore, seemed an innocuous neighbor to the pirates' hidden cove. This is where The Vixen would often lay in waiting for passing ships. The frequent presence of The Vixen had not escaped the scrutiny of French fishermen on these shores.

One fateful morning cloaked in dim fog the tranquility of Flat Island shattered. The Vixen lay poised for action as Eric and his crew prepared for another day of plunder.

Meanwhile, Maria and two sailors were ashore, attending to the upkeep of the log homes. Their routine was abruptly interrupted by the ominous approach of six armed French soldiers emerging from the dense woods, muskets at the ready.

Panic gripped the scene as a desperate pirate lunged for his musket, only to fall to a shot fired by the advancing soldiers. Maria stood frozen, her hands raised in surrender, while another sailor, attempting to defend himself, suffered an injury to his arm.

The crew aboard The Vixen witnessed the unfolding chaos ashore and sprang into action. Eric jumped on the quarter-deck and took command. Frantically, the men opened the gun ports, loading their cannons in a desperate bid to intervene. At the sight of the looming threat from the pirate ship, the French soldiers hesitated, then swiftly retreated.

But Maria was not spared. Seized by the soldiers, she was dragged toward the west coast of the island, where a small French warship lay anchored. With grim determination, the soldiers rowed her aboard the vessel, leaving the pirates on Flat Island in shock and fury.

As the mist lifted, revealing the scars of the morning's turmoil, Eric and the pirates of Flat Island found themselves confronted not only by the might of their adversaries but also by the harsh realities of their chosen path. One of their crew members lay dead on the sandy shore, and another, William, had taken a gunshot to his upper arm and was bleeding. And in the heart of the wilderness, Maria's fate hung precariously in the balance, tethered to the uncertain tides of fortune and the relentless pursuit of justice.

With urgency burning in his veins, Captain Eric wasted no time. Gathering two of his most trusted sailors, he set out across the island, determination etched into every step. The fog that had cloaked the morning now seemed to part before him, revealing a path fraught with uncertainty and peril.

As they reached the western shore, their eyes fell upon the unexpected sight of a small French schooner. It sat anchored, a lone sentinel in the vast expanse of the Gulf of Saint Lawrence behind it, its silhouette casting a shadow of foreboding over the tranquil waters. Though not a warship by appearance, its formidable arsenal of twenty heavy guns betrayed its potential for mischief. This ship could easily sink The Vixen if allowed to fire a full broadside at her.

Eric's mind raced with possibilities. The French, it seemed, had no rightful claim to these waters, yet their presence spoke volumes. Perhaps they sought to disrupt British fisheries or assert dominion where none was warranted. Whatever their motives, Maria now found herself ensnared in their web of intrigue, a pawn in a game of power and ambition.

The ship was too large to navigate the treacherous waters where The Vixen lay anchored. It was a stalemate of sorts, with both sides poised for conflict, each awaiting the other's move.

Eric knew that time was of the essence. With Maria's fate at stake, he was desperately looking for a plan.

As Maria stood before the captain of the militia vessel, her heart pounded with a mixture of fear and defiance. She knew her fate hung precariously in the balance, teetering on the edge of the captain's judgment.

"Bonjour, Madame," the French captain greeted with a courteous but stern nod, his voice carrying the refined accent of a well-educated man.

"Serrault is the name, François Serrault, captain of His Majesty's ship, the Néreïde," he introduced himself with a slight inclination of his head.

Marie returned the introduction with a polite smile, her demeanor composed yet attentive.

"Marie Lindsay," she replied, her tone respectful as she acknowledged the captain's formal introduction.

Monsieur Serrault, the French captain, cut a lean, tall figure upon the deck of his ship. He carried himself with an air of authority and confidence that commanded respect from his crew.

Middle-aged and seasoned by years of maritime

experience, Monsieur Serrault's face was lined with the marks of the sea. His dark eyes, sharp and penetrating, betray a keen intellect and a steely resolve that brook no opposition.

Clad in a tailored uniform adorned with gold braid and insignia, Monsieur Serrault exuded an aura of elegance and refinement, a testament to his status as a seasoned naval officer

"We did not expect a woman on a pirate ship," Captain Serrault remarked, his voice dripping with disdain. "But a woman will hang just as nicely as a man on the gallows, I suppose."

Maria's jaw clenched, her resolve hardening as she met the captain's gaze head-on.

"I am not a pirate, Monsieur," she retorted, her tone steady despite the turmoil churning within her.

Serrault arched an eyebrow, skepticism etched across his features. "You seemed to meddle well with these outlaws," he countered, his voice laced with suspicion.

"I was taken against my will from my hometown of Plymouth in England, and was brought to these uninhabitable shores," Maria explained, her words a plea for understanding amidst the sea of accusations.

The captain's expression softened slightly, though doubt still lingered in his eyes.

"What did you do in Plymouth?" he inquired, probing for any hint of falsehood in her tale.

"I worked at the Minerva, a local inn at the harbor," Maria replied, her voice tinged with nostalgia for the life she had once known.

"One day, the captain of this ship approached me and invited me onboard. When I was on the ship, he set sail and took me here, forcing me to cook and clean for the crew," she concluded.

Her words hung in the air, a fragile thread woven from the fabric of truth and deception.

"Why are you dressed in this pirate garb, Madame?" Monsieur Serrault inquired, his tone now lower with curiosity.

Maria met the captain's gaze, relief washing over her as his tone softened. She straightened her posture, grateful for the opportunity to explain herself further.

"Because it is impossible to live in proper attire on these rough and hostile shores," she replied, her voice steady. "The only dress I had was ripped after a month of enduring the hardships of life at sea, so I took a coat from what was on the ship."

The captain nodded thoughtfully, his expression softening with understanding. "We will see if we have proper ladies' clothes on board," he said, signaling to one of his officers to go below deck in search of suitable garments.

As the officer disappeared from view, Maria felt a glimmer of hope flicker within her. Though her circumstances remained precarious, Captain Serrault's willingness to listen offered a ray of light in the darkness that surrounded her.

Minutes passed like hours as Maria waited with bated breath, her heart pounding in anticipation. Finally, the officer emerged from below deck, a bundle of fabric cradled in his arms.

"We found some clothing that should suffice, Madame," he announced, offering the garments to Maria with a respectful nod.

Gratitude was shown by Maria as she accepted the clothing, her fingers trembling slightly as she examined the garments. Though they were simple and utilitarian, they represented a semblance of dignity and comfort amidst the chaos of her captivity.

"Thank you," she whispered, her voice barely noticeable over the sound of the waves crashing against the hull of the ship.

Maria followed the sailors below deck to a small cabin where she was given privacy to change into her new dress. As she emerged, the fabric flowing around her, she appeared more feminine, her resolve softened by the simple act of donning proper attire, as she stepped on the quarter-deck again.

In the eyes of the officers and the captain, Maria's transformation seemed to mirror a shift in their perception of her. Her once rough appearance of a pirate woman now exuded a quiet strength and grace, her willingness to cooperate and her vulnerability in the face of uncertainty resonating with their sense of empathy and understanding.

With a nod of acknowledgment, the captain turned his attention back to Maria, his gaze lingering with a newfound sense of respect.

"We will need your help; you will share all the information about this pirate ship with us, Madame," Captain Serrault demanded, his voice firm with authority.

"It is my pleasure! I will gladly do that," Maria replied, her tone resolute, "if you promise to take me back to civilization in Europe, and away from these vile pirates."

With her appearance altered and her intentions clear, Maria had succeeded in convincing those around her of her sincerity, even though she already scanned the French ship for potential weaknesses.

In the tranquil evening glow, Maria found herself seated with the captain and the officers, partaking in dinner aboard the vessel. As conversation flowed, the captain turned to her with a direct inquiry.

"Tell me, how many guns does the pirate ship have, and what size?" he asked, his tone expectant.

Maria, well aware that the captain already knew what guns were on board the Vixen, paused, considering her response carefully. "Oh, it probably has around ten cannons, and they're quite large," she replied, her voice measured.

A curious officer chimed in, seeking further details. "What caliber are the guns?" he asked, hoping for a more precise assessment.

"Monsieur," Maria began, her expression earnest, "they are long and very loud. Exceedingly noisy!"

A ripple of amusement passed among the officers at Maria's simplistic description, their eyes rolling at what they perceived as her lack of familiarity with naval gunnery. Yet, beneath their condescension, Maria remained composed, her resolve unshaken by their skepticism.

"How many men are aboard the pirate ship?" Captain Serrault inquired further, his interest piqued.

"I believe there are around ten, including the captain," Maria responded, her voice steady. She knew that the French had likely observed the pirate vessel for some time before orchestrating their attack that morning, and knew exactly how many men were aboard.

The officers exchanged glances, taking note of Maria's estimation. One of them pressed on with another question. "Do they have weapons?" he asked, seeking clarification.

"Oh yes, they are armed with long guns and pistols," Maria replied without hesitation, rendering more useless information.

Her response elicited a nod of acknowledgment from the officers, who now saw that Maria was willing to cooperate. Despite their earlier skepticism, they began to appreciate Maria's efforts even though she brought no value to their mission.

As the dinner conversation continued, Maria's willingness to assist the officers became increasingly apparent, even though her contributions were practically useless to their efforts to thwart the pirates' nefarious activities.

Gathered on the deck of The Vixen, Captain Eric and his crew faced a daunting reality. They were trapped like rats, hemmed in by the looming presence of the waiting French ship. With no viable escape route in sight, they found themselves ensnared in a perilous game of cat and mouse, their every move shadowed by the threat of annihilation.

Desperation hung heavy in the air as Eric and his crew brainstormed strategies, their minds racing with the urgency of their predicament. They knew that attempting to pass the waiting French ship would only invite disaster, as its superior armament stood poised to unleash devastation upon them. The French had twice as many guns and much heavier ones on top.

Yet, to remain idle was not an option. Time was running out, and with Maria's fate hanging in the balance, they could not afford to falter in their resolve.

Maria's newfound freedom aboard the ship granted her the opportunity to gather valuable intelligence. With the captain's trust secured, she moved about freely, her eyes keenly assessing the vessel's capabilities.

The gun deck was right underneath the upper deck. Counting the guns, Maria noted their size and placement. A row of nine 18-pounders on each side, with one 12-pounder situated in both the front and rear on the upper deck. The numbers gave an idea of the ship's firepower. It was a formidable force to be reckoned with.

As she strolled the deck, Maria engaged the sailors in conversations, deftly weaving flirtatious banter into her interactions. Her charm and wit endeared her to the crew, granting her access to their trust. On board, there were a total of 39 crewmen, accompanied by four officers, in addition to the captain. That was four times the men the Vixen had.

In the evening, following another dinner with Captain Serrault and his officers, Maria found herself back in her cabin, her gaze fixed on the shores of the island. She knew that the native inhabitants were likely observing the movements of the French ship from the cover of the dense woods.

With a quick glance toward the dense brush lining the shore, Maria opened the small window of her cabin. With a candle in hand and a piece of cloth as her signal, she began her clandestine communication with the shore, hoping someone there would notice the faint light signal. Every twenty minutes, she repeated the motion, casting her message into the night.

As the hours ticked by and the moon ascended higher in the sky, Maria's vigil continued. Then, in the dead of night, a dark shadow slipped into the water at the edge of the island. Its movement was stealthy, almost imperceptible, like a predator stalking its prey.

Drawing closer to The Vixen with an eerie silence, the shadow took shape, revealing itself to be one of the Micmac natives. Maria's heart quickened with recognition as she hissed to catch his attention. With silent grace, the native approached, gliding beneath her window like a ghostly apparition.

In hushed tones, the native spoke French, and Maria wasted no time in relaying the vital information about the French ship's armament and crew. She implored him to convey this intelligence to Eric, emphasizing her willingness to assist in any way she could, given her newfound freedom to move about the ship.

With a nod of understanding, the native assured Maria that he would return the following night. And just as swiftly as he had appeared, he disappeared into the depths of the water, leaving Maria alone once more with her thoughts and the weight of the night's revelations hanging heavy in the air.

The next morning brought with it a sense of urgency as the French captain dispatched a johnboat to explore the shallow waters east of Flat Island. Their objective: to determine if there was indeed no feasible passage for their larger vessel, allowing them to sneak into the shallow bay and confront The Vixen directly. However, the expedition returned with disheartening news. The sandbanks and shallow waters proved formidable obstacles, with depths insufficient for any vessel exceeding a 10-foot draft.

With their options dwindling and impatience mounting, Captain Serrault contemplated seeking aid from a smaller ship. Fearful that the standoff could drag on for weeks, they weighed their next move with cautious deliberation.

That evening, after another dinner with the captain, Maria wasted no time in resuming her signaling. As she opened her cabin window and sent out her message, her heart raced with urgency. It wasn't long before her native ally reappeared by her side.

In hushed tones, Maria relayed the pressing need for swift action. The French were growing impatient, she explained and were actively seeking ways to outmaneuver The Vixen. Time was of the essence, and they could ill afford to delay their response.

With a solemn nod, the native understood the gravity of the situation. As Maria watched him vanish into the night once more, she prayed that their message would reach Eric in time.

At 2 o'clock in the morning, Maria slipped quietly out of her cabin, the ship enveloped in the hushed embrace of night. With only the guards patrolling the upper deck awake, she took off her shoes and moved barefoot across the planks, her steps guided by a daring plan forming in her mind.

Walking across the deserted gun deck, Maria surveyed her surroundings. The cannons lay dormant, their deadly potential concealed behind closed gun ports and wooden barrel plugs. With a steady hand, she removed one plug and peered into the barrel, confirming her suspicions – the cannons were indeed loaded, ready for the inevitable confrontation that loomed on the horizon.

Worm hooks, sponge rammers, linstocks, and filled sponge buckets stood at the ready next to each naval gun, a testament to the captain's anticipation of battle. Maria's mind raced as she formulated her plan, each detail falling into place like pieces of a puzzle.

Returning to her cabin, Maria waited with bated breath for the following day. As heavy rain cascaded down upon the ship, obscuring her signal from view, she refused to be deterred. With determination burning in her veins, she signaled once more, hoping that her message would reach its intended recipient.

To her relief, the native swimmer emerged from the waves. With a sense of urgency, Maria conveyed her plan – to disable the guns and signal with a red flag from her window when The Vixen could safely depart from her hideout.

With a hand wave, the native signaled that he understood the gravity of the situation. As Maria watched him disappear into the night once more, she expected that her actions would pave the way for their escape from the clutches of their adversaries.

Amidst the relentless downpour, Captain Eric gathered his crew below deck aboard The Vixen, their faces illuminated by flickering lantern light. With Maria's plan to disable the guns of the French ship in motion, tension hung heavy in the air as they awaited the outcome.

"I don't know what Maria has in mind, but if she can disable those guns, it will give us the opportunity to escape," Eric declared, his voice echoing with determination.

James, the quartermaster, added his input, suggesting they

prepare their muskets and pistols as well, in case of an attack from the French men trying to board the Vixen, once they realize their guns don't fire.

"We best be ready to defend ourselves," he warned, his tone grave.

A grizzled pirate of the crew scoffed at the notion. "As if they'd dare to fire in this damn rain," he retorted, his confidence unwavering despite the storm raging outside.

Eric nodded in agreement, addressing his crew with a sense of urgency.

"The rain shows no signs of letting up. We must prepare ourselves. Load your muskets and pistols, and seal the pans with beeswax to prevent the powder from getting wet. We cannot afford any mishaps," he instructed, his voice firm with authority.

With a sense of purpose, the crew set to work, their movements swift and methodical as they readied their weapons for the inevitable confrontation that awaited them. The ship's guns were loaded and the firing mechanism and powder pans of the muskets and pistols were sealed with a layer of beeswax, to prevent the gunpowder from getting wet.

Under the cloak of night, Maria moved with silent purpose, her heart pounding with anticipation as she crept onto the empty gun deck once more. With each step, she felt the weight of her mission pressing upon her, knowing that the success of their escape hinged upon her actions.

Armed with a beaker meant to hold ale, Maria approached the first of the nine portside guns. With steady hands, she removed the tight wooden plug, revealing the barrel's gaping maw. Taking a deep breath, she dipped the beaker into the filled sponge bucket next to the cannon, scooping out two pints of water.

With careful precision, she poured the water into the gun barrel, watching as it disappeared into the darkness within. Closing the plug once more, Maria repeated the process with each of the remaining guns, methodically ensuring that they were all receiving a couple of pints of water.

Moving to the starboard side, Maria replicated the procedure, filling each of the nine guns there. The two pints of water, soaking through the patch and seeping past the cannonball, would render the gunpowder beneath useless, and bake it into the barrel. When the gunner would now attempt to ignite the powder with the glowing linstock, the powder in the pan would ignite, but not the soggy powder mash in the barrel.

As Maria completed her task, a sense of relief washed over her. Though the stakes were high and the risks great, she knew that she had done everything in her power to tilt the scales in their favor.

Maria's confidence swelled as she surveyed her handiwork. With the main guns rendered useless by her cunning sabotage, she knew that even if the French crew were to discover the ruse, it would take considerable time and effort to clear the guns of their waterlogged charges and reload them.

Though the two smaller guns on the bow and stern of the ship remained functional, they posed a lesser threat compared to the formidable firepower of the main cannons. Maria knew that their strategic advantage had been secured, at least for the time being.

With a sense of satisfaction, Maria retreated to her cabin, her mind racing with anticipation for the events that would unfold in the wake of her actions. Despite the challenges that lay ahead, she remained resolute in her determination to see their escape through to the end. And as she awaited the dawn of a new day, Maria found solace in the knowledge that their fate was now firmly in their own hands, the rules of engagement altered by her courage and resourcefulness.

The next morning, the sun still hidden behind the dark rainclouds, Maria's thoughts focused on the lingering threat posed by the two smaller guns on the bow and stern of the ship. Determined to neutralize it, she devised a daring plan.

With casual nonchalance, Maria made her way to the front of the ship, her steps purposeful yet seemingly carefree. As she approached the head, a facility she had never utilized before, she knew that her actions would need to appear inconspicuous to avoid arousing the wariness of the few sailors patrolling the deck.

Maria discreetly surveyed her surroundings, ensuring that she remained unobserved. With practiced stealth, she maneuvered closer to the smaller gun on the bow, its proximity to the head providing her with the perfect opportunity for sabotage.

As she finished her business, Maria casually strolled past the gun barrel, her heart pounding with anticipation. With deft fingers, she attempted to loosen the plug ever so slightly, hoping that the elements, perhaps aided by the heavy rains, would eventually find their way into the barrel and compromise its functionality. The one operational gun left at the stern of the ship she could simply not reach, but it would pose no real danger to the fully functional armament of The Vixen

As the first light of dawn filtered through the cabin window, Maria wasted no time in executing the next phase of her escape plan. With a determined resolve, she retrieved her red underskirt and hung it from her window, the vibrant hue serving as a beacon of hope amidst the gloom of the rainy morning.

Across the island, Eric's vigilant guard stationed on the west coast caught sight of the signal and wasted no time in relaying the message to The Vixen. Racing back to the ship, he shouted to Captain Eric, "The red flag is out!"

Upon hearing the news, Eric sprang into action, his voice carrying authority as he issued orders to his crew. With practiced efficiency, they readied the ship, preparing to set sail despite the relentless rain that pounded against the deck.

As The Vixen slowly pulled out of the bay, the crew was focused on navigating the shallow waters surrounding the island. With each gust of wind and roll of the waves, they pressed onward, their determination unwavering in the face of adversity.

Through the driving rain, The Vixen forged ahead, her sails billowing defiantly against the waves.

As the pirate ship sailed around the northern tip of Flat Island, her presence did not go unnoticed by the vigilant French guards stationed on the deck of the Néréide. With a clarion call, the French ship sprang into action, her crew swiftly raising sails and lifting anchor in preparation for the impending confrontation.

Before The Vixen could fully navigate out of the bay, the French ship pivoted, turning her full broadside toward the approaching pirate ship. On the quarter-deck, the French captain stood, his laughter echoing across the tumultuous sea.

"The pirates must be out of their minds! We will annihilate them!" he bellowed with confidence, his voice filled with scorn.

Yet, as The Vixen's gunports swung open, a sudden hush fell over the French ship. In a swift and decisive move, Captain Eric issued his command.

"Fire!" he sounded, his voice cutting through the tension like a blade.

The thunderous roar of The Vixen's portside guns reverberated across the waves as her first broadside struck the French ship with deadly accuracy. However, to the astonishment of the French crew, their own guns remained silent.

Only two guns fired with a soft thud, their report muffled and feeble. Captain Serrault's rage boiled over as he demanded answers.

"What is this? Why don't you fire, you imbeciles?" he screamed, his fury palpable.

"The gunpowder seems to have gotten moist from the rains," the first officer reported, his voice tinged with frustration.

With their cannons rendered useless, the French captain wasted no time in rallying his crew to prepare for a different kind of battle.

"Get the muskets ready! All men on deck!" he commanded, his tone resolute.

"Fire!" roared Eric, his voice cutting through the chaos as another broadside from The Vixen found its mark on the French ship. Yet, as the smoke cleared, the French crew, assembled on their deck, stood defiantly, their muskets leveled toward The Vixen.

Despite their readiness for battle, the pouring rain had taken its toll on the French muskets, rendering many of them useless. In contrast, the muskets aboard The Vixen, sealed with care and protected from the elements, fired without hesitation. The beeswax had served its purpose.

With a deafening roar, all ten muskets aboard The Vixen discharged simultaneously, their deadly payload finding their targets among the exposed French crew. Panic erupted on the French ship as men fell, their ranks thinned by the unrelenting barrage from their adversaries.

In the midst of the melee, Captain Eric stood resolute on the quarter-deck, his gaze fixed on the French ship.

As The Vixen prepared to unleash another devastating broadside upon the crippled French ship, Captain Eric's keen eyes caught sight of a figure leaping from the stern of the Néréide, and plunging into the churning, ice-cold waters below. It was Maria. In a daring bid for freedom, she had shed her dress and was now swimming completely without clothes and with determined strokes toward the safety of the island shore.

With Maria's escape imminent, Captain Serrault barked

orders to his soldiers, commanding them to open fire. Yet, once again, the relentless rain proved to be the pirates' ally as only one musket discharged its deadly load, its shot missing Maria by a mere two yards. Undeterred by gunfire, she pressed on toward the shore, her resolve unyielding in the face of danger.

With each stroke, Maria drew closer to the safety of the shore, her heart pounding with the exhilaration of her escape, as her limbs became numb in the cold water. She reached the sanctuary of solid ground. A wave of relief washed over her, as the Micmac natives emerged from the woods and cradled her shivering body in a blanket.

Meanwhile, aboard The Vixen, the crew wasted no time in delivering another thunderous broadside upon the beleaguered French ship. As the deafening roar of cannon fire echoed across the water, the masts of the French vessel splintered and collapsed, their destruction signaling the decisive turning point in the battle.

With their adversary crippled and Maria safely ashore, the crew of The Vixen stood united in victory, their spirits soaring. With its masts splintered and its sails in tatters, the once-proud French ship now floated defenseless upon the turbulent waters of the Gulf of Saint Lawrence. Desperate to escape the relentless pursuit of The Vixen, the crippled vessel strained against the currents, its crew laboring frantically to coax any semblance of movement from their battered hull.

Yet, as The Vixen closed in, her cannons roaring once more, the final blow was dealt. Another thunderous broadside found its mark, hastening the demise of their adversary. With each deafening blast, the French ship listed more, tilting dangerously to the post side, its hull breached and water flooding its decks.

In a last desperate gasp for survival, the doomed vessel fought valiantly against the inevitable. The weight of the ocean claimed it as its own, and the once-mighty ship surrendered to its watery grave, sinking slowly beneath the waves.

As the waters closed over the wreckage, a sense of finality descended upon the scene. The battle was over, the pirates' victory hard-won but well-deserved. The Vixen emerged triumphant and soon sailed back to her secret hiding spot, her crew united in their success against a vastly superior adversary.

As the pirates stood again on the shores of their hidden bay, a sense of relief filled the air. Maria's safe return brought a wave of joy, and as she embraced Eric, their bond was strengthened by the trials they had overcome together.

In the quiet of the evening, in their little log home, with glasses of wine in hand, Maria recounted her daring feat of disabling the French ship's guns. With each word, her companions listened intently, their admiration for her courage and resourcefulness growing with each passing moment.

As the night fell around them, they found solace in each other's company, grateful for the comradeship that held them together once more, in the face of great danger.

# 8 THE CAPTURE OF THE POLLUX

In the late 1600s, Irish Catholics came to Newfoundland looking for safety and opportunities. At that time, Newfoundland was controlled by Quebec, which was a French colony, and Catholic. These settlers added to the mix of different cultures already living there. But matters started to change. In 1713, the Treaty of Utrecht was signed, which meant that France gave up control of Newfoundland to Britain, marking a significant change of power. The Catholic Church's influence over the island went from being controlled by the leaders in Quebec to being controlled by leaders in London.

At the same time, more and more people in the French colonies on the North American Continent were becoming Protestant instead of Catholic, which made things even more difficult for the Catholic Church. Sensing the shifting tides of religious allegiance, the Catholic Church soon began to move some of its assets out of the French colonies, anticipating further weakening of its position in the face of Protestant expansion.

As the summer wore on and the winds of fortune continued to favor them, The Vixen and her daring pirate crew embarked on a string of successful raids, plundering five merchant ships and reaping a net gain of between £7,000 and £9,000 with each conquest. With their coffers overflowing and their spirits buoyed by their victories, they prepared to set sail once more, their sights set on returning to England before the harsh winter descended upon the seas. The season had netted Eric and Maria £20,000 and each crew member around £5,000.

As The Vixen bid farewell to their native allies on Flat Island, they set sail once more, their sights set on the northern tip of Cape Breton. Patiently, they waited, scanning the horizon for any sign of opportunity amidst the busy sea lanes of the Cabot Strait.

Despite the obscured visibility, the seasoned sailors of The Vixen remained undeterred, their senses finely attuned to the subtle shifts in the wind and the faint glimmer of distant sails through the mist. With each passing moment, the tension aboard the ship grew palpable, the promise of adventure and riches driving them ever forward into the unknown.

For days, they cruised the waters with a watchful eye, letting half a dozen ships pass by unscathed as they deemed them unworthy of their attention. As the late afternoon descended upon the ocean, The Vixen sailed through the mist, her sleek silhouette cutting through the veil of fog that hung thick in the air. The mist enveloped the ship like a shroud, casting an ethereal glow over the deck as the crew moved about their tasks with practiced efficiency. But then, on the horizon, a silhouette emerged, a large brig flying the colors of France, her sails billowing in the wind as she made her way from Quebec.

With anticipation coursing through their veins, the crew of The Vixen sprang into action, their hearts pounding with the thrill of the chase. Maneuvering with expert precision, they closed in on their target, their cannons at the ready and their blades gleaming in the pale sunlight.

As they drew nearer, the French brig came into full view. She was a good-sized schooner, bout 120 ft long, and her cargo hold promised to be laden with riches from the New World.

As The Vixen closed in on the seemingly unencumbered ship sailing eastward, there was an eerie stillness about the vessel. Despite the lack of visible activity on deck, tension hung thick in the air. The crew of The Vixen exchanged wary glances as they approached, unsure of what they might encounter.

With caution, Captain Eric ordered his crew to prepare for a boarding action. The pirate crew moved swiftly and silently, readying their guns and weapons and securing their grapple hooks as they prepared to make contact with the silent ship.

As they finally drew alongside, Eric peered over the railings with his telescope, eyes scanning the deck for any sign of movement.

The ship's name was Pollux. But to Eric's astonishment, there was little, except the man on the steering and an officer on the quarter deck. With a fierce battle cry, the sailors of The Vixen threw their lines with grappling hooks attached onto the deck of the unsuspecting vessel, her cannons ready to unleash a barrage of shot and shells. But firing seemed not necessary as no resistance was given, and only a small number of sailors emerged on deck with their hands in the air.

Perplexed and unnerved, Eric cautiously stepped aboard the quiet vessel, his senses on high alert for any sign of danger. He sent men down into the ship's cabins to look for hidden crewmembers and the captain.

As the crew of The Vixen searched the silent vessel, their cautious exploration was suddenly interrupted by the reappearance of two members of the pirate crew, pistols drawn, accompanied by the ship's captain and first officer whom they had captured. The captain still wore a linen bibb around his neck. He obviously had been eating dinner below deck.

The pirates, with a menacing air about them, wasted no time asserting their dominance over the situation. Their pistols glinted in the faint sunlight as they directed the captain and first officer to stand before them, their expressions grim and determined. Soon, the captain and the crew members were sitting on the deck with their hands bound.

Meanwhile, another group of unexpected figures emerged from the shadows of the ship: four monks, their presence an enigma amid this unfolding drama. Clad in soutanes, wrapped around their bodies, and held with a belt-like cinture, they seemed out of place among the sailors. Going by their attire, they seemed to be Jesuits. They were followed by a native man in a suit, who seemed to be their servant.

The sudden convergence of these disparate characters added to the tension already thick in the air. The crew of The Vixen exchanged wary glances, unsure of what to make of this unexpected turn of events.

The pirates, with a glint of triumph in their eyes, brandished their pistols menacingly in front of the prisoners, asserting their control over the situation. The monks, on the other hand, remained calm and composed, their serene demeanor a stark contrast to the chaos unfolding around them.

As the tension aboard the silent ship escalated, another pair of pirates emerged from below deck, their faces etched with concern.

"Captain," one of them began, addressing Eric with a sense of urgency, "this ship is empty. There's no sign of cargo, no goods, nothing of value."

The disappointment in their voices was palpable as they relayed the barren state of the vessel they had just explored. Eric, the ever-cautious pirate captain, narrowed his eyes thoughtfully, absorbing the news with a furrowed brow.

As Maria engaged in conversation with the bound captain, the atmosphere on deck remained tense, the exchange between them unfolding against the backdrop of the mysterious ship and its silent emptiness.

"Where are you headed, gentlemen?" Maria inquired, her voice steady despite the gravity of the situation.

"We are bound for Rouen in France," the captain replied, his tone resigned yet determined.

Maria's brow furrowed in disbelief. "And yet, we cannot locate any cargo on your ship," she pointed out, her skepticism evident.

The captain's response was unwavering. "We are sailing empty, Madame," he affirmed, his words ringing with a sense of truth.

Maria's doubts lingered, her incredulity growing with each passing moment. "It is hard to believe that such a mighty schooner would sail the oceans empty," she countered, her gaze unwavering.

The captain's explanation only seemed to raise more questions. "We are indeed empty, Madame. We are taking these gentlemen back to Rouen, to Lycée Pierre-Corneille," he explained, pointing at the monks, his words laden with a sense of duty.

Maria's skepticism turned to warning as she addressed the captain with steely resolve.

"Listen," she began with her voice firm, "if you lie to me and we find gold and riches on this ship, all of you will go down with it. But if you tell us where the valuables are, we may let you go."

The captain's response was swift and unequivocal. "There is nothing of worth on my ship," he repeated.

"I swear by the holy virgin Mary," one of the monks interjected, his voice solemn, "the ship is empty. There is no gold."

Despite their reassurances, Maria remained wary, her instincts telling her that there was more to this situation than what met the eye. With a final glance at the bound captain and the enigmatic monks flanking him, she knew that the truth would only reveal itself with time, and she was determined to uncover it, whatever the cost.

"Empty, you say?" Eric muttered, his voice tinged with both frustration and intrigue. "No cargo, and almost no crew. This doesn't add up."

Eric's mind raced as he contemplated the implications of this discovery. Why would such a large ship sail from the New World to France completely empty? Or was there something more sinister at play?

With a sense of foreboding settling over the scene, Eric turned to his own men, determination flashing in his eyes.

"Search the ship again," he commanded, his voice firm and resolute. "The cabins of the captain and these monks also. Lift up planks, look behind walls. We may not have found treasure, but there's something here worth uncovering."

With renewed purpose, the pirates set about scouring the empty vessel once more, their senses alert for any clue that might shed light on the mystery of the vacant ship. As they delved deeper into its silent corridors and deserted compartments, the truth seemed to elude them, shrouded in the shadows of uncertainty.

Maria's gaze fell upon the heavy golden pectoral cross adorning one of the monks. With a swift motion, she reached out and tore the cross from his neck, the weight of the gold unmistakable in her hand.

"Well, there is at least a little gold," Maria remarked, her tone laced with a mix of frustration and vindication.

The monk recoiled in shock, his expression a mixture of

outrage and disbelief. "This is blasphemy, my child," he protested, his voice carrying a note of indignation.

Before Maria could respond to the monk's objections, the scene was interrupted once more by the reappearance of the pirates from the ship's hull.

"Captain," one of the pirates called out, his voice echoing across the deck, "there is not even a mouse on this ship, let alone cargo."

Eric's expression darkened at the news; his frustration was evident as he grappled with the reality of the situation. It seemed that the mystery of the empty vessel only deepened with each passing moment, leaving more questions than answers in its wake.

Maria exchanged a meaningful glance with Eric, the gravity of the situation weighing heavily upon them both. It was clear that they were facing a puzzle unlike any they had encountered before, and the truth behind the ship without content remained elusive, shrouded in layers of uncertainty and intrigue.

As Eric, Maria, and the two pirates ventured below deck, tension hung heavy in the air, their senses heightened as they delved deeper into the belly of the ship. Eric's grip tightened around the axe he carried, a tool that now seemed more like a weapon in the face of the unknown.

With determined resolve, they searched the cabins, tearing through the wooden planks with Eric's axe in search of hidden compartments or stashes. Yet, despite their efforts, they found nothing but empty spaces, devoid of any sign of treasure or cargo.

Their quest led them to the cargo hold, a vast chamber that echoed with emptiness. Save for a few crates containing sails and rope, the hold appeared disappointingly barren. The were empty burlap sacks stacked in a corner, but nothing of value. But Eric's intuition urged him forward, leading him to a small cargo room tucked away to the side. It was filled with wooden barrels.

"What's in there?" Eric demanded of one of his sailors, his voice edged with anticipation.

"Water, they're full of water," the sailor replied, his tone matter-of-fact.

"Did you check?" Eric inquired, as his voice filled with urgency.

"I opened one of them, yes," the pirate replied, confirming his actions. "It seems to be only drinking water."

Eric wasted no time in taking action. With a swift swing of his axe, he struck one of the barrels, releasing its liquid contents into the room. To his surprise, the next barrel yielded the same result. Water!

But then, as he struck a third barrel, something

unexpected happened. No water emerged from the hole he had created. He shook the barrel; it was heavy. Intrigued, Eric removed the top of the barrel with blows from his axe, revealing its hidden contents: stacks of silver livres gleaming in the dim light of the cargo hold.

A sense of awe swept over the crew as they beheld the unexpected treasure before them. Maria's suspicions had been confirmed, and Eric's instincts had led them to the prize they had sought.

"Look at these sneaky bastards," one sailor exclaimed, his voice tinged with a mixture of disbelief and triumph.

"I knew it," Maria responded, her eyes gleaming with satisfaction.

As Maria ascended to the deck with a handful of silver coins, she confronted the monks, her eyes blazing with accusation as she cast the coins at their feet.

"You just swore on the Holy Virgin Mary that there is no treasure on this ship. What is this?" she demanded, her voice sharp with resentment.

The Jesuit monk met her gaze with unwavering calmness, his demeanor composed despite the tension that crackled in the air. "This is money of the Holy Mother Church, donated by the faithful," he explained, his tone measured and serene.

Maria's expression hardened at his response. "Isn't lying a

grave sin, Father?" she challenged, her voice cutting through the stillness of the deck.

The priest's reply was firm and unapologetic. "In this case, the end justifies the means. I have a responsibility to protect God's assets by all means," he asserted, his words carrying a sense of conviction.

The crew of The Vixen watched in silence, their eyes darting between Maria and the monks as the confrontation unfolded before them. It was clear that beneath the facade of piety and devotion, there lurked a darker truth, one that threatened to unravel the fragile balance between faith and deception.

Maria chuckled darkly as she addressed the monks, her voice tinged with a hint of defiance. "If it fits your agenda, lying is justified. I see. Well, your silver is ours now," she declared, a smirk playing on her lips.

The monk's eyes widened in shock at Maria's brazen declaration. "This is a grave sin, my child. You are stealing from God," he admonished, his tone filled with reproach.

Maria's laughter rang out across the deck. "I have little concern, and I am joyfully stealing from you as well as from God," she retorted, her words laced with a sharp edge of sarcasm.

"Think of the consequences. You will face eternal damnation," another monk chimed in, his voice grave with warning.

Maria shrugged indifferently. "I have faced damnation before, here on earth," she replied with a steely resolve. "I reckon, it will not get much worse in Hell."

The Jesuit monk furrowed his brow in confusion. "Why is that? What have you faced?" he inquired, his curiosity piqued.

Maria's gaze hardened as she spoke of her past. "Try living in a harbor town, with a dead father and a mother who is a prostitute, while you have to work in pub kitchens to eat scraps leftover on the plates by patrons," she recounted bitterly.

The priest nodded solemnly, his expression sympathetic. "Fornication and deceiving married men into adultery is a sin, my child. Perhaps you and your mother invoked the ire of God," he mused.

Maria's eyes flashed with defiance as she countered his words. "Leave my mother out of it! If anybody deserved Heaven it is her. And I am sure I invoked the wrath of God, too, when I was not even 11 years old and gave in to the advances of grown sailors, who bribed me with a piece of bread and a copper coin," she confessed bitterly.

The priest remained unmoved. "A sin is a sin regardless," he explained with conviction.

Maria scoffed at his words. "It is quite interesting how

these sins only apply to us poor, but the King, the dukes and the counts can afford mistresses and commit adultery all day long, and God and the church seem just fine with it," she remarked, her voice dripping with bitter irony.

The conversation aboard the ship grew tense as the priest expounded on the concept of divine providence.

"Everybody shares a lot according to God almighty's will," the priest explained, his voice carrying the weight of conviction. "The king is of God's grace. Had God wanted him to be a pauper, he'd be a beggar. And the poor will reap their reward in Heaven, of this there is no doubt."

Maria's eyes narrowed as she listened to the priest's words, her skepticism evident.

"Your promise of a reward in the afterlife is to keep the poor from the throats of the rich, Reverend," she countered sharply, her tone laced with bitterness. "The church has done nothing to ease the pain of the common man, neither has God. On the contrary, the church blesses exploitation, serfdom, and slavery."

The friar's voice carried over the sound of the waves as he attempted to justify the use of the church's money. "The church uses its money to give alms to the poor," he explained, his tone earnest.

Maria's expression remained unchanged.

"Oh, I am very aware of these alms, as I have received

some in the past myself," she countered sharply, her voice tinged with anger.

"The food is not deemed suitable for your tables anymore, but it is still too good for a pig's trough. And the clothes you give are threadbare robes, which the wealthy have discarded," she continued, her words dripping with scorn.

The friar shifted uncomfortably under Maria's scrutiny, his gaze dropping to the deck below. It was clear that her accusations struck a nerve, challenging the very foundation of the church's supposed charity.

The monk regarded her with a solemn expression. "Are you questioning God's will, my child?" he inquired, his voice somber with concern. "Everything that happens on Earth happens according to His will. Nothing takes place unless the almighty God approves it."

Maria shook her head adamantly. "No, I am not questioning God's will, Monsieur. I am questioning the existence of God," she replied defiantly, her words hanging heavy in the air.

A murmur of shock rippled through the gathered monks as Maria's declaration reverberated around them. "This is blasphemy and a grave sacrilege! It will cost you dearly in purgatory," another monk chimed in, his voice filled with admonishment.

Maria met their reproach with a steely gaze, unyielding in

her convictions. As the echoes of their conversation faded into the sea breeze, it became clear that the clash of beliefs aboard the ship would not be easily resolved.

The deck buzzed with tension as Maria's orders rang out, cutting through the air like a blade. "Go down and bring me some of those big burlap sacks!" she commanded, her voice sharp and authoritative.

A sailor sprang into action, hastening below deck to retrieve the requested sacks. Moments later, he emerged, bearing the heavy burlap sacks in his arms.

"Put the friars in there, and bind the top of the sack tight with a rope," Maria instructed, her tone unwavering as she watched the scene unfold.

With swift efficiency, the pirates seized the bound friars and forced them into the sacks, securing the tops tightly with thick ropes. Confusion and fear flickered in the eyes of the friars as they found themselves trapped within the coarse confines of the sacks.

"What is this? What are you doing?" their leader demanded, his voice tinged with desperation before his head disappeared.

Maria's laughter echoed across the deck. "I will have you drowned in the ocean," she declared, her words carrying a chilling finality. "Our deal was you give me the silver and I let you go. You lied."

The friars pleaded for mercy, their protests falling on deaf ears. "Wait, you can't do that! We are men of God," one of them cried out, his voice tinged with disbelief.

"Oh, but I can. I am afraid, this is the will of God," Maria retorted coldly, her gaze unyielding. "Nothing here happens without his will, right?"

"You are committing murder! It is a grave sin! A deadly sin," the friar protested, his voice trembling with fear as the sack closed over him.

Maria's laughter rang out once more, a bitter echo of amusement in the face of their plight. "It seems to be a deadly sin, indeed. But do not worry, brother. You will reap your reward in the afterlife. In minutes, you will be reunited with God in paradise," she joked, her words dripping with sarcasm.

With a sense of finality, the sailors bound the sacks closed, sealing the fate of the trapped friars as they prepared to cast them into the unforgiving depths of the ocean.

As Maria stood at the railing, her gaze fixed on the sacks containing the screaming friars as they thrashed in the water, a sense of grim satisfaction washed over her. With a cold resolve, she watched as the sacks disappeared into the depths, their cries silenced by the unforgiving sea.

Meanwhile, the pirate crew wasted no time in loading the barrels filled with silver onto The Vixen. The weight of their newfound treasure seemed to add an air of excitement to the crew as they worked swiftly and efficiently.

With the silver securely stowed away, The Vixen set sail, its course set for England. London beckoned as their destination, offering a haven where they could sell and deposit their ill-gotten gains with relative ease.

With over 1,200 pounds of silver in their possession, they were poised to make their mark on the crowded streets of London, where fortunes were won and lost amidst the bustling chaos of the city. A course of 100° east and then 65° northeast would take them directly into the English Channel.

## 9 IN LONDON

As late November enveloped the River Thames in a cloak of heavy fog, The Vixen navigated her way through the mist-shrouded waters, its sails billowing in the chilly breeze. The city of London loomed ahead, its towering spires and swarming streets obscured by the dense fog.

The crew of The Vixen strained their senses, relying on their knowledge of the river and the occasional sound of distant bells to guide their way. The murky waters of the Thames flowed steadily beneath the ship's hull, carrying them ever closer to their destination.

As they sailed further into the harbor of London, the fog seemed to thicken around them, casting an eerie pall over the scene. The faint glow of lanterns and the distant hum of activity hinted at the presence of the bustling city beyond the mist.

With cautious precision, Eric steered the ship through the maze of docks and moorings, his eyes scanning the murky waters for any sign of obstacles. Despite the challenges posed by the fog, he remained steadfast in his determination to safely guide his crew and their precious cargo to shore.

As The Vixen finally slipped into her berth in the heart of London, the crew let out a collective sigh of relief. Their journey had been fraught with danger and uncertainty, but they had finally arrived at their destination.

After successfully mooring The Vixen at a dock and dismissing the crew to enjoy a well-deserved respite, Eric and Maria wasted no time in seeking refuge from the chill of the late November evening. With weary steps, they made their way through the bustling streets of London, their breath visible in the cold night air.

Their destination: The Four Swans Inn, nestled along Bishopsgate Street, promised warmth and shelter from the elements. It was a sizeable three-story building enclosing an inner court, with wooden walkways leading around the courtyard on the second and third floors. As they approached the inn, its cozy glow beckoned to them through the fog, a welcome beacon amidst the darkness of the night.

Pushing open the heavy wooden door, Eric and Maria stepped into the warm embrace of the inn's interior. The air was thick with the scent of ale and roasted meats, and the sound of laughter and lively conversation filled the room.

They exchanged weary smiles as they made their way to the innkeeper, who greeted them with a friendly nod. "A stately room for two, if you please," Eric requested, his voice tinged with exhaustion from their long journey.

The man nodded in understanding, reaching for a key and gesturing toward the stairs. "Right this way, follow me to our best room, Captain," he replied, leading them to their quarters through the teeming inner court of the Inn with a brisk stride.

With the promise of a hot meal and a soft bed awaiting them, Eric and Maria settled into their lodgings at The Four Swans Inn, grateful for the sanctuary it provided amidst the bustling chaos of London's streets.

In a scene bathed in the soft glow of candlelight, Maria knelt before Eric, her movements filled with a potent mixture of desire and longing. With trembling hands, she reached for the zipper of his trousers, her breath catching in her throat as she spoke.

"You know," she whispered, her voice husky with desire, "I've been wet ever since I took care of those monks off the coast of Newfoundland."

Eric's brows furrowed slightly at her admission; his gaze was locked with hers.

"You seem to have a penchant for violence, my dear," he remarked, his tone tinged with amusement and curiosity.

Maria's lips parted in a soft moan as she leaned closer, her curls cascading around her face like a halo of darkness. "Oh, it just feels so good for once to be on the giving end," she confessed, her words dripping with raw passion.

Eric's senses were overwhelmed by the sight of her, her curled hair brushing against her shoulders, the gentle clinking of her silver bracelets filling the air as she moved. He felt her tongue, wet and soft, tracing patterns of desire across his skin, igniting a fire deep within him.

Just as he felt himself on the brink of release, Maria's touch withdrew, leaving him achingly empty. Slowly, sensually, she began to undress him, removing each article of clothing with deliberate care. His jacket, his pants, every layer peeled away until he lay bare before her, exposed and vulnerable.

She unbuttoned her dress and her blouse, a tantalizing tease that left him craving more. As she sat beside him on the bed, she took his hand in hers and guided it beneath the fabric of her dress. His fingers met with warmth and wetness, his touch sending shivers of pleasure coursing through her body.

With a hungry sigh, he delved deeper, feeling the intoxicating heat of her desire enveloping him. Her essence was deep, warm, and impossibly wet, pulling him deeper into the depths of passion with each passing moment. As he explored her, his fingers lost in the depths of her desire, they became entwined in a dance of ecstasy and longing, their connection forged in the flames of desire that burned between them.

As Maria straddled him, a tender intimacy enveloped them, her movements slow and deliberate as she guided him inside her wetness. With each gentle thrust of her hips, the ruffles of her dress brushed against his naked skin, igniting a sensation of warmth and desire that pulsed through his body.

Maria's curves, draped in the soft fabric of her dress, hovered above him like a delicate cloud, her chest rising and falling with the rhythm of their joined bodies. Her vulva, warm and firm, enveloped him with an irresistible force, drawing him intensely into the embrace of her thighs with each passing moment.

As he grew larger and harder within her, a surge of desire rippled through him, the intensity of their connection transcending mere physical pleasure. It was as if something magical, something sacred, lay dormant within her, slowly awakening and intertwining with his essence, creating a bond that transcended the boundaries of the flesh.

It felt as though their souls were merging, their bodies becoming vessels for a deeper, more profound connection that defied explanation. It was a sensation unlike any other, a union of two souls bound together by the irresistible pull of love and desire.

With their passion sated for the moment, Eric and Maria decided to indulge in the pleasures of the palate, their appetites whetted by their earlier exertions. They called upon the innkeeper to arrange for a sumptuous feast to be delivered to their room, along with a bottle of fine wine to accompany their meal.

As they awaited the arrival of their food and drink, Eric and Maria basked in the afterglow of their lovemaking, their bodies entwined in a tender embrace. The soft glow of candlelight cast a warm hue over the room, lending an air of intimacy to their surroundings.

When the knock at the door signaled the arrival of their repast, Eric rose from the bed with a lazy stretch, his movements languid with satisfaction. Maria watched him with a fond smile, her heart filled with a sense of contentment as she took in the sight of her lover.

Together, they shared a feast fit for royalty, savoring each delectable bite and sip of wine as they reveled in the simple pleasure of each other's company. With each shared glance and whispered word, their bond grew stronger, a testament to the enduring power of love and desire.

As the night wore on and the remnants of their feast lay

scattered upon the table, Eric and Maria found themselves lost in each other's arms once more, their bodies entwined in a tender embrace as they drifted off to sleep, sated and content in each other's love.

As the first light of dawn painted the sky with hues of pink and gold, Maria and Eric met with two trusted sailors from their crew at the bustling docks of London. Together, they set about unloading the precious cargo of silver from The Vixen, their movements swift and efficient as they worked to transfer the heavy barrels onto a waiting carriage.

With the silver securely loaded, Maria and Eric made their way through the crowded streets of London, the rhythmic clip-clop of hooves accompanying their journey. Their destination was the Bank of England, where they would exchange their bounty for a handsome sum of coin.

Arriving at the familiar facade of the office on Threadneedle Street, Maria and Eric wasted no time in presenting their cargo to the bankers, who examined the silver with keen interest. After a brief negotiation, they reached an agreement, and the silver was exchanged for a hefty sum of £22,000.

Buoyed by their success, Maria and Eric wasted no time in depositing the rest of their funds into the Bank of England, their share from the summer raids on top of the profit from the silver now totaling nearly another £40,000. It was a staggering sum.

With their wealth safely deposited and their crew rewarded with their share of the silver, Maria and Eric returned to The Vixen, their hearts light with satisfaction.

Throughout the afternoon, Eric took it upon himself to ensure the ship would be in pristine condition in the spring. He found a trusted shipbuilder to arrange for the hull to be cleaned and tarred once more, ensuring The Vixen would glide through the waters with ease. Additionally, repairs were commissioned for the sails and rigging, ensuring the ship would be ready for her next voyage.

As the sun dipped below the horizon and the day gave way to dusk, Maria and Eric stood together on the deck of The Vixen one last time, their hands clasped in a silent acknowledgment of all they had achieved, before making their way back to the Four Swans.

After settling into their accommodations at the hotel, Eric and Maria decided to embark on another excursion to explore the areas surrounding London in search of potential property for their retirement. Boarding a coach once more, they set out on Dover Road, their destination veering toward the picturesque coast.

The pair left the lively city behind. The carriage meandered toward Shooter's Hill. A sense of tranquility washed over them as the rolling countryside unfolded before their eyes in a patchwork of green fields and winding country lanes.

However, their peaceful journey was abruptly interrupted when their carriage was brought to a sudden halt by the menacing presence of three armed robbers, mounted on horseback. The coachman, paralyzed with fear, trembled at the sight of the highwaymen.

With a steely resolve, Eric stepped out of the carriage, his gaze unwavering as he assessed the situation. Inside, Maria remained seated, her heart pounding with apprehension as she watched the events unfold before her.

Despite the danger that loomed before them, Eric remained calm and composed. As the highwaymen's demands echoed through the stillness of the countryside, Eric stood his ground, his gaze steady as he faced the imminent threat. "Hand over your purse, mister," one of the robbers barked, his voice laced with menace.

Eric's brow furrowed in defiance. "Why would I want to do that?" he retorted, his tone unwavering.

The leader of the highwaymen smirked, a cruel glint in his eye. "Because we will kill you and violate the lady if you don't," he threatened, his words dripping with malice.

Eric's grip tightened around his purse, his resolve unyielding. "I do indeed have £2,000 with me," he admitted calmly. "But it is of little use to you, because I most certainly will not hand it over. Trust me, there are easier ways to earn this handsome sum."

The highwaymen erupted into raucous laughter, their amusement ringing through the air. One of them brandished a flintlock pistol, pointing it menacingly at Eric. "What are you going to do now, bigmouth, eh?" he taunted.

Eric's jaw clenched, his eyes flashing with determination. "I am going to kill you," he declared boldly. "You better ride away."

Meanwhile, Maria had quietly retrieved her trusty double pistols, her hands steady as she took aim from the darkness of the carriage. With a silent nod from Eric, she fired a shot that rang out through the stillness of the night, striking the robber with the pistol square in the chest.

As the highwayman tumbled from his horse, Eric seized the opportunity to draw his own pistol, leveling it at the remaining two bandits, one of which was drawing his pistol and trying to point it at the carriage. With Maria's swift and decisive action buying them precious moments, Eric let his pistol speak, shooting the second robber off his horse.

The third robber's bravado wavered in the face of Eric and Maria's determined defense.

"I was not aware that you were armed, and the lady was such a good shot," he stammered, his voice tinged with uncertainty.

Eric's expression softened slightly, a glimmer of understanding in his eyes. "You were warned," he stated firmly, his tone resolute. "But I understand. You are carrying out a dangerous trade. So go about your way."

With a nod of acknowledgment, the robber swiftly turned his horse and galloped off into the enveloping darkness of the night, disappearing into the shadows like a phantom.

As the sound of hoofbeats faded into the distance, Eric and Maria breathed a sigh of relief, the tension of the encounter slowly dissipating. With the threat averted, they turned their attention back to their journey, grateful for the bond of trust and courage that had seen them through the ordeal.

As Eric and Maria continued their exploration of the English countryside in search of the perfect retirement property, Eric's demeanor grew increasingly apprehensive. At one point, as they surveyed yet another manor, Eric's unease bubbled to the surface.

"I think we may need to look elsewhere and leave England behind," Eric remarked, his voice tinged with uncertainty.

Surprised by his sudden change of heart, Maria turned to him with a furrowed brow. "Why do you think that?" she inquired, her concern evident.

"I find it quite depressing, London in particular, the

poverty, the senseless drinking of gin," he responded. "And I feel a little insecure about being recognized one day and facing the gallows," Eric confessed, his tone heavy with worry. "Why take that risk?"

"Where could we go?" Maria asked, her voice tinged with uncertainty.

"The new colonies perhaps. Or even France," Eric replied, his tone contemplative. "Who knows us there? Nobody."

With a heavy heart, Maria nodded in understanding. She could see the weight of Eric's concerns pressing upon him, the fear of a dark and uncertain fate looming over their heads.

With a shared glance, they silently agreed to heed Eric's instincts and return to London, their dreams of finding a retirement haven in England overshadowed by the specter of impending danger. As they made their way back to the bustling city, their thoughts turned toward the future and the unknown adventures that lay ahead.

Back in London, Eric and Maria strolled along the hectic streets, their stomachs rumbling in anticipation of a satisfying meal. They meandered through the labyrinthine alleys, their eyes scanning the rowdy taverns and cozy eateries that lined the cobblestone streets. They were on their way to The Cheshire Cheese on Fleet Street to treat their crew for a hearty dinner.

The tantalizing aromas of savory dishes wafted through the air, tempting their senses and fueling their hunger. The clamor of voices and clinking of glasses filled the atmosphere, adding to the lively ambiance of the city's nightlife.

As night cloaked the streets of London, a vibrant display unfolded as brightly attired prostitutes took to the bustling side streets. While some of the high-class women awaited the attention of potential suitors, the majority actively pursued clients, beckoning them with alluring gestures and inviting words. They surrounded lone individuals, tempting them with promises of companionship.

As the evening progressed, the younger women concluded their transactions and vanished into the shadows, leaving behind the older ladies, typically aged fifty or sixty, who emerged from their dwellings. These seasoned individuals targeted the intoxicated pedestrians, often coaxing them into indulging their desires right there on the crowded streets.

The aroma of cheap gin permeated the air, its effects evident as both men and women succumbed to its intoxicating allure, indulging heavily in its consumption amidst the nocturnal chaos of the city.

They were nearing their destination on Fleet Street, eager to reunite with their crew of twelve. Along a side street, a young woman stood, tears streaming down her face.

Bruises marred her arms, and a scratch showed on her cheek. Sensing her distress, Maria approached and inquired about her well-being.

"It's nothing," the woman murmured. "I just need to earn more money."

"We all do," Maria quipped with a wry smile. "Why don't you join us for a nice dinner and some decent company at the Cheshire Cheese?"

Eric chimed in, extending an invitation. "Come with us. You shouldn't be alone, especially after what you've been through."

"But I've already had a run-in with my two pimps, and they won't be pleased if I dine out," the woman hesitated, revealing her hunger.

"Leave that to us," Eric assured her. "We'll handle it. You need sustenance, and we can provide that."

Grateful for the offer, the woman agreed to accompany them. As they made their way toward the pub, they encountered a sudden challenge from two men.

"Where are you taking my lady to?" one of the men demanded, his tone menacing.

"It's none of your business," Eric retorted, his stance defiant.

"You seem unfamiliar with this territory. I happen to own

this woman," the other man declared, brandishing a dagger and pressing it against Eric's throat.

Just as tension reached its peak, the crew of the Vixen, 12 sailors some in the company of ladies from the streets of London, led by quartermaster Bancroft, rounded the corner.

"Who dares threaten our captain?" Bancroft demanded, his deep voice laced with authority.

Caught off guard by the unexpected appearance of an entire crew of burly sailors, the two men faltered, releasing Eric from their grasp.

"I believe these gentlemen need a stroll by the river," Maria interjected smoothly. "A little swim, too, to cool off a bit, perhaps?"

In an instant, four stout pirates seized the men and whisked them away toward the shores of the Thames. After a swift but effective reprimand in the form of a good flocking, the two assailants were left to float in the river, their threat neutralized.

As the crew regrouped, they entered the Cheshire Cheese pub and claimed a large table. Maria reassured the woman, now identified as Elisa Connor, that she needed not to worry about the two men any longer.

"I'm Maria Lindsay," Maria introduced herself, gesturing to Eric. "And this is Captain Eric Cobham, along with

Mr. James Bancroft, our quartermaster, and the rest of our ship's crew."

"Nice to meet you," Elisa replied, introducing herself in turn once more.

The jolly group settled into the cozy atmosphere of the Cheshire Cheese pub, and the tension from the earlier encounter began to dissipate. Elisa looked around cautiously, still somewhat on edge from her recent ordeal, but the warmth of the place and the company of her newfound allies helped to ease her nerves.

"So, Elisa," Maria began, her tone gentle and understanding, "what's your story? How did you end up in such a predicament?"

Elisa sighed, her gaze falling to the table as she traced patterns in the wood grain with her finger. "It's a long story," she admitted, "but it all started when my family fell on hard times. I had to find a way to support myself, and... well, I made some bad decisions. The two men helped me at first, bought me new clothes and had me sign a paper. Then they demanded that I pay them back or they would send me to debtor's prison. I have been paying for 6 months now, and it's never enough."

Eric listened intently, his expression sympathetic. "We all make mistakes," he said softly, reaching out to clasp Elisa's hand in a reassuring gesture. "The important thing is that you're here now, and you're safe. They will not mess with me and my crew, that I can assure you."

Elisa managed a small smile, gratitude shining in her eyes. "Thank you," she murmured, her voice barely above a whisper. "I never thought I'd find kindness in a place like this."

As the evening wore on, laughter filled the air as stories were shared and friendships blossomed. Elisa found herself opening up to her new companions, a sense of camaraderie growing stronger.

Eventually, the night drew to a close, and Eric picked up the tab for his men.

As the crew scattered outside the pub, and Eric and Maria prepared to head back to the Four Swans, Elisa wandered into a nearby side street, taking a seat on the curb. Concerned, Maria approached her and inquired why she wasn't heading home.

"I have nowhere to go," Elisa replied quietly. "I was living with the two men."

Sensing her predicament, Eric extended an invitation for her to join them at the Four Swans Inn. Though hesitant at first, Elisa eventually relented, agreeing to accompany them albeit with reluctance.

As the three made their way back to the Inn, Elisa walked quietly beside Eric and Maria, her thoughts heavy with the weight of her circumstances. Eric couldn't help but feel a pang of sympathy for her situation.

Maria, seeing the weariness in Elisa's eyes, offered her a reassuring smile. "You're safe here," she said softly. "We'll figure things out in the morning."

Elisa nodded gratefully, feeling a sense of relief wash over her. For the first time in a long while, she allowed herself to relax, knowing that she was in the company of people who genuinely cared about her well-being.

They ascended the creaking staircase to their room.

"I once walked in your shoes," Maria confided to Elisa, her tone soft with empathy.

Perplexed, Elisa inquired, "What do you mean?"

"I used to be a prostitute in Plymouth, working at a harbor pub," Maria explained, her gaze distant with memories. "That was before I met Eric."

"So, Eric rescued you?" Elisa questioned, a glimmer in her eyes.

Maria shook her head gently. "Yes and no," she clarified. "Eric provided me with an opportunity, but ultimately, I had to find the strength to change my circumstances myself. It wasn't solely about escaping the profession; there was a lot I liked about it. It was about reclaiming my autonomy. While being a prostitute had its advantages, such as the relationships I formed with some of my clients, there were negatives. What I despised was the lack of choice, the feeling of being trapped by poverty."

"I understand completely," Elisa murmured, her expression softening with understanding. "It's not the work itself that's the issue; I don't mind doing it. I enjoy it even, at times. It's the exploitation and the sense of being powerless. Despite the relationships I've built, I long for freedom and self-determination."

Maria nodded in solidarity. "Exactly," she affirmed. "It's about having the power to make choices and control over our own lives. That's what matters most."

"But isn't that the case with everything these days?" Eric interjected, his voice tinged with bitterness. "Whether you're forced to walk the streets and pay exorbitant rent to some landlord, or you're compelled to sail on a ship of the King, pressed into service against your will, only to return home broke or maimed, like my father... it's all the same. As a poor man, you may have freedom on paper, but you lack autonomy over your body, because you do not have the means to exercise your freedom."

Elisa listened intently, absorbing Eric's words. "So, what exactly do the two of you do?" she inquired.

"We own a ship, but I must say, it wasn't acquired through conventional means," Eric admitted with a hint of reluctance. "If we hadn't resorted to extraordinary methods, I'd never have been able to afford a ship or become a captain."

Curiosity piqued, Elisa pressed further. "What exactly is it that you do? Tell me!"

"We sail the seas and take what we need," Maria answered with a knowing smile.

"Robbery? Or piracy, even?" Elisa gasped in shock.

"Precisely," Eric confirmed with a nod. Then, he fell asleep.

The next morning, Eric was roused from slumber by soft moans emanating from beside him. Groggy-eyed, he observed Maria and Elisa entwined in a tight embrace. While Maria harbored genuine affection and deep love for Eric, her curiosity about Elisa was undeniable. There was an allure in the idea of Eric watching, as though his presence added an element of excitement to their intimate encounter.

Elisa, receptive to affectionate gestures, reciprocated Maria's kisses upon awakening, their connection immediate and passionate. They snuggled closer, their bodies intertwining in the warmth of the bed.

Maria's kisses grew fervent, igniting a fiery passion between them. In a matter of minutes, they shed their spare shirts and clothing, their naked forms now entwined in the middle of the bed where Eric had lain just moments before. As Eric watched on, surprised yet intrigued, Maria nodded to him, expressing a long-held desire fulfilled.

The women continued to explore each other's bodies, their kisses and caresses intensifying. Before Elisa could fully grasp the situation, she found herself reaching climax, currents of pleasure crashing over her like ocean waves, leaving her feeling simultaneously out of control yet safe in Maria's embrace.

Maria positioned herself on the bed, her head nestled between Elisa's legs, immersed in her ministrations. Briefly glancing back at Eric, she locked eyes with him before arching her back, and presenting herself to him. Eric, overcome with desire, was already aroused, entered Maria from behind as she continued to lavish attention on Elisa, indulging in the sensual pleasure enveloping them.

As Eric reached his climax with Maria, a spasm of pleasure swept through Elisa's body as well, causing her to tremble uncontrollably. The three bodies collapsed together onto the bed in a tangled heap of limbs, their shared ecstasy binding them in a moment of intimacy.

After a brief interlude, Eric rose from the bed and arranged for breakfast to be delivered from the pub below. They indulged in a leisurely meal together, relishing the comfort of each other's company as they lounged in bed, savoring the afterglow of their passionate encounter.

"So, I take it you two will be setting sail again soon?" Elisa inquired sheepishly.

"In a couple of weeks, yes," Eric confirmed.

"Where to?" Elisa pressed.

"Newfoundland, at the northern coast of the New World" Eric replied.

"So, you do this every year, and then come back?" Elisa sought clarification.

"We do, but we'll probably call it quits after another season or two. We've earned enough," Maria interjected.

"I wish I could do that," Elisa sighed wistfully.

"Why not? Why can't you?" Eric challenged.

"I would think the crew would be in agreement. Our ship can realistically accommodate 18, and we have 14 on board with Eric and me. There's no reason why you can't join us," Maria suggested.

"How much does a pirate earn?" Elisa asked eagerly.

"Our crew brings home about £8,000 each per trip. Eric and I make about 5 times that, but we also have to take care of the ship and procure provisions, which isn't cheap," Maria explained.

"That's more than I could ever earn in my lifetime," Elisa mused.

"Just know, piracy isn't all bliss. It's a bloody trade," Eric cautioned.

"I wouldn't mind getting my hands dirty or bloody," Elisa declared with determination.

"Could you cook a decent meal for a crew of 16?" Maria inquired. "I've been managing meals for the crew, but truth be told, I'm growing weary of the task. With so many other responsibilities on board, we could use a seasoned cook," she explained.

"Oh, yes, I'm quite the wizard in the kitchen," Elisa replied confidently.

"Well, I'll discuss it with the crew then," Eric confirmed. "Since every additional crew member may reduce each man's share of the profits, they'll have to agree. This is a pirate ship, after all, and the men have a say too," he explained. "Since I have never led my crew wrong, and all of them already carry a heavy purse, I don't see much objection."

With that, Eric rose from the bed, swiftly dressed, and made his way to the harbor to inspect The Vixen. The ship, finally completed, lay moored at the dock, ready for another adventure.

## 10 THE RETURN TO SAINT LAWRENCE

Upon Eric's recommendation, Elisa had gained the crew's acceptance and now served as the ship's cook.

As The Vixen navigated through the foggy Thames and into the English Channel, Elisa found her sea legs quickly, adapting to her new role as the ship's cook with ease. Maria, relieved of her duties in the galley, focused her attention on other tasks aboard the vessel. As the routine on board the ship unfolded, Eric readied the vessel to set course 283° west toward Newfoundland, soon after leaving the English Channel.

The journey was eventless during the first 2 weeks. However, their trip was met with adversity as a fierce storm descended upon them 300 miles east of the coast of Newfoundland. The howling winds and crashing waves battered The Vixen, straining its rigging.

Recognizing the imminent danger they faced, Eric made the difficult decision to divert their course to the port of St. Johns in Newfoundland for much-needed repairs on the rigging. With the sails damaged, it was crucial to seek shelter and ensure the safety of both the vessel and its crew.

It didn't take long for the repairs to be completed. After three days in port, the Vixen's main sail was mended and the crew stood ready to set sail toward Flat Island. As Eric, Maria, and Elisa ventured into a small makeshift pub for a brief respite, Eric's gaze fell upon a figure across the tavern.

"That's Miller, the scoundrel," he muttered through clenched teeth. "The captain of the fishing vessel I was pressed onto as a child. He's likely the one who murdered my friend, Peter."

Maria regarded the older captain with a steely gaze. "Do you want me and Elisa to bring him on board the Vixen?" she inquired, a hint of determination in her voice.

"It could be fun to take him on a little journey," Eric replied.

"Leave us here, and we'll approach him," Maria suggested, her resolve unwavering.

As Eric departed the small tavern, Elisa and Maria made

their way to the back where Captain Miller, seemingly drunk, sat. They settled at a table opposite him, their laughter and joviality filling the air. It was an uncommon sight in the humble, undeveloped harbor town to see such spirited women.

"You ladies seem to be having a good time," Captain Miller remarked, joining their conversation.

"Oh, always," Elisa responded cheerfully."

"Where are you from?" he inquired.

"We're from London," Maria answered. "Our ship suffered a torn sail in the storm last week, so we had to make a stop here for repairs."

"And where are you headed?" Miller pressed.

"We're bound for Boston," Elisa explained. "We'll be heading back to our ship soon. We need to rest in our cabin for a little while. We'll be setting sail in the morning again."

"I wish I could join," the captain joked with a grin on his bearded face.

"Why not?" Maria playfully invited. "We are always in for a good time."

With laughter ringing in the air, the tipsy captain accompanied the women as they made their way back to The Vixen, the captain in the middle, with a pretty lady on each side.

Amid laughter and playful banter, they made their way up the gangway plank and into the ship. Descending below deck, they headed toward the cabin designated for the ladies. However, their mirth abruptly ceased as Eric, emerging from behind, swiftly struck Captain Miller with the butt of his pistol, rendering him unconscious. With a determined grimace, Eric dragged the limp body of the captain to the brig, where he would be confined until The Vixen would be at sea again.

Dawn approached. The Vixen slipped its moorings and quietly departed from the harbor, setting sail under the cover of the early morning light. With the crew at their stations and the wind filling the sails, the ship began its journey through the Cabot Strait, charting a course around the rugged coastline of Newfoundland. With each passing wave, the port of St. Johns faded further into the distance.

As the afternoon sun cast its warm glow across the deck of The Vixen, Eric summoned two pirates to bring Captain Miller on deck. The enraged captain protested vehemently as his hands were bound and he was secured to the mast.

"What is the meaning of this? I demand to be released!" Captain Miller bellowed furiously.

Approaching him with purpose, Eric, Maria, and Elisa

stood before the bound captain.

"Do you remember me?" Eric asked, his voice dripping with accusation.

"Why should I remember you? Who are you?" the captain retorted, his anger palpable.

"Fifteen years ago, on a fishing vessel departing from Poole, you were the captain," Eric began, his tone cutting through the air. "There was a boy named Peter, just over thirteen years old. His hand was ripped off by a pulley on your ship."

Recognition flickered in Captain Miller's eyes as the memories resurfaced.

"So, what? It was an accident. Accidents happen," the captain rationalized, his voice tinged with defiance.

"He should have never operated this kind of dangerous equipment. And instead of rendering aid, you and your first officer threw him overboard," Eric continued, his words heavy with accusation. "You killed him."

"What choice did I have? You know as well as I do, as a captain, you can't just sail ashore to seek help for some boy. The cost is too high," Miller argued defensively.

"Ah, yeah, the cost. And poor boys like Peter and myself are just expendable to you. Still, you didn't have to kill him," Eric retorted, his voice thick with emotion.

"He was driving the entire crew to madness with his constant cries," Captain Miller countered, attempting to justify his actions.

"I think you're a despicable excuse for a human being," Eric shot back, his voice laced with disgust. "Instead of caring for your crew, you choose to eliminate them. You're not worthy of the title of captain."

"Regardless, it was fifteen years ago. Release me now!" the captain demanded, his tone growing more desperate.

"Hoist him up on a pulley," Maria commanded. Two sailors swiftly obeyed, securing the captain to a rope and hoisting him up until he dangled in midair from the main square sail boom.

"Elisa needs to learn how to shoot," Maria explained, retrieving her two double-barrel pistols from her jacket. She handed one to Elisa, guiding her through the process. "You need to cock it here and pull the hammer back. Then you aim by aligning the two sights with the target, and pull the trigger."

Elisa nervously accepted the pistol, attempting to follow Maria's instructions. She aimed carefully, holding the pistol with both hands and squeezed the trigger. With a loud bang, the shot missed the target, causing Elisa to squeal in surprise.

"Not bad," Maria praised as the crew cheered and applauded. "Take another shot, this time hold steady," she encouraged.

Elisa fired again and missed using the second barrel of the pistol. Maria then handed her the second pistol. With determination, Elisa aimed once more and fired, this time hitting the screaming Captain Miller in the leg as he was suspended in the air.

"Well done, Elisa!" Maria exclaimed, smiling proudly as the crew continued to cheer for her newfound marksmanship.

"Take another shot," Maria encouraged, her confidence inspiring Elisa. Elisa focused intently, aiming with precision, and fired from the second barrel, striking the captain now squarely in the stomach, as he screamed in pain.

Impressed by Elisa's growing skill, Maria had reloaded her first pistol. With practiced ease, Maria took aim and fired, hitting the screaming man in the forehead, ending his life.

"Well done, Elisa! And not bad yourself, Maria," Eric remarked, nodding in approval at their display of marksmanship at a distance of over 30 feet.

The crew enjoyed a satisfying meal prepared by Elisa. The atmosphere aboard The Vixen was relaxed. After dinner, most of the crew retired to their quarters, leaving only the watch and the helmsman on duty. Meanwhile, Elisa, Maria, and Eric gathered in the captain's cabin, where the trio shared the captain's bed.

In the dimly lit cabin, Maria retrieved two smaller flintlock pistols and a dagger from her chest, presenting them to Elisa with a mischievous grin.

"You're a true pirate wench now," Maria quipped playfully, her eyes sparkling with amusement. "Take these and practice every day on the upper deck, so you'll be ready to strike if the need arises."

With a mixture of excitement and determination, Elisa accepted the weapons, feeling a surge of empowerment course through her veins. As she clutched the pistols and dagger in her hands, she vowed to hone her skills and embrace her newfound role with courage and tenacity. With Maria's guidance and support, she knew she would become a force to be reckoned with on the high seas.

"It's a strange feeling, having taken a man's life," Elisa began, her voice tinged with uncertainty. "I feel guilty, quite a bit, actually."

"It's natural to feel that way at first," Maria reassured her.

"Miller deserved what he got. He was a devil!" Eric exclaimed. "He killed a boy over nothing, to preserve some coins. And he has probably done it many times before."

"I do feel great compassion for human suffering, and more so for animals, as they seem more innocent," Maria continued, her tone thoughtful.

"But dealing with scum like Miller... it excites me," she admitted with a laugh. "Killing bastards like him makes me feel alive. It makes me wet."

"Perhaps I'll become like you too one day," Elisa mused, contemplating the implications of her newfound role as a pirate.

If Elisa was honest with herself, she had to admit that having too many objections about the killing of Captain Miller was a bit dishonest. She knew men like him from her 6 months on the streets of London, and they were entitled, brutal, and did not care about the struggles of others. Apart from piracy, Elisa had neither money nor prospects. The only prospect she wanted was making a living and be independent in her choices. She found herself with her hand in her pants thinking of the days that lay ahead and her potential riches.

Elisa came to realize her past folly, recognizing the confines imposed upon her by her circumstances and the constraints that had held her in bondage. But now, on the precipice of newfound liberation on a pirate ship that followed no societal norms, she felt a glimmer of hope.

Approaching her, Maria tenderly cupped Elisa's face in her hands, offering reassurance. "Just be true to yourself, Elisa. That's what I did. That's all that matters," Maria whispered.

With a surge of desire, Maria pressed her tongue into

Elisa's mouth, igniting a fiery passion between them. The girl's senses reeled as Maria's thigh nestled between her legs, eliciting an almost instantaneous response. For the first time, Elisa felt truly seen and loved for who she was.

Anticipation coiled within her like a serpent as Maria's hands ventured further, stoking the flames of Elisa's desire. Meanwhile, Eric observed the scene from a distance, a silent witness to the unfolding intimacy.

Maria's words hung in the air, her touch igniting a fire within Elisa as she whispered softly, her voice barely audible above the gentle rhythm of the waves outside.

"There is something you enjoy about being in charge, about pulling the trigger," Maria murmured, her fingers tracing tenderly along Elisa's skin.

Caught off guard by the intimacy of Maria's touch, Elisa hesitated for a moment before conceding, "Yes, I admit it." Her confession was met with a playful smirk from Maria, who continued to explore Elisa's body with a knowing touch.

Maria's fingers found their way to Elisa's vagina, and as they slipped inside her, Elisa's breath caught in her throat. Sensations of pleasure washed over her, mingling with the salty sea air that enveloped them.

"Are you content, my little Elisa?" Maria softly questioned.

"I am," Elisa confessed softly, her voice laced with desire, "it feels good."

Then, Maria lowered her mouth onto Elisa's chest. With Elisa's nipple still ensnared in her mouth, Maria deftly discarded her pants that she always wore on board the ship, revealing her half-naked form. As Eric watched, he began to succumb to his desires, his actions mirroring the raw passion that enveloped the cabin.

Elisa slid her hands beneath Maria's black captain's coat, savoring the sensation as they traced the contours of Maria's smooth sides. With deliberate slowness, she explored, reveling in the touch. Maria's grip tightened as Elisa moved closer, their bodies intertwining. Elisa shuddered with pleasure as Maria's hands found her nipples, sending a surge of sensation coursing through her.

With a gasp, Elisa reciprocated, her tongue probing the area eagerly as she, lying on her back, positioned herself between Maria's thighs. Amid their intimate exchange, Eric approached, drawn by the scene unfolding before him. Maria seized his penis, guiding it to grasp Eric's arousal. With practiced skill, she lavished attention upon him, her mouth enveloping him in a frenzy of desire.

As Maria's effort intensified, Elisa found herself lost in the whirlwind of sensation under her, her senses overwhelmed by the ecstasy of the moment. Surrounded by the passionate fervor of Maria's movements on her face, Elisa surrendered to the pleasure, lost in the depths of desire, as Eric exploded in Maria's mouth.

Soon, the three slumbered peacefully, entwined in a gentle embrace, as they nestled closer to one another. They remained in this tranquil state throughout the night, undisturbed by the world around them, until the first light of dawn gently roused them from their slumber, awakening to greet the new day.

After another two days of navigating the waters of the Cabot Strait and then following the western coast of the Island of Newfoundland, the lookout spotted Flat Island on the horizon. Despite his familiarity with the treacherous seas, Eric approached the island with caution, skillfully guiding The Vixen around its sandy shores and into the concealed anchorage on the eastern side.

With the anchor securely dropped, the crew disembarked onto the familiar shores of Flat Island. The sight of their three modest log cabins greeted them, standing just as they had left them the previous November. A sense of comfort washed over them as they reunited with their sanctuary, ready to resume their lives in this secluded haven.

As Elisa familiarized herself with the cabin shared by Eric and Maria, she couldn't help but feel a sense of belonging settle within her. The cozy atmosphere and traces of their shared lives spoke to her, and she quickly made herself comfortable in the space.

"So, when do we set sail to plunder ships?" Elisa inquired eagerly, her eyes sparkling with anticipation.

Eric chuckled at her enthusiasm, his voice carrying a note of amusement.

"Patience, my dear," he replied with a smile. "You'll soon join us on your first raid. But for now, we'll take our time and prepare carefully. The seas are vast, and there's plenty of plunder to be had when the time is right."

As they settled back into life on Flat Island, the crew of The Vixen were warmly welcomed by their native friends, the Micmac. Reunited after the winter months, the Micmac relayed that the season had passed without any unwelcome intrusions from ships or outsiders.

Eager to reconnect with their seasonal, native brides, the sailors of The Vixen presented them with gifts from their distant home shores of England: clothes, tools, some jewelry, and trinkets. These tokens of affection served as reminders of their enduring bonds and provided a sense of connection despite the vast distance separating their worlds. With laughter and joy, the crew and their Micmac companions celebrated their reunion, cherishing the old friendship and the mutual respect that bound them together on the tranquil shores of the Island.

After a week of settling back into their routine on Flat Island—cleaning up the log homes, hunting, and fishing—the crew of The Vixen felt prepared for their first encounter. The air was charged with anticipation as they made final preparations, ensuring their weapons were in good condition and their supplies were well stocked.

Their first raid awaited them on the horizon, and they were ready to seize whatever treasures the Gulf of Saint Lawrence had to offer. With spirits high, they looked forward to the adventure that lay ahead, eager to test their skills as pirates once more.

# 11 THE TERROR OF BELLE ISLE

The strait of Belle Isles served as the northern passage for the Gulf of Saint Lawrence, alongside the Cabot Strait in the South. It acts as a dividing line between the Labrador Peninsula and the island of Newfoundland, spanning a mere 11 miles in width. Navigation through the strait posed numerous hazards, including strong tidal currents, interaction with the Labrador Current, unpredictable weather patterns, and extensive sea ice covering the passage for eight months annually. Despite these challenges, some captains, particularly those with time constraints, aside from whaling vessels, favored the strait during the summer months due to its considerable reduction of travel distance from England by approximately 300 miles.

Eric recognized its narrow expanse as an advantageous setting for preying on ships, eliminating the need to linger and wait around Port aux Basques, where past activities had aroused suspicion and led to the discovery of their hiding spot at Flat Island.

Nestled south of Deadman's Cove and northeast of Anchor Point on the Western Shore of Newfoundland Island, lay an ideal hiding spot for The Vixen. The bay provided a sheltered place where the ship could lay in wait.

During fair weather, the bay offered a strategic advantage, providing nearly three miles of unobstructed visibility across the strait. This vantage point allowed the crew to keep a watchful eye on passing ships, ready to pounce upon unsuspecting vessels and claim their bounty.

As The Vixen anchored within the safety of Deadman's Cove, the crew prepared themselves for the opportunities that lay ahead.

As the fog hung thick and heavy over the Strait of Belle Isles, obscuring the horizon in a ghostly shroud, The Vixen sailed onward with purpose under the command of Captain Eric. The crew moved about the deck with quiet efficiency, their eyes scanning the misty expanse for any signs of their quarry. Soon they heard the faint ring of a ship's bell.

With the creak of timbers and the snap of billowing sails, The Vixen cut through the fog, her sleek silhouette slicing through the murky waters like a phantom in the night. The sound of lapping waves echoed against the hull as she forged ahead, her crew navigating skillfully through the treacherous strait.

The pirate ship approached an unsuspecting vessel, looming faintly through the mist. The tension aboard The Vixen was palpable. Captain Eric stood on the quarterdeck with quartermaster James at the helm, his gaze fixed ahead with unwavering determination. His orders were crisp and decisive, guiding the crew as they prepared to spring their trap.

Suddenly, the outline of the target ship materialized before them, its form emerging from the fog like a specter from the depths. With a swift and calculated maneuver, The Vixen closed in on her prey, her crew poised for action. It was not an undesirable whaler, so it was a go.

Amidst the swirling mist, the two ships drew closer, the tension mounting with each passing moment. The crew of The Vixen readied themselves for the impending clash, their hearts pounding with anticipation as they prepared to unleash the fury of their portside guns upon the unsuspecting vessel, which moved southward in the thick fog.

Maria and Elisa joined Eric on the quarterdeck, their pistols poised and ready for action. At Eric's command, the gun ports of The Vixen swung open, revealing the menacing gleam of cannon barrels aimed squarely at their target.

"Fire!" Eric bellowed, and with a thunderous roar, the portside guns unleashed their wrath upon the unwary vessel. As the cannons belched smoke and flame, the pirate crew sprang into action, hurling lines with grappling hooks onto the enemy ship's deck and rigging.

On board the targeted vessel, the crew scrambled to respond, their surprise quickly giving way to defiance. Unlike many merchants who surrendered without a fight, this English captain was determined to defend his ship at all costs.

"Fight!" he roared from the quarterdeck, rallying his sailors to stand their ground. Armed with muskets and knives, they braced themselves for the onslaught of the pirate crew.

Meanwhile, Eric seized his two pistols and leaped onto the enemy ship's deck, his boots pounding against the wooden planks as he led the charge. As he landed, the stern gun of The Vixen unleashed another deafening blast, tearing a gaping hole into the side of the vessel at close range.

With a swift and coordinated assault, the rest of the pirate crew descended upon the ship's deck. Eric's pistols cracked with deadly accuracy, felling two sailors holding muskets in quick succession before he deftly drew his cutlass, ready to engage in close combat.

Maria followed suit, her own shots ringing out as she

targeted the opposing crew members with lethal precision. Reluctantly, Elisa joined the fray, her hands trembling as she gripped her pistol tightly.

As the chaos of battle unfolded around her, Elisa found herself confronted by a sailor brandishing a knife, his eyes fixed on her with predatory intent. He had figured that trying his luck with a woman would be easier than facing a battle-hardened pirate. Maria's urgent command cut through the din of battle, urging Elisa to take action. "Fire! Shoot him! Pull the goddamn trigger!" she screamed, her voice ringing across the deck.

With her heart pounding in her chest, Elisa steadied her aim and squeezed the trigger, the sailor now being only two steps away from her. She felt the recoil jolting through her body as she fired.

The sailor staggered backward, his body crumpling to the deck as the bullet found its mark. Maria nodded in silent acknowledgment of Elisa's decisive action, her eyes flashing with approval.

With six of their comrades fallen and the odds stacked against them, the remaining members of the merchant crew soon realized the futility of further resistance against the seasoned pirate crew. With a resigned defeat, they dropped their weapons, signaling their surrender to their victorious adversaries.

The cargo hold of the captured ship was a treasure trove

of valuable goods, filled to the brim with brand new English Long Land Pattern Muskets, each in pristine condition and recently developed. Eric wasted no time in assessing their bounty, ordering a rough count of the crates containing the rifles. To their amazement, the ship carried a staggering 5,900 rifles—a potential profit that seemed too good to be true at about £3 a gun apiece.

But the riches didn't end there. The hold also contained a plethora of accessories, including bayonets, gunpowder, and bullets, further adding to their spoils. Meanwhile, Maria and Elisa scoured the captain's cabin in search of hidden treasure, uncovering a cache of £1,400 in gold coins—a significant haul in its own right.

With their plunder secured, the crew wasted no time in hoisting the loot onto The Vixen. Despite the considerable distance separating them from their trusted harbor of St. Esprit at Cape Breton, Eric was undeterred. With the promise of lucrative pay from their newfound cargo, he set sail without delay, eager to deliver their spoils to market.

As The Vixen charted a course across the open seas, the crew's spirits remained high, buoyed by the prospect of wealth and adventure that lay ahead. Despite the distance they now faced, their hearts were light and their laughter rang out across the deck.

As the rifles were unloaded and sold, they fetched an impressive £2 and 9 Shillings each, amounting to a total of close to £14,000. The remainder of the cargo, including accessories and other goods, was sold for an additional £5,000. When combined with the £1,400 found by Maria and Elisa in the captain's cabin, the total loot amounted to over £20,000.

The Vixen soon dropped anchor at their hiding spot by Flat Island. With their spoils divided among the crew, each member received a handsome sum of £1,000. Eric and Maria, who took care of the ship and the supplies, gained £8,000. As Elisa held a leather purse with her share of the loot in her hands, her eyes widened in astonishment at the sheer magnitude of their wealth.

"This could rent you a small house in London for a hundred years!" she exclaimed, her excitement palpable.

Eric nodded thoughtfully, considering the possibilities. "Or you could invest it," he suggested. "Buy some property and rent it out. With careful management, it could provide a steady income for years to come."

"Can you do this forever, I mean, plundering ships?" Elisa inquired, her voice tinged with curiosity as she reclined on the bed. "It has to come to an end."

"It's all about balance," Eric responded, his tone measured as he considered her question. "People get caught because they become too greedy. We only operate during certain times of the year, and we limit our activities to avoid drawing too much attention."

Maria nodded in agreement, her gaze thoughtful as she added, "And we're strategic about our targets and locations. We shift our hunting grounds regularly to avoid detection."

"But what about the ships we attack and sink? Aren't they missed?" Elisa pressed, a hint of skepticism in her voice.

"Of course, they are," Eric acknowledged. "But it can take weeks, even months, for them to be reported missing. And by then, we're long gone. Besides, a missing ship doesn't always mean it was sunk by pirates. There are many reasons why a ship can get swallowed by the sea."

Maria chimed in, "Last year, we targeted the Cabot Strait in the south. This year, we're waiting for prey on the Strait of Belle Isles to the north. We stay one step ahead."

"But what about the King's warships? Aren't you afraid of being caught?" Elisa asked, her brow furrowing with concern.

Eric nodded; his expression was solemn. "We've had our encounters with them. Last year, Maria was taken hostage by one. It's a risk we live with every day. But here we are at least somewhat safe because the waters around Flat Island are too shallow for them to follow us."

Maria nodded, her gaze meeting Elisa's. "But we know it won't last forever. We've already amassed enough wealth. After this season, we may just retire and live off what we've gained."

"Where would you go?" Elisa inquired, her curiosity piqued by Maria's mention of their future plans.

Maria sighed, her gaze drifting as she considered the question.

"We had considered England, looking at a nice place, Mapleton Manor in Derbyshire, a couple of years ago. We were exploring the vicinity of London just recently," she explained. "But now, we're thinking about the colonies or perhaps the shores of France. It's just a day trip to London from there."

Eric nodded in agreement, his expression grave as he added, "England is quite dangerous. We always fear the possibility of being recognized by a survivor of one of the ships we raided. The gallows isn't a fate we're longing to meet."

"In either case, all this feels incredible. Not being a victim anymore," Elisa murmured as she reclined on the bed in the cozy log hut, parting her legs invitingly. Without hesitation, Maria closed the distance between them, her eagerness palpable as she nestled her head between Elisa's thighs, impatiently exploring her most intimate depths with her tongue.

A playful giggle escaped Elisa's lips, swiftly followed by a contented sigh as she surrendered to the pleasure coursing through her. With each lap and caress, Maria savored the salty sweetness that filled her mouth, relishing in the intoxicating taste of Elisa's desire. As Elisa's body arched and writhed beneath her touch, Maria held her thighs tightly, matching her movements with an equal fervor.

Before long, Elisa's cries of ecstasy filled the air, punctuated by breathless pleas and fervent curses that only served to fuel Maria's passion further. Sensing her lover's mounting arousal, Maria rose to her feet, a mischievous glint dancing in her eyes as she turned Elisa around to face Eric, who had been silently observing from the doorway.

"Join us! Take her!" Maria commanded, her voice laced with an irresistible allure.

Elisa, her skin glistening with sweat, eagerly complied, her hands instinctively parting her bum cheeks as she pressed her face into the pillow, her body quivering with anticipation. With a firm grip, Eric guided himself into the warmth of her gaping cave, eliciting a cascade of moans and sighs as he moved with a rhythm as old as time itself.

Maria, now assuming the role of observer, leaned against the wall, her breath quickening as she slid her hand beneath the fabric of her skirt, her fingers tracing delicate patterns against her wet lips underneath. Her gaze remained fixated on the entwined figures before her, her pulse rising.

As she watched Eric and Elisa lose themselves in the throes of ecstasy, Maria felt a primal urge let her fingers dive deep within her, a hunger that begged to be sated.

As their passion reached its peak, the room was filled with the symphony of their desire, the sounds of their lovemaking blending into a primal chorus. In the throes of ecstasy, Elisa's voice faded into wordless cries of ecstasy, her body trembling with each powerful thrust until finally, she surrendered to the overwhelming waves of pleasure crashing over her. Immediately, Eric's release echoed through the room, too, like a primal roar from the depths of his soul.

In the following six months, The Vixen lived up to her reputation, striking fear into the hearts of sailors as it plundered, raided, and sunk five more ships along the treacherous waters of the Strait of Belle Isle. Most of the ships were laden with valuable furs, and each conquest added to the crew's wealth, their pockets heavy with the weight of gold coins earned through daring raids.

As November dawned, preparations began for the journey back to England. Eric, the strategic captain, charted a course through the Cabot Strait, opting for the southern route as the Strait of Belle Isle had already begun to show signs of encroaching ice. With winter looming and the seas growing increasingly perilous, time was of the essence.

Their final mission before setting sail for home awaited

them—a calculated raid on one last ship in the Cabot Strait. The promise of additional spoils awaited, ensuring their return to England would be not only triumphant but lucrative. As the crew readied themselves for one final adventure, the thrill of the chase and the lure of riches beckoned them onward, driving their resolve to seize the next opportunity that came their way.

In the waning days of October, The Vixen bid farewell to Flat Island, her temporary sanctuary, as the crew prepared for their next daring venture. With the air thick with anticipation, they set sail, leaving behind the tranquil shores of their makeshift haven.

Navigating the choppy waters of the Cabot Strait, The Vixen prowled like a silent predator, its crew vigilant and ready for the hunt. It wasn't long before their keen eyes spotted a mid-sized brig traveling westward, flying the French flag—a tempting target ripe for the taking.

Under the command of Eric, the sleek pirate ship closed in on the unsuspecting brig with calculated accuracy. To their surprise, the crew of the targeted vessel offered little resistance, their surrender a testament to the fearsome reputation of their would-be captors.

The crew of the captured ship appeared to be in unusually high spirits, their boisterous laughter and carefree demeanor hinting at revelry in the face of a pirate raid. As The Vixen's crew observed them closely, it became apparent that the source of their jubilation lay in the cargo hold—a plentiful supply of fine French brandy, their secret indulgence discovered and liberally sampled.

The crew of the captured vessel had succumbed to the intoxicating allure of their cargo. For The Vixen's men, the sight was both amusing and bemusing—a testament to the unpredictable twists and turns of life on the high seas. Yet amidst the revelry, they remained vigilant, knowing that even in moments of celebration, the tides of fortune could swiftly turn, and the call of duty beckoned ever onward.

With the threat of violence averted, the pirates wasted no time in scouring the brig's cargo hold for spoils. Amidst crates and barrels, they unearthed a treasure trove of 6,000 bottles of fine brandy—Cognac Saulnier Frères, a prized vintage from Saint Amant de Graves in France. There were about 10 barrels of cheap brandy, and 28 barrels of French wine stacked.

The French captain stood before Maria, a jolly figure with still a slight twinkle in his eye, in the face of Maria's pistol under his chin. Despite his middle age, his demeanor exuded vitality and warmth. He was dressed in a traditional French captain's coat, its rich fabric adorned with details that hinted at his seafaring experience. His eyes, though weathered by the sun and sea, held a spark of merriment and intelligence, betraying a lifetime of adventures on the open waters. As he spoke, his voice carried a hint of charm and confidence, befitting a seasoned sailor accustomed to command. He seemed to treat his sailors well.

"Where do you hail from?" Maria asked the captain. "La Rochelle in France," he replied.

"La Rochelle," Maria repeated thoughtfully, her gaze lingering on the captain. "A beautiful port city, I heard."

The captain nodded, a hint of nostalgia flickering in his eyes. "Indeed, it is. But the sea is my true home."

Maria observed him closely, sensing a shared bond forged by their mutual affinity for the ocean. "And what brings you to these waters?" she inquired, her curiosity piqued.

"We were bound for Newfoundland, to trade our cargo of brandy," the captain explained. "But fate had other plans, it seems."

"Indeed, fate can be a fickle mistress," Maria remarked, her tone tinged with wry amusement. "But perhaps our encounter was not entirely by chance. Who knows what opportunities may arise from such unexpected meetings?"

The captain offered her a knowing smile, acknowledging the mysterious ways of the sea. "Indeed, perhaps our paths were meant to cross for a reason," he mused, his gaze drifting out to the endless expanse of the ocean.

"Here's the deal," Maria declared, her voice firm yet measured. "You divulge the location of the ship's money, and you and your crew can sail away unharmed. We'll even leave you a barrel or two of brandy as a parting gift.

But if we discover you've deceived us, and we find the gold on our own, your ship will meet the bottom of the sea along with you and your crew."

After a moment of contemplation, the captain nodded solemnly, acknowledging the gravity of the situation. He gestured for Maria to follow him below deck, where he carefully pried open a loose plank in the cabin's flooring. Behind it lay three satchels brimming with coins, their contents glinting in the dim light. The bounty, concealed within the captain's quarters, totaled 1,500 Louis d'Or gleaming amidst the darkness.

Maria smiled with satisfaction as the captain revealed the hidden treasure. She nodded approvingly, acknowledging his cooperation.

"Thank you for your honesty, Monsieur," Maria uttered, a note of finality in her voice. "You and your crew are free to go. Consider it a gesture of goodwill."

The captain's expression softened with relief, grateful for the leniency shown by Maria and her crew. "I appreciate you keeping your word," he replied, his tone sincere.

As Maria and the captain emerged from the cabin, the crew of The Vixen stood ready to depart, their sails billowing in the wind. With a nod from Eric, they released the captured ship from their grappling hooks and lines, allowing it to sail off into the horizon.

As the two ships parted ways, Maria couldn't help but feel

a sense of satisfaction at the successful conclusion of the season. Their purses were heavy, and the cargo of French brandy promised an additional profit.

With the gold and the brandy safely in their possession, The Vixen was ready to continue on its journey home to England. The crew set sail once more, the ship's hold heavy with plunder, emboldened by yet another successful conquest.

The crew gathered below deck for the evening meal prepared by Elisa. The aroma of the French brandy wafted through the cramped space, adding to the jovial atmosphere. Eric, leaning back casually, broached the topic of their next destination.

"Which harbor in England should we sail to?" he inquired, his tone relaxed.

"Perhaps London again," Elisa suggested, her voice carrying a hint of excitement.

"What about home to Plymouth?" another sailor interjected, nostalgia evident in his tone. "We haven't set foot on our home shore in a long time."

"It's been 5 years since we left Plymouth," another man chimed in, echoing the sentiment.

Eric pondered for a moment before nodding thoughtfully. "I guess that's a long enough time to not raise suspicion," he mused. "Let's vote on it."

With Mr. Bancroft, the quartermaster, facilitating the process, each sailor received a piece of paper and cast their vote into Bancroft's hat. After the last vote was tallied, it was evident that the sentiment was clear. The sailors longed to sail to their home port to meet their friends and families.

"So, Plymouth it is," Eric declared, acknowledging the collective decision with a nod. The next morning, as The Vixen had cleared St. Pierre and Miquelon, he set the ship on course 65° east northeast, sailing toward the port of Plymouth, the harbor where they all had first met over five years ago.

# 12 HOME IN PLYMOUTH

As The Vixen arrived at Lizard Point in South England under the cover of darkness on November 21st, Eric breathed a sigh of relief. The journey had been long and arduous, but they had finally reached their destination. The following morning, they docked in Plymouth, greeted by the bustling activity of the harbor.

While Eric remained on board, Maria and Elisa made their way to the Minerva Inn, where they secured the largest room available.

The inn had changed hands since Maria had last worked there, and few familiar faces remained. However, one person caught her eye – a maid whom Maria had always liked and who had once helped her in a time of need. Seeing that she was heavily pregnant, Maria didn't hesitate to offer her assistance. She handed the maid three gold coins and urged her to go home and take care of herself.

With the ship secured and preparations underway for storage, Eric wasted no time in seeking out a familiar trader known for dealing in spirits. He had a history with the man from his smuggling days and knew that he could turn a tidy profit selling the French brandy they had looted during their voyage. The transaction went smoothly. Eric made his way toward the Minerva with a pocket full of coins and a satisfied grin on his face. He soon joined the ladies in their upstairs chamber.

As the evening wore on, the trio enjoyed a hearty dinner. The cozy atmosphere of the tavern enveloped them, providing a welcome respite from the rigors of life at sea.

Their meal was interrupted by the arrival of a group of drunken petty officers from a ship of the Royal Navy. Eric, ever the gracious host, asked them to sit down, and ordered tankards of ale for each of them, engaging them in conversation as they drank.

"Returning from the sea or going out?" Eric inquired, curious about their mission.

"We're setting sail for Newfoundland tomorrow morning," one of the officers replied, his speech slightly slurred from the ale.

"We're on a patrol mission to hunt for pirates," another officer chimed in proudly.

Eric nodded, understanding the importance of their mission. "That is good," he countered, his voice tinged with concern. "We just returned from St. Johns the other day, and piracy seems to be getting rampant there."

The officers exchanged knowing glances, confirming Eric's suspicions. "Yes, quite a few ships have gone missing there over the summer," one of them admitted grimly. "And the French aren't doing anything about it, so we are going out and putting an end to this mayhem."

Eric nodded solemnly, grateful for their efforts to combat the threat of piracy in the region. "As a merchant captain, I really appreciate your service, gentlemen," he replied, ordering another tankard of ale for the men as a gesture of appreciation.

As they raised their mugs in a toast to solidarity against piracy, Eric felt a sense of gratitude for the information he had just obtained. He was thankful of the fortunate timing of the Royal Navy's patrol mission at this point, as The Vixen laid securely moored at the docks. It seemed, his own raid activities in the Gulf of Saint Lawrence hadn't gone entirely unnoticed.

As he contemplated the situation, Eric realized that while there were undoubtedly other pirates at work in the region, the Royal Navy's efforts to quell piracy would make things more challenging for anyone engaging in such activities.

With this in mind, Eric knew that he would need to exercise caution in his future endeavors. The seas around

Saint Lawrence were a dangerous place, especially with the Royal Navy actively patrolling to root out piracy. It was a reminder to tread carefully and stay one step ahead of those who sought to enforce the law of the sea.

The following day, the crew reconvened aboard The Vixen, and Eric divided the profits from the brandy sale among the men. It was a moment of celebration as each member of the crew received their share, reflecting on the hard work and risks they had taken over the past five years. With their earnings from the brandy sale, each member of the crew had amassed over £10,000. As Eric divided the money among them, it was a moment of great significance. The crew members realized the magnitude of their accomplishments and the wealth they had accumulated through their dangerous work as pirates.

Eric's somber tone set the mood as the sailors and Elisa and Maria gathered around the table for the meeting.

"I have news about The Gulf of Saint Lawrence, our hunting grounds. Not good ones, though. It is getting too dangerous for us there," Eric explained, his voice filled with concern. "We can't risk running into the Royal Navy while we're conducting our business."

His announcement about the Royal Navy's efforts to curb piracy in Newfoundland weighed heavily on everyone's minds.

The quartermaster, ever practical, offered a suggestion.

"Why not sail to the Mediterranean?" he proposed. "There are plenty of opportunities for trade there, and it may be safer than risking encounters with the Royal Navy."

"Where you suggest sailing? We'll be facing off against French galleys or a Man-of-War of His Majesty King Louis," Eric explained solemnly, his voice carrying the weight of the impending danger. "All heavily armed with 24-pound guns."

The idea sparked a discussion among the crew, weighing the pros and cons of such a decision. The Mediterranean offered new possibilities for trade and profit, but it also came with its own set of severe challenges and risks. The English Channel was too dangerous as it was patrolled by the King's ships.

"The English Channel is out," a sailor interjected, his tone wary. "It's crawling with Royal Navy ships!"

"I've always had a hankering to sail the Southern Seas," another crew member added wistfully.

Eric shook his head in disagreement. "The golden age of piracy in the Caribbean has come to an end," he elaborated. "Most pirates there have taken the king's pardon and are leading respectable lives now. Many of those who didn't, were hanged."

"Why not take a break for a while?" Maria suggested, her voice tinged with concern. "What do we have to gain? We all carry heavy purses, and even the poorest fellow among us could live comfortably for the rest of his life."

"True. Why tempt fate?" James Bancroft, the quartermaster, mused thoughtfully. "Luck has a way of running out eventually, there's no doubt about that."

"Indeed," Captain Eric agreed, his voice tinged with wisdom born of experience. "Greed is the downfall of all. Not knowing when to quit, always wanting more."

His words resonated with the crew, a sobering reminder of the dangers of unchecked ambition and the importance of knowing when to step back and be content with what one has achieved.

As they contemplated Eric's words, the crew couldn't help but reflect on their desires and motivations. The allure of wealth and adventure was strong, but so too was the realization that there were limits to what they could attain without risking everything they had worked so hard for.

The crew began to consider the possibility of embracing a more measured approach to their lives at sea, one that prioritized safety and security over the reckless pursuit of riches.

A sailor spoke up, his voice tinged with a sense of gratitude and relief. "I just wanted to escape poverty and a life of crime, ending up on the gallows one day," he explained. "There was no opportunity for a lower-class man like me, and piracy has given me a way out. I have achieved what I wanted."

His words struck a chord with the others, prompting another to share his own aspirations. "My goal was to be able to provide for a family, without having to join the Navy, and perhaps never see my home port again," he explained. "And now I am well set."

These sentiments resonated deeply with the crew, each member reflecting on their reasons for setting sail and the dreams they had sought to fulfill. In the face of uncertainty and danger, they found solace in the realization that they had achieved what they had set out to do – to forge a better life for themselves and their loved ones, free from the specter of poverty and hardship.

As they deliberated, the weight of their financial situation hung in the air. With the maid earning £12 a year, a laborer making £20, and even a skilled engineer receiving pay of not more than £120, the purse of £10,000 which each crew member carried, bore a significant amount of weight. It represented security and stability in a world filled with uncertainty.

Ultimately, Eric knew that whatever decision they made would impact not only their livelihoods but also their safety and well-being. With the future of their ventures hanging in the balance, he suggested to retire for the time being.

"Let's call it quits for now," Maria suggested, her voice carrying a note of finality.

"That's my take, too. We have slid under the watchful eyes of the law for a long time, and we had quite a bit of luck. If we set sail for Newfoundland in March, we will face warships of the Royal Navy, of that I am certain," Mr. Bancroft added.

His words were met with murmurs of agreement from the crew, each member recognizing the wisdom in his assessment.

"We can all build a life now, according to our wishes and desires. We have perspective now," a man remarked, his tone reflective.

"And we can always decide to go back to piracy in some years when the heat has cooled down," the quartermaster injected, his practicality shining through.

"True that," another crew member replied, echoing the sentiments of agreement with Eric's proposal. His simple affirmation spoke volumes, reinforcing a swift decision of the crew.

"Let's put it up for a vote," Eric suggested, opening the decision to the entire crew.

Mr. Bancroft once again let his hat go around, and each sailor threw in a paper, their votes cast in silence. When the tally was counted, it was revealed to be unanimous –

the crew had decided to take a break from piracy, build lives ashore, and maintain the cloak of reputability.

As they looked toward the future, they knew that whatever path they chose to follow, they could always come back together and resume piracy in days of need.

In the quiet of the evening, Eric, Maria, and Elisa settled into their room at the inn, the warmth of the fire casting flickering shadows across the walls.

"What are we going to do now?" Elisa asked, breaking the silence with a note of uncertainty in her voice.

"I will go to port tomorrow and put The Vixen up for sale," Eric suggested, his tone resolute. "It's time for us to move on, and it will give us a nice sum. With her canons, she is worth gold."

"So, we will be shipless?" Maria questioned, her brow furrowing with concern.

"Not necessarily," Eric replied, his voice calm and reassuring. "We can buy something smaller, a ship that can be sailed with just two or three people. A small sloop, perhaps. It wouldn't require as large a crew as The Vixen."

The atmosphere in the room shifted as Elisa expressed her concerns, her voice tinged with uncertainty and vulnerability. She felt her lighter purse compared to the others and feared being left behind as Eric and Maria moved forward.

Maria, sensing Elisa's apprehension, walked toward her with purpose, pushing her roughly onto the bed. With a firm touch, Maria began fondling Elisa's breasts, her actions filled with a mixture of desire and reassurance.

Her hands, forcefully like a pirate's hands, gripped her breasts firmly, right where it counted most. It was as if some primal, instinctual nerve endings she had been unaware of until now had been awakened and ignited by her touch.

"So, you want to be our whore?" Maria whispered, her hand slipping under Elisa's dress to caress her skin.

Elisa's breath caught in her throat as she felt Maria's touch, her body responding to the intimacy between them. "I do," she moaned softly, her fears melting away in the warmth of their embrace.

Maria's question pierced the air, her tone commanding as she addressed Elisa. "Tell me, you harlot, so Eric can hear you! Do you want to be our whore?" she demanded, her eyes locking with Elisa's.

"I do, I love being a whore," Elisa moaned in response, her voice filled with passion and longing. Her admission hung in the air, a declaration of her desire to embrace her role in their relationship fully.

"Eric, come here!" Maria commanded. "This harlot needs

your cock."

As Elisa raised her buttocks and got on all fours, Eric swiftly approached, prepared for the task at hand. He was ready. With a grin, he reached out toward Elisa's butt and entered her from behind, while Maria hovered close by, her face mere inches away from Elisa's, as she squatted beside the bed.

Advancing further, his fingers tugged at her hair gently, parting it like torn silk, as he pressed himself into her vagina. She beckoned him closer with a subtle curl of her finger, and he obliged, pushing into her to meet her passionate demands.

As Elisa skillfully aroused him, he gazed admiringly at her powerful back, where the lines of her shoulders met, emphasized by the delicate straps of her dress. At this moment, Maria, still squatting, took Elisa's dangling beasts into her two hands, kissing her.

"Say it!" Maria demanded. "Say that you're a filthy whore, a harlot! Say it!"

"I am such a filthy harlot," Elisa responded obediently, meeting Eric's gaze as she spoke.

"Say you are our whore," Maria urged, her voice tinged with anticipation.

"I am, I am your whore, your filthy harlot!" Elisa exclaimed, her excitement palpable.

Eric, spurred on by the charged atmosphere, eagerly interjected, adding to the fervor of the moment, "Harlot, how does that feel now?" as he pounded her behind.

"It feels so good," Elisa moaned, as Eric ejaculated, completely disappearing into her.

As her words echoed in the room, Elisa felt a sense of liberation wash over her, her heart pounding with anticipation of the intimacy and connection they would share.

"We would never leave our little harlot behind," Maria whispered softly into Elisa's ear as they lay together in bed, spent from their passionate encounter.

The following day, Eric made his way to the harbor to meet with a ship broker, tasking him with selling The Vixen. He also examined several smaller sloops in the 35-40 ft. range, suitable for accommodating 3-4 individuals comfortably but manageable enough to be sailed by 1-2 crew members.

It was still undecided where the trio wanted to settle. Eric suggested sailing along the coasts of France and Spain to see if something suitable caught their eyes—somewhere away from England, but also close enough to return if needed.

It didn't take long for The Vixen to be sold, fetching another £22,000. As a gesture of goodwill, Eric distributed £500 of the proceeds to each crew member.

He also gave £1,000 to Elisa, knowing she had the least amount of money among them. It left Eric and Maria with £14,000 for a new ship, which was more than enough.

Soon, Eric found the perfect boat. Her name was Duchess and she was a beautiful 39-foot one-mast sloop with a shallow 5-foot draft. The vessel's main cabin was lined in dark, expensive wood and boasted a well-equipped galley, a comfortable head, and two, small separate bedrooms. Being more a pleasure yacht than a workhorse, the vessel seemed ideal for accommodating 2-4 people in style and comfort. And she was for sale at the docks for £4,800.

Eric had two small 1-pound swivel guns installed one on the port side and one at starboard. While these guns were not powerful enough to sink a ship, they were perfect for firing grapeshot to keep hostile crews away, should they decide to attack The Duchess.

Eric brought along four French St. Etienne muskets and six pistols from The Vixen, in addition to their regular arms. This arsenal should be sufficient to deter any smaller, aggressive vessels they might encounter along the French coast or the Bay of Biscay, off the coast of Spain. Provisions of salted meat, bread, wine, brandy, and strong 160-proof whiskey were loaded onto the ship.

One brisk January morning, Eric and Maria gathered with their old pirate crew at the Minerva tavern for a bittersweet farewell dinner. Emotions ran high as they reminisced about their adventures together, sharing laughter and tears. Eric reassured the crew that he would return to England from time to time to catch up with everyone. Each member of the crew had developed plans for the future.

Amidst the farewells and good wishes, it was revealed that another sailor was planning to relocate to London with his new bride, seeking new opportunities in the bustling city.

As for Mr. Bancroft, the seasoned quartermaster and elder statesman of the crew, he had decided to retire completely from the seafaring life. With the wealth accumulated from their pirate endeavors, he would live comfortably, enjoying a well-deserved rest in his golden years.

One sailor was preparing for marriage, while another had established a cozy inn near Underwood, to the east of Plymouth. This inn would serve as a gathering place for the crew, a home away from home where they could reconnect and ensure each other's well-being in the years to come.

After a hearty meal accompanied by plenty of ale, the crew of The Vixen bid their farewells, each sailor dispersing to their paths. Eric, Maria, and Elisa ascended the stairs to their shared quarters for one final night together in the familiar surroundings of their abode.

The following morning, they would prepare to embark on their journey, setting their sights on the coast of Spain as their first destination. From there, they planned to sail northward along the picturesque shores of France, in search of a permanent place to call home.

## 13 LEAVING ENGLAND

As the first light of dawn began to paint the dreary, foggy sky of Plymouth, Eric, Maria, and Elisa stood on the docks, ready to embark on their new adventure aboard The Duchess. The ship sat patiently, moored and awaiting their command.

With practiced hands, Eric raised the main sail, the fabric billowing in the gentle morning breeze. Maria took her place at the helm, her eyes fixed on the horizon ahead.

"215° southwest," Eric instructed, and Maria adjusted the ship's course accordingly.

The journey ahead would span 160 miles in this direction before they would make a turn southward toward Oviedo in Asturias, nestled along the northern coast of Spain.

With the sails unfurled and the wind guiding them, The Duchess glided gracefully through the waters, leaving the port of Plymouth behind. As the sun rose higher in the sky, painting the sea with golden light, the trio settled into the rhythm of life at sea, their hearts filled with anticipation for the adventures that awaited them.

The trio knew that their voyage to Oviedo would be a short one. With a distance of 450 miles to cover still, they estimated that it would take them a total of three to four days of continuous sailing under full canvas.

As The Duchess cut through the waves, each day brought new challenges and discoveries. They navigated by the stars at night, with Maria expertly guiding the ship's course while Eric and Elisa manned the sails and kept watch for any signs of danger.

Despite the occasional rough seas and unpredictable weather, the journey was filled with moments of wonder and beauty. They marveled at the vastness of the ocean, the breathtaking sunsets painting the sky in hues of crimson and gold, and the gentle rhythm of the waves lulling them to sleep each night. New beginnings awaited them at warmer shores.

Five days later, Eric, Maria, and Elisa arrived at Oviedo in Asturias aboard The Duchess. They disembarked and walked to the Cathedral of San Salvador, taking in the grandeur of the historic landmark.

After a meal at a local tavern, the trio returned to their ship and stocked up on provisions for their journey ahead. With fresh supplies on board, they set sail eastward along the Spanish coast, navigating the waters as they progressed toward their destination on the French coast.

As the Duchess sailed past Bilbao, ready to turn north toward the French harbor of La Rochelle, a small one-masted lugger seemed to be trailing them, creeping closer with each passing moment. Eric squinted through his telescope, observing the ship's movements with growing unease.

"They're getting closer," he muttered to himself, his grip tightening on the telescope.

With a furrowed brow, he counted the figures on the approaching ship: five sailors, a man likely the captain, and another man at the helm. That's seven! Eric's heart quickened. He knew trouble was brewing.

Hurriedly, he gathered the muskets and unplugged the swivel guns on deck, loading them with precision. Each movement was deliberate, a testament to Eric's experience as a pirate captain himself. The tension on the deck was palpable as Maria and Elisa joined him, their eyes reflecting a mix of anxiety and determination.

"We've got company," Eric announced grimly, his voice cutting through the air. "Basque pirates, most likely.

They're faster than us, and they're aiming to board."

Elisa's voice trembled as she spoke, "What should we do? There are only three of us!"

"Don't worry, ladies. Maria, they'll probably pass to our left, away from the coast. So, you take charge of the portside gun and grab a fuse. You've handled naval guns before, so you know what to do," Eric instructed. "Wait for my signal and target the crew only. Our grape-shot should knock some of them out right away."

Elisa, you take the helm. Follow my lead, and we might just make it out of this," Eric explained. "Maintain the course I specify. When I signal for a change, execute it immediately."

Maria nodded, her fingers tightening around the handles of her trusty pistols. "I'm ready," she declared, her resolve unwavering.

Elisa swallowed hard, her hands gripping the wheel with determination. "Tell me what to do when they come on board, Eric. There seems to be more than us on that ship."

"Be not afraid, they will not board The Duchess, I will make sure of this. They think they are approaching a small, civilian sailing vessel. The fact that they go after such a small ship means they aren't very experienced, and they seem unaware that we are battle-hardened pirates ourselves," Eric replied with a faint smile.

With a steely resolve, Eric instructed each of them, outlining their roles in the impending confrontation. Maria stood poised by the small naval gun, her eyes trained on the approaching pirates. Elisa focused intently on Eric's commands, as her hands were steady on the wheel, maintaining course.

Down below, Eric prepared a makeshift deterrent, soaking a cloth in potent whiskey. He uncorked three 160-proof whiskey bottles, stuck the soaked rags in the lids and wrapped them around the bottles. Though reluctant to waste the precious liquor, he knew it might buy them precious moments in the face of danger.

With everything in place, Eric set the Duchess on a northward course, adjusting the sails with precision. The wind blew through the rigging as Elisa steered the ship, her movements guided by Eric's instructions.

As the tension mounted and the enemy ship drew nearer, Eric's gaze never wavered. With grit and determination, the small crew braced themselves for the inevitable clash, ready to defend their vessel against whatever threats lay ahead.

As Eric had foreseen, the pirate vessel made its move, edging closer to The Duchess on the port side. With each passing moment, the gap between the two ships narrowed, until the faces of the pirates were visible, their intent clear. Five men stood tall on the deck, armed to the teeth with muskets and pistols, their eyes fixed on their target.

The lugger surged forward, now a mere 20 yards away from The Duchess, closing in for the attack. Eric stood firm on the deck, his hands steady as he ignited the soaked wrappings of his whiskey bottles, the flames of Eric's torch flickering ominously in the gathering dusk. Maria stood at her portside gun, fuse in hand, as Elisa held the helm.

"Maria! Aim for the crew on deck, and hold. - Fire!" Eric ordered, his voice cutting through the tension. Maria steadied herself, her eyes focused on the enemy ship, her grip firm on the gun.

With a swift motion, she lowered the smoldering fuse onto the powder pan of the cannon. In an instant, a deafening roar filled the air as the small naval gun unleashed its deadly payload of grape-shot, sending two of the pirates crashing to the deck below.

With the pirate ship now almost parallel to The Duchess, Eric seized his chance, hurling the burning bottles of whiskey with precision. One after another, the bottles arced through the air, crashing onto the deck of the pursuing vessel as they burst, spilling their flammable content over the wooden planks of the pirate lugger.

As expected, the fire erupted upon impact, engulfing the deck in a blazing inferno fueled by the potent spirits.

Eric immediately took hold of a loaded musket and fired

a shot, which missed, as both ships rocked in the waves. Then another. Missed again! The third musket shot finally sent a sailor on the pirate ship down to the planks. The pirates had now lost three of their seven men, while the remaining crew was trying to put out the fire.

Amidst the chaos and confusion, the pirates' curses echoed across the sea as the flames licked at their ship, devouring everything in their path. The air was thick with smoke and the scent of burning wood as The Duchess sailed on, leaving the burning vessel of their would-be assailants in their wake.

Eric peered through the dim light, and his eyes locked onto the figure of the pirate captain standing defiantly on the quarter-deck of the burning ship. Despite the chaos unfolding around him, the young Basque man exuded an air of fierce determination, his dark skin and hair stark against the backdrop of flames, which his men were about to extinguish.

With a commanding voice, he barked orders at his crew, who scrambled frantically to douse the spreading fire on deck. Despite their efforts, some of the flames raged on, casting an eerie glow over the scene of destruction.

Eric watched in silence, his gaze unwavering as he observed the unfolding drama. Though their paths had crossed in a moment of conflict, he couldn't help but feel a twinge of empathy for the young pirate captain, caught amid a battle he seemed destined to lose. After all, Eric himself had walked in his shoes before.

As the pursuit persisted, Eric knew they were far from safe. With a steely determination, he barked out orders, his voice cutting through the tension like a blade.

"Maria! Over to the starboard gun!" he commanded; his eyes were fixed on the relentless pursuers.

With a swift motion, Eric drew his dagger and sliced through the outhaul rope of the mainsail, causing the mainsail of The Duchess to flap wildly in the wind. The sudden loss of speed slowed the ship considerably, allowing the pirate ship to gain ground once more and pull ahead in an instant.

But Eric wasn't finished yet. With a calculated maneuver, he directed Elisa to alter their course sharply to the left, throwing the pirate ship off balance.

"Elisa, hard to port, left heading 300°!" Eric commanded urgently.

With a swift motion, Elisa spun the ship's wheel, altering their course as directed. The Duchess swung to the left, and the stern of the pirate ship drifted into the firing range of Maria's starboard gun.

"Maria, target the man at the helm! Fire!" Eric's command rang out, and Maria wasted no time in obeying. With a deafening roar, the swivel gun erupted, sending a deadly barrage of musket balls toward the pirate captain and the helmsman.

The shot found its mark, sending the man at the helm sprawling, his grip on the wheel lost. As chaos erupted aboard the enemy ship, flames began to spread rapidly, devouring the sails and rigging with frightening speed.

Minutes passed like an eternity as The Duchess sailed on, leaving behind a trail of destruction and flames in her wake. With its crew decimated and the helmsman dead, the pirate vessel was soon reduced to a smoldering wreck, consumed by the relentless fire.

Their pursuers were vanquished and danger lay finally behind them. Eric, Maria, and Elisa breathed a collective sigh of relief. Though the ordeal had been harrowing, they had emerged victorious once again.

After swiftly turning the ship into the wind and fixing the cut mainsail outhaul line, Eric took charge of the cleanup efforts on deck, while Maria and Elisa worked together to tidy up the ship's surroundings. Once the immediate tasks were completed, they stowed away the muskets and pistols below deck for safekeeping.

Wasting no time, Eric proceeded to clean the two swivel guns, ensuring they were pristine, plugged and ready for any future encounters. With his hands stained with soot from the task, he then steered The Duchess back onto her northern course before descending into the cabin.

Inside, Elisa was already busy preparing a meal, her

movements fluid and practiced. Maria, her face smeared with gunpowder residue from the naval guns, sat at the table, a faint smile playing on her lips.

"You see, it's all under control. It's easy when you know what you're doing," Eric chuckled as he entered the cabin.

"We sent those scoundrels packing, didn't we?" Elisa laughed, her knife expertly slicing through a pile of carrots in the galley.

"You're a true hero, Eric," Maria remarked, admiration gleaming in her eyes. "You deserve a reward."

With a mischievous grin, Maria unbuttoned her dress, letting her heavy breasts fall out of her blouse. She revealed a playful glint in her eye as she motioned for Eric to lay down on the hard cabin floor.

"Lie back and relax," she commanded, her smile widening as Eric obediently complied, a sense of contentment settling over the small crew of The Duchess as they enjoyed a moment of respite after their last dangerous encounter.

With a deft movement, Maria unbuttoned Eric's pants, revealing the warmth of his skin beneath. He was rock-hard and ready. Her touch sent shivers down his spine as she straddled him, the warmth of her moist vagina embracing him. As his hands slipped over her breasts, Maria's breath caught in her throat, the anticipation palpable in the air.

"Join us," she commanded, her voice husky with longing, as she glanced over at Elisa who was still engrossed in preparing supper.

Elisa, drawn in by the magnetic pull of their shared desire, didn't hesitate to comply. With a coy smile, she also unbuttoned her blouse, exposing the soft curves of her breasts as she approached Eric and Maria.

Without a word, Elisa lifted her skirt and settled onto Eric's face, her presence adding to the growing intensity of the moment. Eric immediately released Maria's breasts and Elisa's hands took over, tenderly twisting her nipples.

As the passion between them intensified, Maria's hands roamed over Elisa's breasts, her touch sending a thrill through her body. With a shared hunger for connection, they surrendered to the heat of the moment, the women's lips meeting in fervent kisses.

With Maria riding Eric and their bodies moving in synchrony, Eric caressed Elisa's vulva with his mouth, his lips tracing every curve of her thighs with a tender reverence, as Maria was riding him with movements that grew faster and faster. They became lost in the depths of their desire. The boundaries between them melted away, leaving only the raw intensity of their shared passion.

As the waves of pleasure washed over them, Eric reached the pinnacle of his ecstasy, releasing himself into Maria's vulva. With a shared sigh of contentment, they collapsed together, their bodies entangled in a blissful weave of limbs.

For a moment, they lie there in the aftermath, basking in the warmth of their connection. But their reverie was abruptly interrupted by Elisa's exclamation of dismay.

"Damn it!" she shrieked, scrambling to her feet. "The roast in the oven is burning!"

Maria and Eric couldn't help but burst into laughter at the sudden shift in focus.

"Well, if dinner is the only thing that's burning, we'll count ourselves lucky," Maria remarked with a grin. "After all, we did let an entire ship go up in flames today."

"And it seems our flames of desire have been extinguished for now too," Eric chuckled.

With their laughter still echoing in the cabin, they gathered around the table to enjoy their slightly charred roast with carrots and a generous pour of red wine, as The Duchess sailed through the night toward the harbor of La Rochelle.

A day later, The Duchess had made significant progress, sailing 170 miles northward and finally pulling into the bustling port of La Rochelle. With practiced skill, Eric moored the ship at the dock, securing it tightly before he and his companions disembarked onto the solid ground of the harbor.

Their purpose was clear: search for a suitable property to call their own. After a brief walk, they found lodging at an inn nestled at the foot of the Tour de la Chaîne, overlooking the Port of La Rochelle. The inn provided a comfortable respite from their journey, offering a temporary sanctuary as they set about their task.

In the afternoon, the trio ventured out into the lively streets of the city, their footsteps echoing against the cobblestones as they made their way through the busy alleys and streets. Their destination was the office of a Jewish merchant and property dealer, renowned for his expertise in the local land market.

With determination in their hearts and a clear goal in mind, Eric, Maria, and Elisa entered the merchant's office.

"What can I do for you, Mesdames et Monsieur?" the merchant inquired politely as they entered his office.

"We are in search of a new home, an estate, something not too far from the sea, but also secluded," Eric explained, his voice carrying a hint of anticipation.

"We hail from the shores of England and plan to sail home on occasions, to do business. We own a boat and are planning to keep it," Maria added, her words echoing Eric's sentiments.

The merchant nodded thoughtfully, his brow furrowing as he considered their request. "Please sit down. Let me see what I can do for you," he replied, reaching for a stack of papers on his desk.

With a practiced hand, he began to sift through the documents, his eyes scanning each one with a discerning gaze. As he delved into his extensive network of contacts and listings, Eric, Maria, and Elisa waited.

"A cousin of mine has a stately castle for sale in Nantes. It has 30 bedrooms though," the man explained, his tone thoughtful.

"That's a bit too large for us," Eric replied, considering the practicalities of such a sizable property.

"Well, if you value a smaller abode and the closeness to London, there's a more affordable château for sale about 20 miles south of Le Harve and only 10 miles to the sea. From there, it is a sea voyage of a mere 140 miles to London," the man elaborated. "The estate has property and acres, side buildings, and even a small chapel."

"This sounds very interesting, a day trip to my hometown of London," Elisa exclaimed, her eyes bright with excitement.

"What price are we talking?" Eric inquired, his interest piqued.

"The castle is called Château de Fauguernon, and it once

belonged to a Marquis," the merchant continued, providing further details. "A duke is selling it and it's priced at 125,000 Livres," he added. "But I'm sure with good negotiation skills, it can be had for less."

"How much is this in English money?" Maria asked, eager to understand the value in terms she was familiar with.

"Let me see, Madame," the merchant replied, quickly calculating the conversion on a scrap of paper. "It's about £12,500 or 11,500 Guineas," he confirmed.

"That's well within our budget," Eric remarked, exchanging a satisfied glance with Maria and Elisa.

"How do we go about it?" Eric asked, his brow furrowed with concern. "Le Havre is over 450 sea miles away from our current location."

"This is not a problem," the merchant reassured them, his tone confident. "I will give you a letter of recommendation, and you take it to my partner in the port of Le Havre. He will then show you the property and connect you with the seller."

"Very pleasant to do business with you," Eric agreed warmly as he shook the Jewish merchant's hand.

The man quickly produced ink and a quill from his desk, swiftly writing in Hebrew onto a piece of paper. With a flourish, he sealed it with wax and inscribed the address before handing it over to Eric.

Furnished with the letter and a newfound sense of optimism, the trio left the merchant's office and made their way back to their lodging for a hearty dinner. The next morning, they would set sail for the port of Le Havre on the shores of Normandy, eager to embark on the next chapter of their journey in pursuit of their new home.

# 14 THE CHATEAU IN NORMANDY

The Duchess sailed gracefully into the harbor of Le Havre in Normandy, the air heavy with fog and the faint patter of rain. As the trio disembarked, the letter of recommendation tightly in hand, they made their way through the mist-shrouded streets until they found the small office of the Jewish trader whose address was written on the sealed letter.

Entering the modest establishment, they were greeted warmly by a man dressed in traditional Jewish attire. With a respectful nod, Eric handed him the letter, watching as the man's eyes scanned the contents with interest.

"Ah, I see this is from my partner in La Rochelle," the man exclaimed, his face lighting up with recognition. "You are looking to buy an estate. Very well, I have the right homestead for you."

With a sense of anticipation coursing through their veins, Eric, Maria, and Elisa followed the trader out into the misty streets of Le Havre, eager to discover the property that could soon become their new home.

As the first light of dawn broke over the horizon, Eric, Maria, and Elisa found themselves settled comfortably in a carriage, accompanied by the Jewish merchant who, in anticipation of a good commission, had agreed to guide them on their journey. After crossing the Seine and with the wheels of the carriage turning, they embarked on the 20-mile trip southward, their excitement mounting with each passing mile.

The road stretched out before them, winding its way through the picturesque countryside of Normandy. Pastures of green grass swayed gently in the early morning breeze, and the distant call of birds filled the air with a sense of tranquility.

As they traveled onward, the landscape gradually transformed, giving way to rolling hills and lush greenery. The scent of wildflowers hung in the air, mingling with the earthy aroma of the countryside.

With each passing moment, their excitement grew, fueled by the prospect of discovering the château that could soon become their new home.

The small Château de Fauguernon, Normandy, located five miles to the north of Lisieux, stood proudly atop a gentle hill. Its stone walls, some of which were built in the 12th Century, were rising majestically against the backdrop of the surrounding countryside. It was surrounded by acres of lush greenery, exuding an aura of rustic elegance and grandeur.

As Eric, Maria, and Elisa approached, they were greeted by the sight of a magnificent entrance gate, hinting at the splendor that lay beyond. Tall cypress trees lined the driveway, their branches reaching toward the sky in a silent salute to the beauty of the estate.

The small château itself was an example of medieval beauty, with its graceful turret and intricately carved facade bearing witness to centuries of history. The stone walls were adorned with ivy, adding a touch of natural charm to the structure, flanked by a small stone chapel.

Within the grounds of the estate, manicured gardens stretched out in every direction, their vibrant blooms adding splashes of color to the verdant landscape. Several outbuildings and stables stood wrapped around the property. A tranquil pond shimmered in the sunlight, its surface reflecting the azure sky above.

As they stepped inside, they were greeted by a small foyer adorned with wood-paneled walls, the air redolent with the scent of aged wood and polished stone. Ornate chandeliers cast a warm glow over the space, illuminating the intricate details of the rustic furnishings that adorned the room.

From the simple attractiveness of the reception room to the coziness of the private chambers, every corner of the Château exuded an air of rough and rustic sophistication. It was a place where history and modest luxury converged, offering a glimpse into a world of opulence and charm.

As Eric, Maria, and Elisa explored the estate, they knew that they had found more than just a house – they had found a home where they could create new memories and embark on the next chapter of their lives together.

After their initial exploration of the Château, the trio settled into a small inn in the quaint village of Quilly-le-Vicomte. With anticipation coursing through their veins, they eagerly awaited word from the owner, hoping to finalize the purchase of their new home.

Owned by Louis d'Orléans, Duke of Orléans and Chartres, the estate had been on the market for two years, with no buyer in sight. Bold and determined, Eric saw an opportunity. He proposed a daring offer of 70,000 Livres to the duke, represented by a servant. Negotiations ensued, and after some back and forth, a deal was struck. The duke was willing to sell Fauguernon to Eric for 80,000 Livres, or £6,000, a sum that Eric readily agreed to.

With the assistance of a notary, a contract was drawn up, and Eric wasted no time in completing the transaction, paying the agreed-upon price in full. In the blink of an eye, they were now proud owners of a small estate in Normandy, their dreams of finding a new home finally realized.

As they walked the grounds of Fauguernon for the first time, their hearts filled with a sense of joy and excitement. They could already envision the countless memories they would create within its walls and the adventures that awaited them in this beautiful corner of the world.

Their new estate was secured and their hearts were filled with excitement for the future. But Eric, Maria, and Elisa still had one important task at hand – finding a suitable home for their beloved ship, The Marquise. While the bustling harbor of Le Havre offered convenience, it lacked the privacy and seclusion they desired.

Determined to find the perfect slip, they set out once again, this time in search of a smaller, more secluded harbor. Guided by the advice of locals, they journeyed to the coast on the south side of the Seine River, where they eventually stumbled upon Trouville-sur-Mer, a charming village nestled along the rugged coastline.

With its quaint charm and picturesque setting, Trouville-sur-Mer proved to be the ideal location for their needs. With merely 500 inhabitants, it offered the privacy and tranquility they longed for. After exploring the area and speaking with the locals, they soon found a small, secluded harbor where they could rent a permanent spot for The Marquise.

With the arrangements made, they returned to Le Havre the next day, driving the carriage back to the vibrant port city. Checking out of their inn, they bid farewell to their temporary stay, their hearts filled with anticipation for what awaited them in their new home at Château de Fauguernon.

On that foggy morning, with visibility limited and the air thick with mist, Eric, Maria, and Elisa embarked on their ship, bidding farewell to the bustling harbor of Le Havre. The waters of the River Seine inlet stretched out before them as they set sail southward, the silhouette of the port city fading into the distance behind them.

The journey across the inlet was short, a mere six miles, but it felt like a significant step toward their new life. As Eric studied the nautical chart spread out on the table, he remarked, "It's not far from England, less than 90 miles across the Channel to Portsmouth, and a mere 220 miles to the harbor of London."

Elisa couldn't help but feel a sense of awe at the realization that they were so close to their homeland, yet it seemed like worlds away amidst the vast expanse of the sea. With a sense of determination, they pressed on, navigating through the fog until they reached their destination.

Finally, The Duchess was moored at the small harbor of Trouville-sur-Mer, its tranquil waters offering a sense of serenity amidst the mist. With practiced skill, they transferred their few possessions onto a waiting carriage and began the journey inland to their new home, the Château de Fauguernon.

As they journeyed through the rolling hills of Normandy, Maria and Elisa couldn't help but marvel at the beauty of their surroundings, while Eric looked ahead with a sense of anticipation for the adventures that lay ahead in their new home.

With their new home secured and plans in motion, the trio wasted no time in getting to work on their new estate. The castle was almost empty, and there was much to be done. Immediately, they set about their tasks with determination and purpose.

The first order of business was to acquire horses and a carriage, essential for transportation and managing the expansive fields surrounding the small castle. With the help of a local horse dealer, this was quickly accomplished, and soon they were equipped with the means to navigate their new domain.

Next, Eric turned his attention to hiring farmhands to assist in the maintenance of the estate. As he surveyed the village, his gaze fell upon a middle-aged man who bore the unmistakable air of a seasoned sailor. Intrigued, Eric approached him.

"So, you've spent time at sea, Monsieur?" Eric inquired, his curiosity piqued.

"Aye, ten years in His Majesty's navy aboard an 80-gun ship of the line," the man replied proudly, his voice tinged with the salt of the sea.

"Then I take it you can handle the duties of a sailor?" Eric asked, impressed by the man's experience.

"Oh, indeed, Monsieur. There's no task on a ship or a farm I cannot do," the man assured him with a confident nod.

"Captain Eric Cobham," Eric introduced himself with a smile.

"Bernard Garnier," the man replied, extending a calloused hand. "A pleasure to meet you, Monsieur."

"We've recently acquired the castle of Fauguernon," Eric explained. "I'm in need of someone to manage the property, and sometimes sail our ship, and your familiarity seems well-suited for the tasks at hand."

"I was raised on a farm, Monsieur, and am experienced in all manner of farm tasks," Monsieur Garnier replied eagerly.

"Excellent. Report to me first thing tomorrow morning, and we'll get started," Eric said with a nod of approval.

With Bernard's experience and willingness to work, Eric knew he had found the perfect addition to their team. He wasted no time in explaining their situation.

Meanwhile, Maria and Elisa embarked on their own mission, taking a carriage to the nearby town of Lisieux to hire a carpenter. Elisa, in particular, had a specific request in mind – a large bed, uncommonly large, to accommodate her desire to sleep with Eric and Maria in one bed.

As they discussed their needs with the carpenter, Maria and Elisa couldn't help but feel a sense of excitement for the future. Each decision made and task accomplished brought the trio one step closer to turning their new home into a place of comfort and belonging.

With six horses stabled and a carriage at the ready, along with the employment of four farmhands and a capable manager, and with furniture steadily arriving, the Château de Fauguernon began to take on the appearance of a true home.

Maria and Elisa hired two maids, Monique and Lisette, and a cook as well. The chef claimed to have worked in the kitchen of the Duc de Chartres before. "We are going to live like real French ladies!" Elisa exclaimed, her excitement palpable.

"We will, my dear," Maria replied. "With maids, stable hands, and even our chef, we won't have to prepare meals anymore."

The servants and the manager were overjoyed by Eric's generosity and fair treatment. Recognizing their hard work and dedication, Eric decided to pay them comparably well for their services, making sure their families were taken care of as well. Additionally, he and Maria made the compassionate decision to provide them with accommodation in the side buildings of the castle free of charge.

Having experienced poverty themselves, Eric and Maria were keenly aware of the struggles faced by those less fortunate. With grateful hearts, they gladly shared their newfound luck and wealth with their new employees, ensuring that everyone within their household was cared for and valued. Their kindness and generosity fostered a sense of community and unity within the château, creating a harmonious environment where everyone could thrive.

With the arrival of furniture and the diligent work of the farmhands and manager, the Château de Fauguernon began to take shape as a true home for Eric, Maria, and Elisa. Each day brought new deliveries and progress, and soon the estate was teeming with activity.

One particular day, as Eric oversaw the unloading of a large bed from the carpenter's cart, he couldn't help but be taken aback by its size.

"Aye, master, this is quite a massive bed you have produced there," Eric remarked, his astonishment evident.

"Monsieur, it was made according to the two ladies' wishes and plans," the carpenter explained respectfully.

"Oh, well, I will not get involved, then," Eric replied with a smile, recognizing Maria and Elisa's desire for a bed that would accommodate all three of them comfortably. With a sense of amusement, he stepped back, content to let the women's preferences guide the furnishing of their new home.

As the bed was carefully placed in one of the grand bedrooms of the château, Eric couldn't help but feel a sense of happiness.

With each passing day, the Château de Fauguernon felt more like home, a sanctuary where they could build a life filled with love, laughter, and shared dreams.

Sometimes the three of them would ride out together, exploring the picturesque countryside surrounding their château. However, more often than not, Eric would rise before daybreak to venture out hunting on his own, his trusty musket by his side.

Eric liked hunting on horseback in the forests surrounding the small castle. His hunts proved fruitful, and he regularly returned to the small castle with a bounty of game. The kitchen was furnished with an array of culinary delights, including pheasant, deer, elk, and wild boar, providing them with hearty meals One day, he returned triumphant, bringing home a huge boar. They eagerly anticipated their first stately dinner prepared by the new chef.

The meal was nothing short of grand. The chef's skill was evident in every dish, and it was clear he had not exaggerated about his experience working in the kitchens of the duke. The dinner began with a delicious soup, followed by a refreshing salad. The centerpiece was the wild boar roast, cooked to perfection and bursting with flavor. For dessert, they enjoyed a selection of fresh fruits, and no French meal would be complete without a serving of fine French cheese.

To accompany the meal, they uncorked a bottle of the finest French wine, sourced from the extensive cellars of the château. To their surprise, the previous owner had left them with over 500 bottles of the finest wines and some fine French brandy, which seemed forgotten in the old dungeons below, and had collected layers of dust over the years.

The grand bedroom was finally complete, and for the first time, they would occupy their oversized bed. As they retired to their abode for the night, Elisa couldn't contain her excitement. She immediately shed her dress and began jumping up and down on the luxurious bed.

"Get in here, you two!" she exclaimed, extending an invitation to Maria and Eric. "This is what we needed. Gone are the days of sleeping in the cramped ship's cabin."

"Oh, come on, Elisa. It wasn't all that bad," Eric remarked with a playful grin.

"Well, beds do seem to be made for one or two, at most. There seem to be few relationships of three, like ours," Maria observed, a smile playing on her lips.

"But ours is the best," Elisa declared with conviction. "We have the best of both worlds – love, companionship, and passion."

"And cock and fanny," Maria laughed.

"Exactly," Elisa chimed in, her eyes sparkling with agreement. "We have something truly special, something that many could only dream of."

"Two ladies! I'm not going to complain," Eric responded with a grin, his tone lighthearted and filled with affection.

Maria and Eric needed no further encouragement. Without hesitation, they too discarded their clothes and joined Elisa on the sumptuous bed, reveling in the newfound comfort and space.

As Elisa stood illuminated by the lamplight, her nude form was accentuated by the black embroidered cotton stockings held up by garters around her thighs. With a sensual grace, Elisa rolled the stockings down, revealing more of her skin. She opened her arms, exposing her ample breasts, as Eric gently turned her around to face Maria, offering her for inspection.

"Lie down," Maria commanded, her voice carrying authority. Elisa obediently slid down onto the bed, anticipation coursing through her veins. "On your back," Maria instructed, a mischievous glint in her eye as she held a bottle of wine in her hand.

Eager to indulge in the moment, Elisa complied, stretching out on her back as Maria approached with the bottle. With a playful cry, Elisa exclaimed, "Ow, Maria! It's too big!"

Gradually, Elisa began to relax, her body responding to the emphatic skill of Maria's hands. As Maria's touch grew more insistent, Elisa's flesh shook and quivered under her ministrations. Maria rubbed her skin with practiced expertise, coaxing Elisa's body to yield to her touch.

With a skilled hand, Maria reached for the bottle, her movements fluid and confident. She used the bottle as a tool, applying just the right amount of pressure to provide relief and pleasure to Elisa's tense vulva muscles. As the tension melted away, and the bottle slid inward, Elisa surrendered to the sensations, allowing herself to be swept away by the waves of pleasure that washed over her.

Eric approached Elisa with a gentle demeanor, offering her his hard cock. Elisa accepted it willingly, her fingers taking it with a firm grip. Gradually, their embrace evolved, and Elisa's lips found their way to Eric's manhood, the touch of her mouth gentle yet eager.

Meanwhile, Maria continued her skilled manipulation with the bottle between Elisa's thighs, her movements precise and purposeful. As the sensations intensified, Elisa's mouth's grip on Eric tightened, her breath growing ragged with each passing moment. The combination of Maria's expert touch and Eric's tender presence enveloped the woman in a whirlwind of pleasure and desire. Elisa screamed like she had never before, as she erupted.

"Turn over," Eric instructed Maria as she placed the used bottle on a nearby table. Maria complied without hesitation, gracefully shifting onto all fours atop the expansive bed. As Maria positioned herself, her mouth instinctively sought out the warmth of Elisa's thighs, her lips gently caressing the delicate skin around her vulva. Her eyes closed in bliss.

Maria's lips formed an involuntary smile, her body surrendering to the sensations coursing through her. Meanwhile, Elisa's hands moved with purpose, tracing a path down Maria's body until they reached her breasts. With skilled precision, Elisa's fingers began to massage and knead Maria's flesh, eliciting soft suctions from her lips.

As Elisa's hands explored Maria's body, her palms gently rotating over her nipples, she felt a surge of arousal coursing through her. With deliberate movements, her hands traced down Maria's flanks, igniting a fire within her as Eric entered Maria from behind.

Maria's body immediately responded, eager to return to Eric's thrusts. Her feet were now pointed like a ballerina's, toes curling in ecstasy. Eric's strong hands gripped her hips firmly as he thrust deeper into her, his passion driving him onward. With each movement, Maria's cries echoed through the room, a wail of ecstasy and desire.

Without hesitation, Maria surrendered to the pleasure, her cries mingling with the sounds of their lovemaking. Suddenly, time seemed to stand still as peace settled over the trio, enveloping them in a cocoon of sleep connection.

As midnight approached, the exhausted trio drifted deeper into a peaceful slumber, their bodies entwined in the aftermath of their passion. When they awoke the next morning, they were greeted by the gentle light of dawn filtering through the curtains. It had been a night filled with passion, pleasure, and intimacy, a fitting beginning to their new life together in their grand bed at the Château de Fauguernon. It had been a good night.

## 15 AN ACT OF PIRACY

One brisk morning, Eric set out on horseback for a hunting excursion, while Maria began her day attending to the affairs of their estate. Her search for Monique, her maid, proved fruitless. In the side building where Monique and her young daughter resided with the other servants, only the child was found.

"Where is your mother?" Maria inquired gently.

"Men took her away," the child replied somberly. "It happened yesterday, two men."

Maria's concern deepened. She marched with purpose to the manager's house, seeking Bernard Garnier. Finding him in the yard, she wasted no time.

"Bernard, the child just informed me that her mother, Monique, was taken away," Maria exclaimed.

Bernard's gaze fell in embarrassment. "Yes, Madame, two gendarmes came and took her to prison," he admitted reluctantly.

"What for? What has she done?" Maria's voice betrayed her growing agitation.

"It was unpaid debt, Madame," Bernard replied, his tone apologetic.

"Why were Monsieur Eric and I not immediately informed of this?" Maria's frustration boiled over.

"We did not wish to inconvenience you, Madame," Bernard offered in explanation.

Maria clenched her fists. "I must be informed of such matters in the future," she insisted firmly.

"I will ensure it, Madame," Bernard promised.

"And what of Monique's daughter? Is anyone caring for her?" Maria demanded.

"Lisette is tending to her needs," Bernard assured her.

"Good. Do you know where Monique was taken?" Maria pressed on.

"I believe to the prison in Pont-l'Évêque," Bernard replied.

Later, when Eric returned from his hunt with two hares in his bag, Maria recounted the distressing events.

Eric's face darkened. The news of Monique's arrest gnawed at him like a relentless itch. His jaw clenched, and his grip on the reins tightened as he listened, the hares forgotten in his saddlebag.

"I will take care of this," Eric declared, his voice edged with determination. "This cannot be left unaddressed."

Maria nodded in agreement, her own anger still smoldering. "We must ensure that things like this do not happen again and that Monique's little daughter is cared for."

Eric had the carriage readied. Soon, Eric, Maria, and Elisa set forth to Pont-l'Évêque, the little town 10 miles away where Monique was held.

When they arrived at the prison gates, Eric and Maria were met with stern-faced guards who eyed them with suspicion. But their noble bearing and attire, combined with their unwavering resolve brooked no argument. They demanded to see the warden, which was swiftly arranged. Eric wanted to understand the circumstances of Monique's arrest.

The prison warden was a tall figure, his demeanor reflecting years of authority and command. Lean but imposing, he carried himself with a rigid posture that demanded respect from both inmates and staff alike. His features were weathered, etched with lines that spoke of the challenges he had faced in his role.

Dressed in the uniform of his profession, a dark navy blue coat adorned with brass buttons, he exuded an air of stern professionalism. His gaze was sharp and penetrating, capable of quelling any hint of disobedience with a mere glance.

"What can I do for you, Mesdames et Monsieur?" he asked.

"My name is Captain Eric Cobham," Eric began, his tone firm yet composed as he addressed the warden. "I recently purchased the castle nearby from His Grace, the Duke of Bourbon. One of my servants, Monique Dubois, has been taken from my home without my knowledge."

The warden, a figure of authority in the dimly lit office, listened attentively before motioning for a guard to investigate. Moments later, the guard returned with a piece of paper, which the warden examined carefully.

"Yes, we do have an inmate by that name here," the warden confirmed, his voice resonating with a sense of duty. "She was imprisoned on behalf of a ship owner in Le Havre, for unpaid debt. The ship owner's name is Fouche, Pierre Fouche, living at Quai de l'Ile in Le Havre. She owes him money, and he chose to have her prosecuted."

"How much debt does she owe?" Eric inquired, his brow furrowing with concern.

The warden referred to the paper once more. "According

to our records, it amounts to 19 Livres, plus interest, totaling 21 Livres. It seems, the debt was incurred by her estranged husband, who is currently missing. However, under the law, she is held liable."

"What madness is this? This is petty debt. She needs to be set free!" Eric demanded, his voice echoing off the stone walls. "Why was this woman even taken from my home, and her child left without care, without so much as a word of explanation? She is in my service."

The prison official, taken aback by Eric's fury, stammered out a response. "It was a matter of law, Monsieur," he explained hastily. "She was detained at the behest of her creditors, and under French law, a wife is liable for her husband's debt. This may sound unfair, but I do not make the laws."

Eric's gaze hardened. "And what of her daughter? Who will care for her in her mother's absence?"

Maria stepped forward, her voice like steel. "What do I need to do? Tell me. How can you even allow such injustice?"

"This is not my problem, Madame. I am only a warden, responsible for the daily operations of His Majesty's prison. The law is the law, and I am only applying it."

"This is so unfair, this poor woman, what can we do?" Elisa exclaimed, her voice filled with empathy.

"Well, the debt has to be paid with the magistrate in town, unless that is done, I cannot release her," the warden explained matter-of-factly.

Eric reached into his coat pocket and withdrew a purse. With deliberate motions, he placed two Louis D'Or onto the table, covering the debt almost twice over. Then, he added another two coins and slid them across the desk toward the warden.

"Here, these are for you, to cover your inconveniences. Can you please arrange for the debt to be paid, Monsieur?" Eric's voice was resolute, his gaze unwavering.

The warden's face lit up with surprise and gratitude. Two Louis D'Or was more than what he earned in three months. Without hesitation, he swiftly summoned an officer and instructed them to take the money to the magistrate for the settlement of Monique's debt.

The warden, elated by the unexpected windfall of the two gold coins, wasted no time in fetching a bottle of Armagnac, pouring generous servings for everyone present.

"If there is anything I can do for you in the future," he declared, raising his glass, "do not hesitate to approach me directly."

Eric, Maria, and Elisa settled into the dimly lit office, the warm glow of the brandy easing the tension in the air.

They chatted amiably, the somber atmosphere of moments ago replaced by a sense of camaraderie.

After an hour of conversation and shared drinks, the officer returned with the paper from the magistrate, along with 8 livres in change. Eric handed the officer two livres and placed the remaining coins on the table before the warden.

"Here, Monsieur, make sure the inmates in this prison get a good meal today," Eric stated firmly.

The warden's eyes widened with gratitude as he swiftly collected the silver coins, a glimmer of appreciation in his gaze.

Moments later, two guards escorted Monique into the room. Tears welled up in her eyes at the sight of her employers. Maria wasted no time in embracing her tightly.

"It's all good, Monique. Your debt has been paid, and your daughter is well taken care of," Maria reassured her, her voice gentle and comforting.

"I didn't know about the debt, Madame, I swear," Monique explained tearfully. "It was something my worthless husband did before he ran away. I didn't have the money to pay for it."

"We know, Monique," Elisa reassured her, placing a comforting hand on her shoulder. "It's all settled now, Monsieur Eric took care of it."

With the ordeal finally behind them, Eric spoke up, his voice filled with warmth and compassion. "Let's go home," he said, his words a soothing balm to Monique's troubled heart.

Soon, the four of them found themselves seated in the rocking carriage, the horses' hooves carrying them swiftly back to the castle. As they journeyed homeward, the weight of the day's events gradually lifted.

As the evening descended and the trio settled into their grand dining room for dinner, Maria's anger simmered just beneath the surface, threatening to boil over. Her frustration and indignation at the injustice faced by Monique burned brightly within her.

"I want this Fouche bastard punished for what he has done to Monique and her little daughter," Maria exclaimed, her voice tinged with fury.

Eric and Elisa exchanged solemn glances, understanding the depth of Maria's outrage. Eric nodded in agreement, his jaw set with determination.

"He is a ship owner, probably worth thousands of Louis, and yet he has a poor single servant woman thrown into debtor's prison for an amount he probably spends on dinner every day," Maria continued, her words laced with contempt. "And to think, her child would be left on the streets if we had not taken care of her."

The injustice of it all hung heavy in the air, casting a

shadow over the opulent surroundings of the dining room. Maria's impassioned plea for justice echoed off the walls, a crisp reminder of the stark disparity between the privileged and the marginalized.

"I will see what I can find out," Eric replied, his tone firm and resolute. "We are members of the pirate trade, after all, and he operates ships," Eric mused, a smile tugging at the corners of his lips. "It would be surprising if we could not find a way to pay him back."

The glint in Eric's eyes spoke volumes, hinting at a plan already forming in his mind. With his background as a pirate, he knew the ins and outs of maritime business, and he understood the vulnerabilities of those who sailed the seas for profit.

The next morning, Eric made his way into the small town of Quilly-le-Vicomte, his steps purposeful and determined. He knew exactly who he was looking for—a no-good cutthroat who had been lurking around the outskirts of the castle, unwanted and uninvited.

Entering the town's tavern, Eric's keen eyes quickly spotted his target, lounging at a table in the dimly lit corner. Eric ordered two beakers of wine. With a steely resolve, Eric approached the man, his presence commanding attention despite the rowdy atmosphere of the tavern, as he put one beaker in front of the man.

"Go to the Quai de l'Ile in Le Havre," Eric began, his

voice low and authoritative. "There is a five-story house belonging to one Monsieur Pierre Fouche. I need you to find out about his activities—when he leaves the house, who he associates with, and any other pertinent information."

Eric slid four silver coins across the table, the promise of payment gleaming in the dim light of the tavern. "If you come back with the requested information, I'll give you another four," he added, his tone leaving no room for negotiation.

The cutthroat nodded, a greedy glint in his eyes as he pocketed the coins. Quickly he emptied the beaker with the wine. With a smirk, he rose from his seat, eager to carry out Eric's instructions and earn his reward. Immediately, he disappeared into the bustling streets of the town.

A week passed, and the man Eric had sent returned to the castle with the desired information. Monsieur Fouche, it seemed, followed a predictable routine. Still unmarried, he left his grand five-story house every morning at 8 o'clock sharp, making his way to a nearby tavern for breakfast before heading to his dockyard in the harbor.

As Eric shared the news with Maria and Elisa, the latter's face lit up with a mischievous glint in her eyes.

"Oh, leave this bastard to me. I'll extract all the information we need from him," she declared confidently.

The following day, the trio found themselves in Le Havre, with Elisa dressed in her most elegant attire. Positioned strategically near Monsieur Fouche's house at the Quai de l'Ile, Elisa waited patiently until precisely 8 o'clock in the morning.

As if on cue, a servant opened the gate, and Monsieur Fouche, large and dressed in an expensive coat, emerged from his residence. Elisa feigned a stumble, gracefully falling to her knees with a faint cry. Predictably, Monsieur Fouche noticed her distress and rushed to her aid.

"Oh, Madame, what happened? Can I be of assistance?" he inquired with concern.

"Oh, Monsieur, you are such a gentleman," Elisa replied, her voice filled with gratitude. "I must have tripped over my dress on these rough cobblestone streets."

"I hope you are not hurt, Madame," Monsieur Fouche replied earnestly. "You most certainly need sustenance. Can I treat you to a nice breakfast? I am on my way there anyway."

"Oh, that would be wonderful," Elisa exclaimed, her acting skills on full display. And so, the pair made their way to a small tavern, where Monsieur Fouche hovered attentively over Elisa, oblivious to her true intentions.

"Monsieur, what does such a generous gentleman like yourself do?" Elisa inquired with feigned innocence.

"Oh, I own ships, mostly West Indiamen, and also Guineamen," Monsieur Fouche explained proudly.

Curious, Elisa pressed the meaty merchant further, "And what are Guineamen?"

"Well, Guineamen are mostly slave ships," Monsieur Fouche answered matter-of-factly. "They sail from the coast of Africa on the middle passage to the colonies with slaves. And West Indiamen bring riches from the Caribbean and the colonies here."

Elisa gasped, her facade of innocence crumbling. "Isn't that cruel, putting all those poor slaves on a ship and taking them away from their lands?" she asked, her voice tinged with indignation.

Monsieur Fouche chuckled patronizingly, brushing pearls of swear from his bald head. "Oh, no Madame, these are animals, they have no soul. They are there for us, even the Bible says so. And, may I tell you, the slave trade is very profitable," he explained, his words dripping with arrogance.

Elisa's expression hardened, but she maintained her pretense. "Ah, I see, these animals can be traded then," she replied coolly. "I wish I could see such a big ship once."

Monsieur Fouche's eyes gleamed with eagerness. "That is not a problem, Madame. I cannot show you a slave ship, as they sail to the Americas but I gladly invite you on one of my ships. One of my West Indiamen, the Martinique, will be coming to Le Havre in 6-8 weeks from the New World, laden with riches from the shores of the Caribbean. She has probably already left the harbor and is en route to the Canaries as we speak."

Elisa forced a smile, masking her disgust at Monsieur Fouche's callous attitude toward human life. Little did he know, she was already formulating a plan to ensure that justice would be served.

"Oh, that is so exciting!" Elisa exclaimed, her voice filled with feigned enthusiasm. "Is this a big ship?" she asked innocently.

"Oh yes, Madame, 950 tons, one of the biggest in the trade, full of sugar, tobacco, and even some silver," Monsieur Fouche explained proudly.

"Will we meet soon again?" the ship owner inquired eagerly as Lisa readied to leave.

"Unfortunately, Monsieur, I am on my way to my castle in the countryside tomorrow, but I will gladly take you up on your generous offer when I return. I will be back in 6 weeks in Le Havre," Elisa replied smoothly.

"Yes, please, Madame, visit me at my house, and I will show you my ships," Monsieur Fouche begged, his eagerness palpable.

As Elisa bid farewell, her mind raced with plans and

schemes. Monsieur Fouche's unwitting breakfast invitation had provided her with the perfect opportunity to gather evidence against him and put a dent into his despicable trade in human lives.

As Eric, Maria, and Elisa drove back to the Château de Fauguernon, Elisa couldn't contain her excitement any longer. Bursting with anticipation, she exclaimed, "Guess what I found out?"

"What is it?" Maria asked eagerly. "Tell us."

"This fat bastard is a slave trader," Elisa revealed, her voice filled with disgust. "Human lives mean nothing to him if he can line his pockets. But I have information!"

Eric and Maria exchanged concerned glances, their anger simmering beneath the surface at the revelation.

"In 6-8 weeks, one of his West Indiamen, the Martinique, will be sailing into the harbor of Le Havre, coming from Port-au-Prince," Elisa continued, her voice trembling with determination. "She is 950 tons and laden with sugar, tobacco, and silver."

"Almost a thousand tons! This is a mighty big ship," Eric exclaimed, his brow furrowed in concern. "It's too big for The Duchess and our three crew members to tackle alone."

Maria nodded in agreement, her expression reflecting the weight of the situation. "Besides, where would we even put all the cargo on the Duchess?" she added, voicing the practical concerns. "And we can't possibly sail the Martinique back with just the three of us. A ship of that size needs a crew of at least ten to maneuver her properly."

"That's true," Elisa chimed in, her mind already racing with potential solutions.

"And considering the size of the Martinique, she likely has a crew of at least twenty sailors, if not more," Eric mused.

Eric sighed heavily, the enormity of the task ahead settling over them like a dark cloud. "We'll need to come up with a plan," he said determinedly. "But for now, let's focus on gathering more information and figuring out our next move."

"Remember the East Indiaman we captured in the Irish Sea?" Eric asked, his voice tinged with nostalgia. "That was our biggest haul ever. It brought over £40,000. And this West Indiaman is even bigger."

"Oh, I remember it well," Maria replied, a fond smile gracing her lips. "She was the first real ship we took."

"Port-au-Prince, that's a long trip to Le Havre," Eric mused, his mind already plotting their course. "Almost 5,000 sea miles. I am quite sure she takes the southern route, sails to the Canary Islands, and takes on fresh water."

"Yes, he mentioned the Canaries," Lisa exclaimed.

"Good! I bet she then will sail north, along the French coast, passing the lighthouse by Pointe Saint Mathieu. We only need to lay in waiting there," Eric concluded confidently.

"But how do we capture her?" Maria asked, her brow furrowed in thought. "We have no reliable pirate crew."

"Why don't we call our old crew?" Elisa suggested, her eyes bright with excitement. "We could fake an emergency on The Duchess, stop the Martinique, and raid her. I reckon our men won't mind another gold-filled purse."

"Then we sail her to Marseille and sell both ship and load," Eric laughed, the thrill of the upcoming adventure coursing through his veins.

The next day, Eric wasted no time. He penned a letter to the tavern near Underwood East of Plymouth, where his old crew gathered on occasions. Instructing them to arrive at the castle no later than in five weeks, Eric knew that with their expertise and skills, they stood a chance at pulling off their most daring heist yet.

As word of their old captain's call reached England, the crew wasted no time in heeding the summons. Sensing the promise of a lucrative haul, most of them embarked on the 190-mile voyage from Plymouth to Le Havre, arriving at the Château de Fauguernon within the designated five-week timeframe.

Maria and Elisa had already made preparations, ensuring that quarters in the main house were ready to accommodate their returning comrades. Ten men of their old crew had answered the call, and their arrival brought about a joyous reunion.

Wine flowed freely, ale was plentiful, and great roasts were prepared by the chef and served to the crew every night. The camaraderie among the crewmembers was palpable as they reminisced about past adventures and eagerly anticipated the one that lay ahead.

The next morning, it was time to arm themselves for the impending mission. Eric distributed the crew's weapons, ensuring that each man received a new Saint Etienne rifle, a cutlass, a dagger, and a pistol. With their arsenal at the ready, the men led by Eric made their way to the Harbor of Trouville, where The Duchess lay anchored. Though the small ship struggled to accommodate the full crew of ten, the sailors were accustomed to making do, often sleeping on makeshift planks.

With everyone aboard, The Duchess set sail, covering the 150 miles south to the lighthouse of Pointe Saint Mathieu in less than a day. There, they waited patiently, scanning the horizon for any sign of their target.

Days stretched into a week, and The Duchess let several ships pass by, biding their time for their designated prey.

Then, on the 11th day in the late afternoon, the lookout spotted the Martinique, slowly sailing north under heavy load, making barely 5 knots. Excitement coursed through the crew as they prepared to enact their carefully laid plans. The stage was set for their most daring heist yet.

Like a silent predator, The Duchess, sailing under the French flag, glided into the pathway of the West Indiaman, her movements calculated and deliberate. Then the ship hauled in sails. On deck, Eric had ignited a smoke can, the billowing clouds simulating a fire, while Elisa and Maria, portraying the image of damsels in distress, stood on the quarterdeck in their light, deep-cut dresses, waving their hands frantically. Below deck, the pirate crew remained hidden, poised for action.

As The Duchess came to a halt directly in the path of the West Indiaman, the larger ship slowed to a crawl before finally stopping, maintaining a distance of 30 yards. An officer from the Martinique called out, his voice carrying across the water, "What is the matter, Mesdames?"

"We were having a fire on board, but I believe it is out now," Maria yelled back, her voice carrying the perfect blend of distress and relief. "We are from Le Havre."

"This is where we are headed to, Mesdames," the officer replied, now joined by the captain. "Can we offer you any help?" the captain asked, genuine concern evident in his voice.

"We lost all our drinking water putting out the fire," Eric, disguised in the garb of a French noble, exclaimed, playing his role to perfection. "If you could help us out..."

"Of course," the captain replied, his sense of hospitality overcoming any suspicion. "Please come on board."

With practiced ease, The Duchess pulled alongside the Martinique, and Eric, followed by the two ladies, boarded the larger ship via a ship's ladder. The captain greeted them warmly, inviting them for a dinner amid their misfortune. As they sat below deck dining with the captain and two of the ship's officers, the night fell, casting a cloak of darkness over their clandestine operation. The stage was set for the next phase of their audacious plan.

The evening progressed and the dinner continued. The pirate crew had remained hidden below deck, patiently awaiting their moment to strike. Maria, seizing the opportunity, excused herself from the table under the guise of using the galley. Ascending to the upper deck of the West Indiaman, she spotted one of her sailors on board The Duchess who signaled her, "We are ready."

With a nod of acknowledgment, Maria descended back into the dinner room, while the pirates boarded the ship one by one, via the ladder which was still hanging off the Martinique's reeling. Below deck, Maria confirmed to Eric with a brief nod, that the time for action had come. In an instant, Eric drew two pistols, while Maria and Elisa retrieved their trusty pistols concealed beneath their skirts.

The sudden appearance of the weapons shocked the captain of The Martinique, who instinctively sprang up from the table, reaching for his rapier. Before he could react, a shot from Maria's pistol sent him crashing to the floor, dead.

The sound of the gunshot served as the signal for the pirate crew, who emerged from their hiding places on deck. Swiftly and efficiently, they overpowered the unarmed merchant crew, binding them with ropes, and lining them up on deck.

Under the cover of darkness, the pirates swiftly took control of the West Indiaman, their actions precise and decisive. With their captives subdued, they set about securing the ship and preparing to sail her to their desired destination: Marseille, the place where they had sold previous loads of plunder.

Maria and a sailor descended back to The Duchess, their mission clear: to trail the massive West Indiaman to the harbor of Marseille, so they all could sail back to Le Havre after the deal was concluded and the Martinique was sold. With the crew of the captured ship safely adrift in a rescue boat about three miles off the French coast, Eric, Elisa and the remaining nine men assumed their positions on board the captured ship. Both vessels set sail, their bows cutting through the dark waters of the

Mediterranean as they embarked on their journey to the bustling port of Marseille.

The night sky stretched endlessly above them, a canopy of stars guiding their path as they navigated the open sea. Onboard The Duchess, Maria and her fellow sailor worked tirelessly, ensuring that their vessel was kept at a short distance from the larger but slower West Indiaman.

14 days later, as the first light of dawn began to break on the horizon, the silhouette of Marseille's harbor loomed in the distance, beckoning them forward with the promise of adventure and opportunity.

Under the deck of The Duchess, the crew celebrated their well-deserved payday. Eric and Maria, as the captain and the leaders of the operation, received £18,000. Each of the sailors, plus Elisa, received their share of the remaining £24,000, amounting to £2,250 each. Additionally, each member of the crew was rewarded with a pound of silver coins from the chest they had seized on The Martinique. This was more than any raid had ever brought in.

With their pockets now heavy with wealth, the crew prepared to set sail for Le Havre once again. However, this time, their journey would be swifter and smoother. Freed from the burden of the heavy cargo-laden ship, The Duchess surged through the water at a remarkable speed of nine knots, cutting through the waves with ease.

As they made their way toward Le Havre, anticipation filled the air, mingling with the satisfaction of a successful venture and the promise of a prosperous future ahead. The trio parted from their old pirate crew in Le Havre, as the sailors made ready to travel back to their homes in Plymouth, England.

Back at their own home at the castle, Eric, Maria, and Elisa summoned Monique into their chambers, the maid whose unfortunate fate had spurred their most recent raid.

Maria, with a hint of sincerity in her voice, inquired, "How much is Monsieur Eric paying you per year?"

The maid hesitated for a moment, taken aback by the unexpected question. "He is paying me £35 in English money per year," she replied, her voice tinged with surprise.

Maria furrowed her brow, considering the response. "Is that a good pay?" she asked, genuinely curious.

"Oh yes, Madame," Monique replied, a hint of gratitude in her tone. "Normally, we only earn between £4 – £14 per year. And we can live at the castle for free. It is a good pay. The servants of the duke don't earn half that."

"We have a surprise for you," Eric interjected, his voice warm as he handed her a small leather purse filled with coins. "Here is £100 for you and your daughter, so she can go to school. We hope you will stay with us."

Tears welled up in Monique's eyes as she accepted the unexpected gift.

"I will always remember what you have done for me when I was arrested," she replied, her voice trembling with emotion. "I will always be loyal to you."

Moved by the moment, Eric then called all the other 12 servants and workers one by one, presenting each of them with a bonus of £25 for their hard work and dedication. As they expressed their honest appreciation, a sense of gratitude filled the room, strengthening the bond between the household members and their generous employers.

Mischievous as ever, Elisa couldn't resist the opportunity to deliver a subtle blow to Monsieur Fouche, the slave trader and owner of The Martinique. Armed with a plan, she made her way to Le Havre and knocked on the man's door, feigning interest in his long-gone ship.

"Monsieur, I am following your generous invitation to see your great West Indiaman," she announced with a smile, upon his answering the door.

The expression on Monsieur Fouche's face turned from surprise to eagerness as he welcomed her inside. "Oh Madame, I am glad you came," he said, his voice tinged with excitement. "But the ship is over six weeks late; I fear she's been lost at sea. Perhaps you will still join me for dinner, Madame?"

Elisa, however, wasn't one to play along with false pleasantries. "I am very disappointed, Monsieur," she replied coolly, her tone dripping with sarcasm. "I believe you are fooling me. I'd rather abstain."

With that, she turned on her heel and strode out of the house on Quai de l'Ile, leaving Monsieur Fouche red-faced and embarrassed in her wake. It was a small victory, but for Elisa, it was a satisfying moment of poetic justice.

## 16 A LIFE IN FRANCE

Eric, Maria, and Elisa had returned to the Château de Fauguernon after their sea adventure, eager to wash off the scent of the ocean in a soothing bath. As evening fell, they gathered in their shared grand bedroom, ready to unwind and share stories of their day.

Elisa, feeling a bit tipsy from the wine, regaled them with tales of her encounter with Monsieur Fouche, the ship owner and slave trader she had visited in Le Havre.

"He wasn't sure if the West Indiaman would still arrive," she chuckled, recounting her conversation with the merchant. "I told him I was disappointed because he was likely just a boaster," she added with a mischievous grin.

Eric and Maria couldn't help but join in Elisa's laughter, their bellies aching from the shared amusement. "Can you show us the stupid face he made?" Maria asked, her eyes twinkling with delight.

Elisa obliged, making a comical grimace that sent them all into fits of laughter once again. "He's still waiting for the ship?" Eric inquired; his amusement was evident in his voice.

"It certainly sounds like it," Elisa replied, her laughter still bubbling over.

"But who knows? The ship is probably already at a harbor in Turkey, and the profits from its cargo are lining our coffers," Maria joked, adding to the lighthearted atmosphere in the room.

As the laughter subsided and they all settled onto the large bed, Elisa broke the moment with a mock scowl. "I need it now!" she exclaimed, her tone playful yet insistent.

Maria, always the dominant one, replied, "Very well, you may kiss my lady parts!"

As Elisa took her hand and sensually sucked the ends of her fingers, a shiver of anticipation coursed through her body. Then, with a bold move, Elisa shifted her head between Maria's legs, pressing her tongue against her hand in a teasing gesture.

Meanwhile, Eric leaned in to kiss Maria, their lips meeting in a moment of intimacy. Yet, amidst the passion, Maria sensed a shift in Eric's demeanor. Suddenly, with surprising agility, he moved to straddle her chest, his weight pressing down on her breasts as his knees pinned her beneath him.

His weight was mostly supported by her forearms, and Maria felt a sense of helplessness and excitement beneath his powerful presence. With her breath catching in her throat, she surrendered to the sensation of being held down by Eric, her body tingling with anticipation for what would come next.

As Elisa continued to stroke Maria's pubic area with her tongue, a wave of pleasure washed over her, sending a thrilling sensation coursing through her body. Maria's focus shifted entirely to Eric, her sole desire now to please him and ensure that this night was a success for all three of them.

With a single-minded determination, Maria took Eric's penis into her mouth, greedily sucking on it with fervor. As she felt the hot sensation of his flesh against her lips, she became consumed by the intoxicating pleasure of the moment.

In a bold gesture, Maria instinctively clamped her thighs around Elisa's head, silently urging her to increase the intensity of her actions. It was a silent communication, a wordless plea for more, as Maria surrendered herself completely to the pleasure of her lust.

Maria, emboldened by desire and passion, freed one arm from beneath Eric's knee. With a sense of curiosity, she trailed her hand along the length of his cock, tracing the prominent veins that ran beneath the surface of his skin. As she reached the tip, she lightly stroked it with her fingers, feeling the heat and hardness beneath her touch.

With a daring move, Maria held Eric's penis loosely with her lips, her mouth exploring every inch of his shaft. Then, overcome by a surge of boldness, she moved her head up slightly, taking his length into her throat, about halfway along. She pressed her head against him, her throat accommodating his size as she reveled in the sensation of fullness and intimacy.

Meanwhile, she felt Elisa's tongue between her labia, adding to the overwhelming pleasure that coursed through her body. Lost in the moment, Maria surrendered herself completely to the ecstasy of their shared passion, her senses alive with the intoxicating sensations of desire and arousal.

As Maria reached the pinnacle of pleasure, her body quivered with ecstasy, Elisa's tongue still teasing her senses, firmly clamped between her legs. After a moment of pure bliss, Maria broke into a quick giggle, her eyes locking with Eric's as she felt the force of lust still coursing through her veins.

Suddenly, Maria sensed a surge of dominance overtake her, fueled by the intoxicating rush of desire. "Go, take Elisa!" she commanded, her voice dripping with urgency and passion.

Eric, obedient to Maria's command, turned his attention to Elisa, who was still held between Maria's thighs. Maria now clamped her head with force locked between her legs. With a swift motion, Eric swung off Maria's chest and rose to his feet behind Elisa, his desire evident as he gazed upon her glistening labia. His hands found her hips, feeling the softness of her muscles beneath his touch.

Sensing Eric's presence behind her, Elisa shifted back, inviting him to take her. With a single decisive movement, Eric entered her, his arousal evident as he plunged halfway into her welcoming warmth. He felt her wetness engulfing him, her body responding eagerly to his touch.

With each thrust, Eric felt Elisa's body yield to him, her wetness enveloping him as he moved deeper inside her. With each movement, he could feel her arching back, her desire matching his own as they surrendered to the passionate rhythm of their encounter.

Elisa climbed onto Maria's thighs, seeking to wrap her arms around her spread legs. Maria, in turn, held her captive, their connection intensifying with each moment of intimacy. As Eric continued to thrust with increasing force, he felt Elisa's vulva contracting around him, a sign of her mounting pleasure.

With each movement, Eric pressed harder against her, driven by the primal urge to satisfy their desires. Then, as Elisa reached the peak of ecstasy, she fell into a state of total relaxation, her cries muffled by the embrace of

Maria's legs.

In the aftermath of their passionate encounter, they lay together in the stillness of their massive bed, illuminated by the soft glow of candlelight. Maria's cheek brushed against Elisa's vulva, her lips greedily lapping up the remnants of Eric's passion. In this moment of quiet intimacy, they were bound together by the unspoken bond of their deep love for each other.

At this time, Eric, Maria, and Elisa's lives were full of joy and adventure, woven with the threads of friendship and shared passions.

At the Château de Fauguernon, the trio found solace and excitement. Regularly, they would embark on expeditions aboard The Duchess, sailing into the tranquil embrace of the open sea. Fishing became not just a pastime but a cherished ritual, where laughter mingled with the gentle lapping of waves, while the summer sun painted the sky in hues of gold.

While Maria and Elisa reveled in the tranquility of their home, Eric often found his thrill amidst the verdant embrace of the surrounding forest. Mornings were his domain, where the earthy scent of dew-kissed foliage mingled with the crisp morning air. With musket in hand, he would disappear into the woods on horseback, becoming one with nature, his senses attuned to the slightest rustle, the faintest whisper of movement.

Their lives were not solitary endeavors but rather a mixture of shared experiences, enriched by their erotic endeavors. The presence of their devoted employees made life pleasant. The manager, Monsieur Bernard, a former seaman himself, ensured the smooth operation of their estate. Bernard Garnier cut a distinguished figure amidst the rustic small castle. With a weathered countenance etched by years of salty sea breezes and a gaze that held the wisdom of past voyages, he commanded respect and admiration from all who crossed his path.

Once a proud seaman of the Royal French Navy, Monsieur Bernard bore the indelible marks of a life lived upon the waves. His frame, though now tempered by age, still retained the lean strength of a seasoned sailor, each sinew a testament to the trials and triumphs of his seafaring days.

His attire spoke of a man who carried himself with authority—an old, tailored coat adorned with brass buttons, and a tricorn hat perched jauntily atop his head, a nod to his maritime heritage.

But it was in his demeanor that Monsieur Bernard truly shone. Beneath the stern facade of a seasoned disciplinarian beat a heart of gold, his every action guided by a steadfast dedication to the well-being of the small castle and its inhabitants. With a voice rich and resonant, he dispensed his wisdom with a quiet authority, each word carrying weight.

In Monsieur Bernard, Eric, Maria, and Elisa had found not just a manager, but a mentor—a man whose knowledge and compassion enriched the servant's lives immeasurably. They looked upon him with gratitude and admiration.

The farmhands tended to the land with loving care, coaxing forth the bounty of the earth. And the servants, with their ever-watchful eyes and deft hands, ensured that the chateau ran like a well-oiled machine.

Everybody in Eric's service was paid two times the going wages, so happiness permeated every corner of Château, a testament to the bonds that bound its inhabitants together. Beneath the vaulted ceilings and amidst the sprawling gardens, laughter echoed, friendships flourished, and memories were forged that would stand the test of time.

In this haven of tranquility, Eric, Maria, and Elisa found not just a home but a sanctuary—a place where the simple joys of life went hand in hand with the timeless beauty of nature. They had found their small paradise.

One summer day, beneath the azure skies that stretched over the Château de Fauguernon, a ripple of the ordinary was disturbed by the arrival of two unexpected visitors. At the grand gates stood two girls, their youthful faces obscured by the dust of the road, clad in tattered rags that spoke of a life filled with hardship. Dressed in ripped dresses, and merely ten years old, they gazed up at the imposing chateau with a mixture of trepidation and hope.

Monsieur Bernard, with his ever-watchful eyes, allowed the girls into the court of the estate. However, it was Elisa, with her keen sense of observation, who first caught sight of the newcomers. Intrigued by their presence, she sought answers from Monsieur Bernard, her curiosity burning bright.

With a heavy heart, Monsieur Bernard revealed the plight of the girls—they were among the many children displaced by the closure of an orphanage in Lisieux. Eric, Maria, and Elisa listened with scorn as he recounted the tale of misfortune that had befallen the children.

Eric wasted no time in issuing directives. He commanded Monsieur Bernard to provide the girls with clothing, nourishment, and a bed. Eric understood all too well the trials of the less fortunate, and in their innocent eyes, he saw reflections of his past struggles. He once had walked in their shoes in the streets of Poole in England.

With a sense of purpose, Eric, Maria, and Elisa dressed in their stately attire and embarked on a journey to the city of Lisieux, their carriage cutting through the verdant landscape. Along the cobblestone streets of the city, they bore witness to the harsh realities of life, as more homeless children roamed the alleys.

Their quest led them to the doorstep of the orphanage, where they were met by the weary faces of the ladies in charge. With heavy hearts, they listened as the women recounted the story of financial ruin—a tale woven with threads of loss and desperation.

Unable to pay the accumulated 120 livres to fulfill the contract with the church, the orphanage stood on the precipice of eviction, its fate hanging in the balance. The main benefactor, an old, wealthy lady whose generosity had sustained them, had passed, leaving behind a void too vast to fill. With each passing day, the specter of eviction drew closer with each day passing. Their finances were depleted and they found themselves unable to meet their financial obligations to the church, which had once sold the property to the orphanage.

Now, the church and the destitute orphanage were embroiled in a legal battle, as the church had brought the matter before the magistrate. The magistrate granted the debtor a mere ten days to either settle their debts or vacate the premises. Only three days remained, as the specter of eviction loomed ominously overhead, casting a shadow of uncertainty over the future of the orphanage and the children it sheltered.

With just three days remaining until the magistrate's deadline, Eric, Maria, and Elisa knew that time was of the essence.

Determined to exhaust every avenue in their quest to save the orphanage, the three made their way to the grand Lisieux Cathedral. Within its hallowed halls, they were received by a reverend whose countenance bespoke a deep familiarity with the plight of the orphanage. With a heavy heart, the priest explained the grim reality—they were powerless to intervene, as the fate of the orphanage lay in the hands of the Bishop of Bayeux, the Most Reverend Paul d'Albert.

Despite their fervent pleas, the priest could offer no solace, for the bishop had adamantly refused to grant an extension of time. With the sands of the hourglass slipping away, the trio realized that their hopes of appealing to the bishop directly would be dashed by the merciless passage of time.

Undeterred by the seemingly insurmountable odds, the trio resolved to explore alternative avenues for salvation. Venturing into the lively streets of Lisieux, Eric sought out the office of Monsieur Martin, an advocate renowned for his commitment to justice.

Advocate Martin cut a striking figure amidst the bustling streets of the town. He stood tall and imposing, with a demeanor that exuded confidence and authority, and even a hint of nobility.

His attire, impeccably tailored and adorned with the subtle elegance befitting a man of his stature, spoke volumes of his professionalism and attention to detail. A crisp suit in the deep hue of midnight hugged his frame with tailored precision, while a silk tie, carefully chosen to complement the ensemble, added a touch of understated sophistication.

But it was in his eyes that Advocate Martin's true strength lay. Behind the polished veneer of his exterior burned the fiery intensity of a man driven by a fervent dedication to the pursuit of justice. With each glance, his piercing gaze seemed to strip away the layers of falsehood, laying bare the raw truth that slumbered beneath.

Under the veneer of professionalism, Advocate Martin harbored a heart of gold. Compassionate and empathetic, he approached each case not as a mere legal matter, but as a deeply personal crusade for justice. His clients were not just names on a docket but individuals whose lives he sought to defend and protect at all costs.

As Eric, Maria, and Elisa stepped into his office, they were greeted not just by a lawyer, but by a beacon of hope. With a warm smile and a firm handshake, Advocate Martin welcomed them into his domain, ready to lend his expertise to their cause and fight alongside them in their quest to save the orphanage from impending doom.

"What can I do for you, Mesdames et Monsieur?" the advocate inquired with a polite nod as Eric, Maria, and Elisa entered his office.

"We have a problem with the orphanage in town; the church wants to close it in three days," Eric replied with a sense of urgency lacing his words.

The advocate's brow furrowed in concern. "Yes, I have

heard about this. It is indeed an injustice, but there is little I can do," he lamented.

Maria, ever resourceful, interjected, "Would money help? From what we have heard, it is merely 120 livres that are needed."

A glimmer of hope flickered in the advocate's eyes. "Oh yes, madame, if someone pays the 120 livres before the deadline expires, I can go to the magistrate and settle the debt," he explained, his voice tinged with cautious optimism.

With a determined resolve, Eric reached into his coat and produced a purse, its contents spilling forth onto the table with a satisfying clink. He put 10 gold Louis d'Or onto the advocate's desk. "I assume this is more than sufficient to pay for the debt and for your services, Monsieur," he stated, his gaze unwavering as he pushed the gold coins toward the advocate.

The lawyer's eyes widened in astonishment at the sight of the generous sum. "Oh, yes, Monsieur, thank you very much, more than enough, indeed," he exclaimed gratefully, swiftly pocketing the coins.

But Eric had another request, one born of a desire to ensure the orphanage's continued well-being.

"I would also like to have my two ladies, Madame Lindsay and Mademoiselle Connor, to be put in charge of the orphanage from now on. This way, we can make sure that it is well-funded, and tragedies like this will not happen in the future," he explained earnestly.

The advocate nodded in understanding. "I can certainly make this happen," he assured them, his voice infused with a sense of determination.

"I am not too familiar with Biblical teaching but from what I recall the Christ taught us to take care of the poor and of orphans. Why is it that the church evicts homeless children? How can such an atrocity even be allowed?" Elisa demanded, her voice tinged with indignation.

The advocate sighed, his expression reflecting the weight of centuries of injustice.

"Well, Madame, the system in France is not always just," he admitted with a resigned shake of his head. "And the magistrates often align themselves with the wealthy establishment, turning a blind eye to the plight of the poor. They are always hesitant to take sides against the Second Estate—the church."

"I sometimes wish I could be a magistrate," Eric mused aloud, his frustration palpable.

"Why can you not?" the advocate queried, his eyes gleaming with a glimmer of possibility.

Eric hesitated, considering the implications of the advocate's suggestion. "I am not even French; we are English," he explained.

The advocate waved away his concerns with a dismissive gesture.

"That seems not to be a problem," he countered. "Our queen is Polish, the King of Spain is French, and the King of England, George, is from Hanover in Saxony. You are a member of the landed gentry, Monsieur, which means you are eligible to serve as a magistrate."

Eric's eyes widened in astonishment at the revelation. The barriers that had once seemed insurmountable now appeared to crumble before him, opening up a world of possibilities previously unimagined.

With newfound determination burning bright within him, Eric realized that perhaps, just perhaps, he held the power to enact change—not only for the orphanage but for all those who had been marginalized and forgotten by society.

"And how would I go about it, becoming a magistrate?" Eric asked, his tone tinged with a hint of uncertainty.

The advocate regarded him thoughtfully before responding. "Well, there are multiple paths one could take. The fastest and most powerful way is to be appointed by His Majesty the King, or more likely, by his Chancellor, Monsieur Henri François d'Aguesseau in Paris."

Eric absorbed this information, his mind already spinning with possibilities. To have the authority to enact change from within the system, to be a voice for the voiceless—it was a prospect that both excited and daunted him in equal measure.

"Where would I even go?" Eric inquired, his curiosity piqued.

"To Paris," the advocate replied, his tone matter-of-fact. "You would need to go to the Palais de la Cité, located on the Île de la Cité in the Seine River."

Eric nodded, absorbing the information. The prospect of traveling to the heart of the kingdom filled him with both excitement and trepidation.

"Could you perhaps accompany me?" Eric ventured, a note of hesitation in his voice. "For a compensation, of course."

The advocate considered the request for a moment before nodding in agreement.

"Why not? I have to travel to Paris anyway in two months' time," he replied with a reassuring smile.

With the journey to Paris now within reach, Eric felt a surge of anticipation coursing through his veins. As he prepared to embark on this new chapter in his life, he knew that he would not be alone. With the advocate by his side, he would navigate the corridors of power with confidence.

"We can take my ship and simply sail up the Seine," Eric

suggested, a glint of excitement in his eyes. "This way, we can save ourselves a long carriage trip."

"I would very much love this," the advocate replied, his enthusiasm mirroring Eric's own. "We would indeed save a lot of travel time."

With the plan in place, the trio and Monsieur Martin reached an agreement to embark on their journey to Paris in September. The prospect of sailing along the Seine, with its picturesque landscapes and storied history, filled them with anticipation for the adventure that lay ahead.

As they finalized their arrangements, Eric couldn't help but feel a sense of exhilaration at the thought of charting a course toward their shared goal.

The following day, Maria and Elisa made their way to the orphanage, their hearts buoyed by the knowledge that they had secured its future. As they crossed the threshold, they were met with the wide-eyed gazes of the children, whose innocence tugged at their heartstrings.

With smiles that radiated warmth and kindness, Maria and Elisa approached the ladies who had tirelessly operated the orphanage. They explained that the debt had been settled, and with it, a new chapter had begun. Maria and Elisa gently conveyed their intention to assume responsibility for the orphanage's operations, ensuring that it would be well cared for and supported.

With gratitude shining in their eyes, the ladies welcomed

Maria and Elisa's offer with open arms, recognizing the benefits of the alliance. Together, they could forge a partnership built on a shared purpose, determined to provide a nurturing environment for the children in their care.

From that day forward, Maria and Elisa dedicated themselves wholeheartedly to their newfound role. Once a week, they would journey to Lisieux in their carriage, their hearts brimming with anticipation for the tasks that lay ahead. They would oversee the orphanage's affairs, procuring food and attending to expenses with meticulous attention to detail.

Through their commitment, Maria and Elisa became beacons of hope for the orphaned children of Lisieux, leading them toward a future filled with promise and possibility.

# 17 PARIS

The Duchess, with her majestic sails billowing in the breeze, gracefully pulled out of the harbor of Trouville-sur-Mer. Under the command of Captain Eric, she charted her course eastward, her bow cutting through the gentle waves of the Channel as she entered the inlet of the River Seine.

As the coastline of Normandy receded into the distance, Maria and Elisa retired to their cabin, their excitement palpable as they anticipated the adventures that awaited them in Paris. With laughter and chatter filling the air, they settled in, eagerly discussing their plans for the journey ahead.

Meanwhile, Monsieur Martin, the advocate, found refuge in a small cabin adjacent to theirs. With a stack of legal documents spread out before him, he immersed himself in his work, his brow furrowed in concentration as he prepared for the challenges that awaited him in the bustling capital.

As the Duchess continued her journey, gliding along the tranquil waters of the River Seine, she carried with her a sense of anticipation and possibility.

The ship slowly navigated its way along the meandering waters of the Seine, its course charted with precision by Captain Eric. He was well-versed in the intricacies of the sea as well as in the hidden dangers that may lurk in coastal waters and rivers. Along the banks, quaint villages and picturesque countryside unfurled like a canvas, each bend in the river revealing a new vista of rolling hills, verdant forests, and charming hamlets.

The four passengers aboard the ship found themselves swept up in the romance of the journey, their senses filled with the sights, sounds, and smells of the river. The air was charged with the scent of river water mingling with the earthy aroma of the surrounding countryside, while the gentle lapping of waves against the ship's hull provided a soothing backdrop to the journey.

On deck, Maria and Elisa gathered to watch as the landscape shifted and changed with each passing mile. They exchanged anecdotes from their days at the Gulf of Saint Lawrence, marveling at the rural beauty that surrounded them.

As the ship drew closer to Paris, the excitement among

Eric and the women reached a fever pitch. The city's iconic landmarks—the spires of Notre-Dame Cathedral, the grand facades of the Louvre and the Palais-Royal—loomed ever larger on the horizon, signaling the approach of their destination.

And finally, as the ship glided beneath the arched bridges that spanned the Seine, it came to rest in the busy port of Paris, its arrival heralded by the clamor of voices and the bustle of activity along the riverbanks.

The short journey along the Seine was over. It had been not merely a means of transportation—it had been an experience to be cherished, a journey that spoke to the allure of travel and exploration, which had unveiled new sights even to seasoned seafarers like Eric, Maria, and Elisa.

As Monsieur Martin disappeared into the bustling streets of Paris to attend to his important legal business, Eric, Maria, and Elisa stepped foot onto the piers of the city, their senses immediately inundated by the sights, sounds, and smells of the astir metropolis.

With a sense of awe, they embarked on a leisurely stroll through the labyrinthine streets of Paris, their footsteps echoing against the cobblestones as they meandered past grand boulevards and hidden alleyways alike.

The city revealed itself in layers, each corner yielding a discovery—an ornate fountain tucked away in a quiet square, the tantalizing aromas wafting from a nearby bakery.

Together, they marveled at the architectural splendor that surrounded them. They wandered through buzzing marketplaces, pausing to admire the vibrant displays of fresh produce and artisanal goods.

As the three navigated the unfamiliar streets, they found themselves immersed in the riches of Parisian life—encountering locals going about their daily routines, artists capturing the city's essence on canvas, and visitors from far and wide soaking in the atmosphere of the French Capital.

After an enchanting stroll through the streets of Paris, Eric, Maria, and Elisa decided to indulge in an evening at the esteemed Comédie-Française theater, nestled on the Rue des Fossés. With anticipation coursing through their veins, they eagerly took their seats in the opulent theater, ready to be transported to another world by the magic of the stage.

As the curtains rose and the lights dimmed, they found themselves captivated by the drama unfolding before them, swept up in the artistry of the actors and the timeless allure of the theatrical arts. For hours, they were immersed in a world of intrigue, passion, and emotion, their spirits lifted by the transcendent power of storytelling.

The following day, a Sunday bathed the city in golden sunlight. The trio embarked on a leisurely carriage ride into the picturesque countryside surrounding Paris. Their destination was a charming guinguette—a rustic tavern nestled just beyond the city limits, where wine flowed freely and laughter filled the air

Here, amidst the verdant splendor of the countryside, they savored a delicious meal accompanied by glasses of fine French wine, their senses intoxicated by the heady aromas and flavors of the region. With each sip and bite, they reveled in the simple pleasures of good food, good company, and the beauty of the natural world.

Back in the city, the trio wandered through the bustling streets, their footsteps echoing against the cobblestones as they took in the sights and sounds of Paris at dusk.

Eric, Maria, and Elisa found themselves strolling down the crowded streets, their senses assailed by the vibrant atmosphere of the Palais Royal Gardens. The area was a hive of activity that pulsed with life and energy. The arcades lining the courtyard teemed with shops, cafes, and even brothels, their colorful facades casting a lively backdrop against the elegant architecture of the palace.

A wooden palisade detached the courtyard from the rest of the palace, creating a sense of seclusion and intimacy akin to a small town nestled within the heart of Paris. Here, amidst the hustle and bustle of daily life, even a circus had found its home, adding an air of whimsy and spectacle to the scene. Prostitutes, following a certain hierarchy, had set up shop in the area of the Palais Royal, their presence a testament to the dynamics that permeated every corner of Parisian society. Clients could peruse pictures of the girls on offer, selecting their companions with a mix of discretion and desire.

As they continued along the Rue de Bagneux, Eric, Maria, and Elisa caught sight of a brightly lit brothel. A man stationed at the entrance beckoned them forth with a welcoming gesture, inviting them to step inside and partake in the pleasures that awaited within.

"I would really like to go inside," Elisa exclaimed with a mischievous glint in her eye.

Curiosity piqued, they exchanged a glance before reluctantly accepting the man's invitation.

"Wouldn't hurt to see what our old profession is like here in Paris," Maria chimed in, her curiosity piqued. "I've always heard about the skills of French ladies of the night."

"Let's enter then," Eric agreed with a chuckle. "Maybe we can have some entertainment and amusement. It seems the entire city here is having fun!"

With their decision made, they approached the entrance of the brightly lit brothel, their hearts pounding with anticipation. As they stepped inside, they were greeted by Madame Bienfait, an older but still striking woman who exuded an air of authority and elegance.

Bonjour, I am Justine Bienfait. Welcome, Mesdames et Monsieur," the madam uttered with a warm smile, her voice tinged with a hint of allure. "Please, come in and make yourselves at home. Allow me to show you our finest accommodations. May I ask, what is it that you seek?"

"Ah, just some general and innocent fun is fine," Maria replied with a coy smile, her cheeks flushing slightly.

"Of course, Madame," Madame Justine replied with a knowing nod. "Allow me to guide you to the boudoir of Mademoiselle Denise. She will ensure that you have a delightful experience."

As they followed Madame Justine deeper into the brothel, Eric, Maria, and Elisa couldn't help but feel a sense of excitement building within them. What adventures awaited them within the walls?

With a graceful sweep of her hand, Madame Justine led the trio up the grand staircase, their footsteps echoing softly against the polished wood. As they ascended to the upper floors of the brothel, the air was heavy with anticipation, each step bringing them closer to their destination.

Upon reaching Mademoiselle Denise's boudoir, Madame Justine paused at the door and gestured for them to enter.

"Here you will find everything you desire for a pleasurable evening," she remarked with a knowing smile before bidding them farewell.

The three entered the boudoir. Their senses were immediately assailed by the heady scent of incense and the soft glow of candlelight.

"And, did I mention, we charge by the hour?" the madam explained as she opened her hand.

Eric nodded in understanding and reached into his pocket, withdrawing a gleaming Louis d'Or. With a gracious smile, he handed the coin to the madam, a gesture of appreciation for her hospitality and discretion.

"Thank you, Madame," Eric replied, his tone polite.

With a final nod of acknowledgment, the madam bid them farewell and departed, leaving Eric, Maria, and Elisa alone in the softly lit room. As they settled in, they knew that the hours ahead held the promise of excitement, intimacy, and the kind of forbidden pleasures found within the walls of Madame Justine's establishment.

A side door opened. Mademoiselle Denise glided into the room, her presence as captivating as it was alluring. Dressed in a light, flowing dress that accentuated her every curve, she exuded an aura of effortless charm and sophistication.

"Ah, bonjour," she greeted them with a warm smile, her

voice like music to their ears. "Couples are my specialty, and I am delighted to see you here."

Mademoiselle Denise stood before them, a vision of beauty and understated allure. Her petite frame exuded an air of grace and poise, her movements as fluid as a dancer's as she walked across the room.

With her golden locks cascading in gentle waves around her shoulders, she possessed a noble beauty that seemed to radiate from within. Her features were delicate and finely sculpted, her porcelain skin flawless and luminous in the soft candlelight.

Despite her diminutive stature, Mademoiselle Denise commanded attention with an innate sense of confidence and self-assurance. Her eyes, a shade of azure blue that sparkled with intelligence and mischief, held a captivating allure that drew others in with their magnetic gaze.

Though her figure may have been petite, it was no less alluring. Her aura exuded a subtle sensuality that left a lingering impression on all who beheld her. And though her breasts may have been small, they were perfectly proportioned to her slender frame, adding to her overall charm and femininity.

But it was not just her physical beauty that captivated those around her—it was the aura of warmth and kindness that emanated from her every pore. With a genuine smile that lit up her face and a voice that carried a melodic lilt, Mademoiselle Denise welcomed Eric, Maria, and Elisa into her presence with open arms, ready to guide them on a journey of pleasure and exploration that would leave them breathless with desire.

Maria and Elisa exchanged a glance, their anticipation mounting as they realized that they were in the presence of someone who possessed not only beauty but also a rare talent for pleasure.

"We are pleased to meet you, Mademoiselle Denise," Eric replied, his voice tinged with excitement. "We are looking forward to a delightful evening in your company."

With that, they settled in, ready to embark on an unforgettable journey.

"May I explain, we are not entirely novices at this. We are pretty much colleagues, from England, if you know what I mean?" Maria smiled.

Mademoiselle Denise's eyes widened in surprise at Maria's words, a knowing smile tugging at the corners of her lips.

"Ah, then we are in for a delightful evening indeed," she replied with a playful twinkle in her eye.

With a sense of camaraderie and excitement, Maria and Elisa approached Mademoiselle Denise, their movements fluid and practiced. With a deftness born of experience, they expertly untied the laces of her dress, revealing the tantalizing curves of her slender figure beneath.

As the fabric fell away, Mademoiselle Denise stood before them, her skin glowing in the soft candlelight, her gaze alight with anticipation. With a subtle nod of approval, she allowed herself to be enveloped in their embrace, surrendering to the pleasures that awaited her.

Eric watched with a mixture of fascination and desire, his pulse quickening at the sight of the intimate tableau unfolding before him. At that moment, they were not just strangers brought together by chance—they were kindred spirits, united in their pursuit of fulfillment.

As Maria reclined upon the plush bed in the boudoir, her senses ablaze with anticipation, Mademoiselle Denise moved with a grace and confidence that left no doubt as to her expertise. With a sensuous flick of her hair, she positioned herself between Maria's spread legs, her lips eagerly seeking out the sweet warmth nestled between her thighs.

Meanwhile, Elisa, emboldened by the passion that filled the room, shed her dress with practiced ease, allowing her breasts to fall out of her silk blouse. With a newfound sense of freedom and abandon, she leaned over Maria, her lips meeting hers in a passionate kiss that sent shivers of pleasure coursing through their bodies.

As their mouths met in a fervent embrace, Elisa's hands roamed eagerly over Maria's body, her fingers trailing along the curves of her breasts with a touch that was both tender and demanding. With each caress, she elicited soft moans of pleasure from her, the sound of a symphony of desire that echoed throughout the room.

With a primal urgency burning within him, Eric wasted no time in giving in to his desires. His hands moved with a fevered determination; he swiftly unbuttoned his pants, his arousal evident as he positioned himself behind Mademoiselle Denise.

Grasping her hips with both hands, he guided himself into her with a hunger that bordered on desperation. As he entered her, a low groan of pleasure escaped his lips, the sensation of her warmth enveloping him and sending waves of ecstasy coursing through his veins.

With each thrust, he surrendered to the primal rhythm of their bodies, their movements synchronized in a dance of passion and desire. The room filled with the whispers of their labored breaths and the soft, rhythmic sounds of their loving, a symphony of pleasure that echoed off the walls of the boudoir.

In the heat of the moment, Eric and Mademoiselle Denise became lost to the world around them, their bodies moving in a whirlwind of sensation and desire, as Elisa still fondled Maria's breasts, while Denise, in exchange, was still pleasing Maria. All four now moved in perfect harmony.

As the waves of pleasure ebbed away, leaving them sated and content, Eric reached into his pocket and withdrew a gleaming Louis d'Or, a token of appreciation for the unforgettable experience they had shared with Mademoiselle Denise. With a gracious smile, she accepted the coin, her eyes alight with satisfaction.

"Merci, Monsieur," she said, her voice a melodic whisper as she bid them farewell.

With a sense of fulfillment and contentment settling over them, Eric, Maria, and Elisa made their way back to the piers where the Duchess awaited, moored gracefully against the gentle lapping of the river.

They climbed aboard the ship, their hearts still racing with the memory of their passionate encounter, yet also filled with a profound sense of peace and satisfaction.

The next morning, as the early sun cast its golden glow over the city of Paris, Monsieur Martin returned with news that filled Eric with anticipation. Securing an appointment at the office of the Chancellor was no small feat, and Monsieur Martin's cousin's connection had proven invaluable.

"Now remember, Eric," Monsieur Martin cautioned, "when we are the Place of Justice, the Chancellor is an official of the King. Conduct yourself accordingly."

With a sense of purpose and determination, Eric and Monsieur Martin made their way to the Palace de Justice, where they were to meet with the esteemed Chancellor. They waited in the grand office, the air crackling with anticipation. It took merely five minutes, and they were greeted by the arrival of the King's Chancellor, Henri François d'Aguesseau himself.

Bowing deeply in a show of respect, Monsieur Martin rose from his seat, and Eric followed suit. "Messieurs," the Chancellor greeted them warmly, his voice carrying an air of authority tempered by geniality.

"François Martin, Advocate in the Parlement de Rouen," Monsieur Martin introduced himself with a polite nod, "and this is Monsieur Cobham."

"Ah, you must be the cousin of Monsieur Jean Martin then," the Chancellor remarked, his keen gaze falling upon Monsieur Martin.

"Yes, Monsieur, I am," Monsieur Martin confirmed with a respectful nod, acknowledging the familial connection that had paved the way for their meeting with the high official.

A smile played at the corners of the Chancellor's lips as he nodded in understanding. "Jean is a valued man," he replied warmly. "You come from good stock, Monsieur Martin."

As the meeting unfolded, Eric couldn't help but feel a sense of gratitude toward Monsieur Martin for his resourcefulness and initiative. With his cousin's help, they had gained access to the highest echelons of power in Paris.

"What can I do for you, Messieurs?" the Chancellor inquired, his gaze moving between them with interest.

"Monsieur Cobham is a member of the landed gentry in Pays d'Auge, Monsieur Martin explained, paving the way for Eric to present his case to the esteemed official. "He would like to serve as a magistrate in Lisieux. There is a vacancy, as the old Magistrate is 72 years old and ready to retire."

"So, Monsieur Cobham, how is it with your loyalty to His Majesty King Louis?" the Chancellor inquired, his tone measured and curious.

"I fully submit to the supreme authority of His Majesty the King," Eric replied with unwavering conviction, "and I am willing to defend his rule among my peers and the people."

The Chancellor nodded in approval at Eric's response, his expression thoughtful as he considered the young man before him.

"And what makes you desire this position?" the Chancellor pressed on, his gaze steady as he awaited Eric's answer.

"In Lisieux, I have witnessed great injustice due to the magistrate's complacency and disregard for the King's laws," Eric explained, his voice tinged with resolve. "With the help of Monsieur Martin, I am willing to remedy this and restore the laws of the King for the benefit, advancement and prosperity of all of His Majesty's subjects. It is my duty as a member of the landed gentry to uphold justice and ensure that the rights of the people are protected."

His words resonated with a sense of purpose and determination, leaving no doubt as to his sincerity and commitment to the cause. And as the Chancellor listened intently to Eric's impassioned plea, he was convinced of the sincerity of the young man's dedication.

"Well then, be here tomorrow morning to receive your appointment letter," the Chancellor conveyed. With that, he stood up, briefly nodded, and left the room.

With hearts buoyed by the promise of a new beginning, Eric and Monsieur Martin made their way back to the ship, eager to share the news of Eric's appointment with Maria and Lisa. As they reunited on the deck of the Duchess, excitement filled the air as they recounted the details of their encounter with the Chancellor.

"We need to celebrate this," Maria exclaimed with a radiant smile, her eyes shining with pride and joy.

Agreeing wholeheartedly, the four of them decided to mark the occasion with a hearty dinner at a nearby restaurant. Amidst laughter and camaraderie, they toasted to Eric's newfound role and the adventures that lay ahead.

The next morning, Monsieur Martin wasted no time in retrieving the sealed appointment letter for Eric from the

Palace of Justice, a tangible symbol of his new responsibilities and authority.

As evening fell, the Duchess set sail once more, her course set for Le Havre. Gliding gracefully down the Seine, they passed through the ancient city of Rouen, its storied landmarks standing sentinel along the riverbanks.

With each passing mile, they felt a sense of exhilaration and anticipation building within them, their hearts filled with the promise of new horizons and adventures yet to come. And as they sailed toward their home port of Trouville-sur-Mer, they knew that they were embarking on a journey that would forever alter the course of their lives.

They arrived at the Château de Fauguernon, after dropping off Monsieur Martin at his home in Lisieux. It had been a good and successful voyage.

Eric, Maria, and Lisa savored the delicious meal prepared by the chef. Their spirits were lifted by the recent elevation of Eric and by the joyous atmosphere of their home. As the plates were cleared away and the evening wore on, they took a bottle of heavy French Bordeaux and retired to their shared bedroom, eager to continue their celebration in the privacy of their own quarters.

With a sassy glint in her eyes, Maria shed her dress with playful abandon, her laughter echoing through the room as she flopped onto the bed with a dramatic flair.

"I've never been taken by a magistrate," she exclaimed with a mischievous smile, her words laced with teasing anticipation.

Beside her, Lisa joined in the laughter, her playful spirit infectious as she propped herself up beside Maria.

"Me neither. I heard they have magical powers," she chuckled, her eyes twinkling with excitement as she watched Eric begin to shed his clothes.

With a sense of playful abandon, Eric joined the two women on the bed, his heart light with laughter and joy. He was a magistrate now, he could finally do right by the people, something he had always wished for.

As they came together in a tangle of limbs and laughter, they knew that this night would be one to remember—a celebration of newfound beginnings and the enduring bond of love that held them in unison. And as they surrendered to the pleasures of the moment, their laughter mingling with the caressing whisper of the wind in the trees outside, they knew that they were exactly where they were meant to be.

In the warmth of their shared embrace, Eric, Maria, and Lisa felt a bond that transcended mere physical intimacy. There was no room for jealousy, want, or covetousness among them, for they had found in each other a connection that went beyond the surface, reaching deep into the recesses of their souls.

They reveled in the joy of their shared companionship, knowing that their bond was unbreakable, forged through shared experiences on the rough streets of Plymouth and London, the high seas, and the bloody trade of piracy. They had shared laughter and tears and had stood next to each other with cutlass and pistol in hand. Each one complemented the other, their strengths and weaknesses blending together seamlessly to form a whole.

Their love for each other knew no boundaries and no limitations imposed by society's narrow definitions of acceptability. In their embrace, they celebrated the beauty of diversity and the richness of human connection, unfettered by the constraints of prejudice and discrimination.

In their unity, they found strength, support, and unconditional love. There was no need for competition or comparison, for they celebrated each other's victories as if they were their own, offering solace in times of sorrow. Beyond the conventions and taboos of societal norms, they had soared and stood liberated from the chains of expectation and conformity.

Against all odds, they had taken what they desired, together, with the imagination of their minds and swords in their hands. They had transcended the heavy shackles of their past. In their union, they had found a sanctuary where their true selves could flourish, unencumbered by the judgments of the outside world.

Together, they would navigate the trials and tribulations of life with unwavering solidarity, their hearts intertwined in a bond that could weather any storm. Eric would be a magistrate for the people. Maria and Elisa would manage the orphanage in Lisieux. And as they drifted off to sleep, wrapped in each other's arms, they knew that they were truly blessed to have found such rare and precious companionship in each other.

With each passing moment, they reveled in the freedom to express themselves authentically, to love boldly and without reservation. Theirs was a love that defied categorization, transcending the narrow confines of traditional relationships to embrace the boundless possibilities of the human heart.

And as they lay together in the moonlight, their laughter ringing out in the night, they knew that they were pioneers, forging a path of love and acceptance for all who dared to follow in their footsteps. For in their unity, they had discovered the true essence of freedom—the freedom to love, to be, and to thrive in a world that too often sought to confine and control.

*The End*

# ABOUT THE AUTHOR

Alexander De Chastelaine has lived and worked in in France, England, Switzerland, Germany, and the Middle East. He has traveled most European, Asian, Middle Eastern, and Middle American countries extensively, researching historic and archeological facts. The author currently studies the history of Florida and the Caribbean, speaks 4 modern languages, and reads several ancient languages like Latin, Classical Greek, and Hebrew.

# THE TERROR OF SAINT LAWRENCE

Made in the USA
Columbia, SC
03 October 2024